# Tricia LaVoice

Latte to Chardonnay

This book is a work of fiction. Names, characters, events, dialogue and incidents are a product of the author's imagination or used fictitiously.

ISBN: 978-1-7350314-0-8

Cover art design by Olivia Milton
Interior design and composition by Olivia Milton
Content Editing by Full Bloom Publications
Proofreading by Audrey Shepard
Website design by Trisha Hibbs
Author Photo by Robert LaVoice

For More information visit:
www.lattetochardonnay.com

## Dedicated to:

*My Crazy Ass Bitches, Coffee Clutch, Circle Goddesses, Avon Warriors, and to all my other girlfriends who have shared their secrets, and kept mine, helping each other keep it all together and exciting. Special thank you to Mary Jo who has been there with me from the beginning.*

# The Latte TO Chardonnay Club

## PERMANENT CONDITIONS:

- A weekly date night
- Sex once a week, but try really hard for twice
- Spouses may NOT refer to you as "Mom" or "Mother"

## MONTHLY CHALLENGES:

*One point for every time you complete the challenge*

- Challenges are chosen each month by a different member of the group
- Members must respect each other's choices
- Keep challenges mainstream

## BONUS CHALLENGES:

*Three points for every bonus challenge completed*

- Chosen by the member who picked this month's challenge
- Spicier
- Optional

## WINNINGS:

Besides a healthy and fun love life, the winner gets a $25.00 Starbucks gift card from each member!

CLUB MEMBERS: Lisa, Allison, Meagan, Rose

## Meet Allison

♀ Smart

♀ Devoted Wife

♀ Part-time Job at Waxing Salon

♀ Stay At Home Mom

*Spouse ♥ Tom*

*Children ♥ Emma, Julia, Tommy, Henry*

## Meet Rose

♀ Sweet

♀ Innocent

♀ Naive

♀ Stay At Home Mom

*Spouse ♥ Frank*

*Children ♥ Jasmine, Lily, Violet, Daisy, Dahlia*

# Meet Lisa

♀ Bold

♀ Vulgar

♀ Real Estate Agent

*Spouse ♥ Gomez*

*Children ♥ Mary Jane,*

*Adam*

# Meet Meagan

♀ Young

♀ Neurotic

♀ Editor

♀ Hard-working

♀ Single Mom

*Children ♥ Mickey*

Latte TO Chardonnay

# Latte: The Club

"Yes, I'm in front of my computer now," Lisa said as she stepped out of her car and headed to the door. She and Allison pulled up simultaneously, and Allison waited for her on the steps. Lisa gave Allison an "I'll be one minute" hand signal to wait while she finished up her phone call.

"Okay, so all I have to do is give you my credit card information and remote access to my computer, and you'll fix my computer problem I didn't even know I had?... I see, I see..."

Lisa rolled her eyes at Allison as she continued talking into her phone. "I have an idea. Why don't you lick my dirty crotch? Get a real job, loser."

She clicked "End" on her call and smiled at Allison. "Good morning."

They wiped their feet twice on the mat, gave a soft knock on the door, and walked in, removing their shoes immediately. Rose never asked them to do this, but it was a natural response to her 6000-square-foot, perfectly clean home filled with overstuffed, white shabby chic furniture, plush white carpet, and plants. Lisa always felt like she was entering an intervention for Pessimist-aholics when entering Rose's house. The only color you would find was on the endless inspirational box art hanging throughout the house. The sign on the front door read, "Life does not have to be perfect to be wonderful." The foyer was covered in a combination of professional photography of Rose's family, all in white, and more signs. Three uniform signs proclaimed: "Never let the things you want make you forget the things you have," "Everything is going to be alright—maybe not today, but eventually," and "You cannot prevent the birds of sorrow from flying over your head, but you can prevent them from building nests in your hair." One wall was covered in photos, and a huge white sign with black cursive writing simply read, "BREATHE."

"What does she think? Suddenly, we'll all forget how to breathe and pass out in her foyer?" Lisa asked Allison, who caught herself breathing deeply.

Rose was so committed to life and happiness that Lisa would have nicknamed her Mary Poppins if her real name did not already lend itself to so many fantastic opportunities for ridicule. Allison and Meagan loved Rose for her innocence and commitment to see the world only as wonderful, but Lisa struggled with Rose's rose-colored glasses and did not try to hide it. Lisa, Allison, and Meagan had been a threesome since their oldest, now in 8th grade, were in kindergarten. Rose moved her girls from St. John's to the local public school years later. Allison immediately took a liking to Rose, but Lisa wanted nothing to do with someone named Rose Garden with five daughters named Jasmine, Violet, Lily, Dahlia, and Daisy. "It's not her fault that she was named Rose as a baby or that she fell in love with a man named Frank Garden—although she could have kept her maiden name. But it's one hundred percent her fault that her family sounds like a bad wedding bouquet."

"I think it sounds sweet," Meagan said.

"It sounds like she's a perennial nut job."

"She loves annuals too."

Lisa was reluctant to allow Rose into their inner circle until Rose became head of the fundraising committee for the school auction one year and thought it wouldn't hurt to get a little closer to the richest woman in town. Over time, they became a foursome, and Rose grew on Lisa like a vine.

As Allison and Lisa walked down the hallway towards the laughter, Lisa spotted a new sign on the wall. It was a quote from Audrey Hepburn: "To Plant a Garden is to Believe in Tomorrow".

Someone—Rose—had crossed out "Plant a" and written in thick black marker, "Love Frank." Now the sign read, "To Love Frank Garden is to Believe in Tomorrow."

"Ugh, I'm going to puke," Lisa said, turning the sign upside down.

"Lisa, quiet. Rose will hear you."

"I hope she hears me. By the way, you smell like sperm. You had sex and didn't shower, right?"

Lisa was an expert at detecting when her friends had sex. Allison was holding a tall latte and looking disheveled. Under no circumstances would Allison be drinking a tall latte unless it was her second coffee of the day. Allison's morning grande latte ritual was as predictable as rain in Seattle. Therefore, if Allison was drinking a tall, that meant she had already had her grande—and that only happened if Tom, sweet loyal Tom, had left it beside her bed.

"She is so spoiled," Lisa and Meagan frequently repeated.

Tom knew nothing made Allison happier than to wake up next to her Starbucks. He left them religiously for her on the weekends, but on a weekday it must have been a "thank you"— a sex "thank you." Tom may have been sweet and loyal, but he was also a man driven by the desires and satisfaction of his penis. Lisa believed that ninety percent of all men's behavior was penis- driven. She also felt that she missed her calling as a detective and now had to settle for watching "murder porn" (that was what her husband Gomez called her investigative murder shows) and stalking her friends' sex lives. It was pure enjoyment for her to watch them become self-conscious about smelling like sex, particularly if the opportunity arose at a public event. Allison was notorious for getting Tom in the bedroom before any Saturday night gala. She thought it decreased the pressure to have sex after the event, when the sex wasn't that good anyway, considering all of the alcohol in their bloodstreams. Lisa got Allison every time and relished watching her sit tight-legged all night, walking to the restroom as if she were holding a sheet of paper between her thighs. The girls thought Lisa had a nose like a grizzly.

This morning Allison chose to ignore Lisa and kept walking down the long hall to the kitchen. As they passed the exercise room, it was Allison who had the outburst. "Oh, my God! Now I have seen it all."

Dandelion, Rose's five-pound Pomeranian, was wearing a little pink doggie sweat jacket and running on the family treadmill while Ana, Rose's housekeeper, spotted her. Lisa looked in and calmly called out to Ana, "You have rights, you know?" Ana flipped Lisa off. She and Dandelion loathed Lisa and never tried to hide it.

Ana had moved from Florida to Connecticut as a young child. Her mother had practically raised Rose from the time Rose was a baby until Rose went off to college. Ana's mother returned to the Keys but Ana chose to stay with Rose. They were like sisters, and Ana was very protective of Rose. Although Rose put her through college to earn her teaching degree, Ana opted to work for Rose, using all she learned to tutor the girls. She was quiet as a mouse when others were around. Lisa was always asking her questions, but Ana ignored her. She loved her books and walks in nature, and she loved Rose and the girls.

Meagan had already arrived and was sitting with Rose at the kitchen table. She was wearing professional attire and sipping a cup of green tea beside a bottle of B complex vitamins. Lisa observed this from the corner of her eye, Meagan's classic giveaway, and stored the gem for later.

Meagan was the baby of the group, sweet as could be and neurotic as shit—but not neurotic in an annoying way, like the person who calls you two minutes after sending you a text to ask if you got the text. It was more in a self-punishing way, worrying about others and if she had done something wrong. Even as an adult, she avoided walking on sidewalk cracks, fearing for her mother's back. Green tea, dandelion, chicory root, walnuts, garlic, apples, and B complex were all part of her daily ritual after a night with more than one glass of wine. Milk thistle was reserved for morning hangovers after bingers, which luckily were not often. Meagan allowed herself three glasses of wine on Friday and Saturday nights. She abstained during the week except for Wednesday nights, when she would have a glass with the girls during their weekly Zoom call. After extensive internet research, she believed this routine was acceptable for a healthy liver. However, whenever she broke this treaty with herself, she was full of guilt and worried that she would develop cirrhosis, so she showered her liver with love. Lisa knew that Meagan would never break her self- inflicted treaty unless that piece-of-shit boyfriend of hers was over at the house looking for sex. Lisa and Allison were convinced he was married, but Meagan assured them he just liked to sleep in his own bed. Her reasoning for never having seen his apartment was just as naïve: "He hates where he lives, but he's moving to a bigger place soon. He says he'll cook me dinner as soon as he settles." The girls had been hearing that for a full year.

Lisa spotted the string tied around Meagan's waist under her tent shirt and pulled it as she walked in. She lifted her own shirt, exposing the muffin top hanging over her jeans, and smacked her belly twice. "This here is the beautiful byproduct of some delicious nachos and the best margaritas ever. Gomez and I had a blast at that new Mexican restaurant downtown. Worth every calorie."

Allison followed close behind and pulled Meagan's shirt back down over the string. Meagan was full of what she called "creative ways" to watch her calories—the string reminded her not to overeat. She also carried around peppermint spray, sniffing as often as possible to trick her brain into believing she was full. Having read an article that claimed the color blue was an appetite suppressant, she now surrounded herself with shades of blue when eating. Her kitchen was painted blue, the refrigerator light was blue, her plates were blue, and her napkins were all blue. Even her wine glasses were blue. When strictly dieting, she added blue food coloring with a dose of magnesium and vitamin D and B12 to a squirt bottle and sprayed her food before eating. During these more intense periods, Lisa refused to dine with her. Meagan was a beautiful woman but always battling her weight. She cringed every time someone said to her, "You're just big-boned." In her obsession to Google, she read that the average weight for a 5'4" woman was 108 to 132 pounds. Meagan fluctuated between 140 to 145—always the girl who looked like the "before" picture in a diet ad. She wasn't looking to be model-thin. She just wanted to be average.

Meagan's situation differed from the happy marriages of the three other women in the club. She was a single mother on her own with a half-assed boyfriend. She came from a large Catholic family, the second to the youngest of eight children. Although her family was very religious, beer and wine had substituted for water and milk in the home where she grew up. Every Sunday after church, her aunts and uncles would come to the house and play poker. The drinking started at noon and went way into the night, always ending with relatives shouting and stumbling out the door. As a child, she had loved this Sunday ritual, playing with her cousins and running around free and wild with little adult supervision. But as she grew older, she witnessed first-hand the effects of alcohol abuse. Both her parents were still struggling with alcoholism. Meagan was not even in junior high when she started lying to the teachers about her mother being wheelchair-bound and unable to attend any school events. She signed their names on school documents, got herself to and from school, and was working to pay her own way by sixteen.

The day after graduation, Meagan moved to Nashville with a couple of friends looking to start a band and be discovered. Their apartment became a hangout for drifters searching for self and stardom. It was there she met Mikey's dad, the boy with long, golden hair who mesmerized the room with his gentle voice and amazing guitar skills. Meagan was not one to sleep around, but as he stared into her eyes with his emerald greens while singing "American Pie," she felt as if she had loved him her whole life. They made love all night long, as dusk became dawn. He was gone in the morning, after leaving a sweet note and a daisy by her bed. "Forever, you will be an angel in my soul making my journey of discovery that much sweeter. Peace and love, Mike the 3rd." And that was that. She had no way to locate him or even know where or who he was.

When she discovered she was pregnant, Meagan moved back home and lived in her sister's basement. She spent the next six years working to pay rent, taking night classes for a Bachelor's degree, and raising a baby. She promised herself she would never complain about her situation. She chose it and owned it. Once she finished college, she accepted a job in Manhattan at a startup publishing company with flexible hours and she moved to a small town in Connecticut, where the schools were good and the commute tolerable.

And then the unthinkable happened. Shortly after Mikey's tenth birthday, his wandering hippie dad turned corporate, found Meagan, and wanted to be part of Mikey's life. Meagan couldn't be mad at him for deserting them because he hadn't known about Mikey until years later, when he had stumbled upon a mutual friend from Nashville. But she had been Mikey's only parent his whole life, and there was no room for another parent in her mind. Still, she could not deny her son the chance to know his father. Mikey was over the moon when Meagan told him his father had found him.

At first, they took it slowly. There were lunches, and Mike showed up at Mikey's ball games. Over time, Mikey started sleeping over at Mike's place and eventually began spending a weekend or two there each month. Mike sought Meagan's advice and respected all her motherly wishes. But then, he became very involved, wanting to be part of every parenting decision. Meagan did not think he was a jerk or a bad father, but she wasn't used to co-parenting or the aggravation that came with it. Then came the day she had dreaded. Two weeks before eighth grade started, Mikey asked to live with his father for the school year. Meagan was heartbroken. She resented Mike, knowing it was his idea, but pretended to be okay with it all.

Although Meagan's circumstances were different from the other women in the club, all four members were there for the same reason: to encourage one another to stay healthy and alive. Allison, Lisa, and Rose had their marriages, and Meagan had her search for a soulmate.

On the day they had officially formed the club, Lisa had made everyone sign a privacy contract swearing honesty and total secrecy, and then demanded a ritual. It didn't matter that they had been friends for years—she said it was no different than a dating couple needing a ritual to commence their marriage. She had given them each a dog tag with their names on one side and *L to C* on the other. "Since life happens between the latte and chardonnay," she explained, "we will call our club, 'Latte to Chardonnay.'" A simple prick to the index finger and an exchange of blood and we are officially, 'The Latte to Chardonnay Club!'"

Meagan adamantly refused to swap DNA, which Lisa ignored. However, once Allison and Rose joined Meagan's protest they opted for an old fashion girl scout pledge.

Countless teas from around the world graced the center of the table, along with perfectly homemade scones, muffins and an abundance of fruit. A selection of sugars, milks, and honey was offered. Of course, everything was organic, non-GMO, and gluten-free. Kisses and hugs were exchanged. Allison took a seat while Lisa walked around the kitchen, reading more inspirational signs.

"What can I get you?" asked Rose, rising to pour tea.

Rose always looked like she was on her way to the Kentucky Derby. Her golden locks were perfectly curled and her makeup just right. This morning, Rose wore a white dress with red dahlias trailing down the side. Much of her clothing included flowers. Her ability to weave a flower motif into every aspect of her life was both impressive and trite. In the house, candles smelled of wildflowers, and bathroom soaps left your hands scented with lavender and lilac. If you rode in her car, your clothes and hair absorbed her jasmine deodorizer. Rose always smelled of the exquisite Chanel Gardenia perfume on her wrists. She never spent much money on herself, regardless of how hard the girls tried to convince her to treat herself, but Frank bought her nice things. Every birthday and Christmas, he gave her the Gardenia perfume.

Allison and Meagan thought she smelled like a dream. Lisa was just relieved she didn't wear some god-awful rose-scented fragrance. Lisa twitched at the smell of roses. They reminded her of her Aunt Agnes, who smelled like cheap rose spray and had three huge moles growing out of her face—the face that Lisa was forced to kiss every time they visited. It haunted Lisa as a child. She had always protested visiting her aunt, even though Aunt Agnes bred apple head chihuahuas and the house was full of puppies.

Lisa continued walking around the kitchen, quietly reading signs to herself. "Nothing is Impossible. The word itself says 'I'm Possible.'" "Difficult Roads Often Lead to Beautiful Destinations."

"Rose, do you really believe all this crap?"

Allison placed her hand on Rose's hand. "Ignore her. She's an angry woman."

"You want to hear some shit?" Meagan asked. "I was over at Lyndsey's yesterday, and she and her girlfriends were comparing 'push presents,' a fricking gift your husband gives you for pushing out a baby."

Lyndsey was Meagan's sister who did everything right. She was a generation younger than Meagan and annoyed the shit out of her. Meagan had been the family baby, a role that came with many perks, until one day the "Oops Baby" had arrived and stolen her thunder. Although Lyndsey was now a perfect size four, she had been heavy at birth, leaving their poor mother on crutches for weeks. Meagan never forgave her and assumed this was why her mother drank so much.

"I applaud the millennials and their zest for life. You know they take babymoons now," said Allison as she placed half a stick of salted butter on her cranberry scone. "That's a vacation before the baby is born."

Dandelion had found her way to the kitchen and was sniffing inside Lisa's handbag on the floor. Lisa grabbed her bag and snapped at the dog. "Asshole."

Dandelion showed her teeth before turning and prancing out of the kitchen.

"We all got gifts when we gave birth," said Rose. "We just didn't have names for them." She glanced at Meagan and quickly caught herself. "Well, nothing special."

Meagan smiled at her, appreciating the effort.

"The only things I got from pushing were hemorrhoids and stitches," said Lisa as she searched her bag for all its contents.

"I thought you had C-sections?" Allison asked.

"Yeah well, I still had to push Gomez off my gurney. Blubbering idiot."

Meagan felt a headache coming on and began to rub her temples.

"They are so self-absorbed. Who would want to go on a stupid babymoon anyway, all fat and unable to drink?"

"Yeah, but think how good the sex is when you're pregnant," said Allison. "I love those baby hormones."

Lisa walked up behind Meagan and rubbed the back of her neck. "Not me. You can bang me halfway around the world when I'm pregnant, and I'm not coming."

Meagan wanted to reprimand Lisa for being vulgar in the morning, but her headache was starting to subside and she didn't want Lisa to stop massaging her.

"Okay, throw down your calendars and cards bitches. I have to get to the office", Lisa said. "Is everyone going to back-to-school night tomorrow?"

"Frank is handling the elementary school, and I'm going up to the junior high," said Rose. She placed her Starbucks gift card in the middle of the table. "I feel terrible because I also missed the fourth-grade picnic and Frank had to take Dahlia to meet the new teacher."

"I missed it too, but why did they need to throw it in the middle of summer?" Allison tossed her card on top of Rose's. "Tom's getting in late tomorrow. Rose, can you ask Frank to take fourth-grade notes for me, please? It's so ridiculous they have all the grades on the same night. How do they expect us to be everywhere at once?"

"Most people only have one or two kids, so it's only a problem for you farm-animal-breeding types," said Lisa. She smiled at Allison and smacked her card on the table.

Rose and Allison pulled up their iPhone calendars while Lisa and Meagan went old-school and pulled out day planners.

Meagan glanced at Allison. "Good choice this month. That was fun."

"Nine times for me this month. Beat that!" Allison beamed. They had agreed upon three mandatory conditions for the club: One hundred percent sex once a week but try hard for twice, a weekly date night, and no spouses calling them "Mom" or "Mother." But the real fun was in their monthly challenges.

Rose laid her phone on the table, "seven."

"Oh, that's better than me. I only got to six this month," said Meagan. "Can we Zoom after back-to-school night, and you guys can fill me in on what to expect for eighth grade?"

Rose was always trying to make Meagan feel better about her relationship. "Yes, we can Zoom, and don't forget you get to double your score since your boyfriend lives so far away."

Meagan dropped her head. "I did double it."

Lisa gloated, holding her calendar high over her head. "I win, I win. Fifteen nights, bitches. I got my sorry, tired ass in lingerie fifteen times!"

Allison pushed the cards towards Lisa. "Well, technically you should only be able to count the nights you wore it and had sex because of it. There's no way I'm walking in the bedroom in lingerie and Tom isn't reading that as an invitation."

Lisa and her husband, Gomez, had come up with a schedule that worked for them both: sex every Wednesday night after her call with the girls and Saturday night. He was not to ask for it any other night, and she was never to refuse on those nights. Also on those nights, it was Gomez's job to make sure the kids were in bed or somehow too preoccupied to disturb their parents. Gomez was to pour Lisa a glass of wine and meet her in the bedroom. Once he had washed up, he was supposed to engage Lisa in what she called "reconnecting talk," but Gomez found this challenging. He could not understand why a woman he had been married to for over a decade needed to get to know him constantly.

On the first Thursday of each month, Lisa and Gomez checked into the Howard Johnson two towns over. Lisa loved these nights so much that she would go every Thursday night if possible. Gomez used his company discount making their indulgence affordable. Lisa packed them a picnic dinner and wine. She brought music, lingerie, and candles. Gomez was in charge of supplying a medicine bag filled with sex toys, in which Lisa of course approved. Only "No one gets hurt" toys were permitted, so his bag contained things that vibrated and tickled.

Lisa also made rules about the type of sex they had. She had already given him his thrill of a lifetime on their tenth wedding anniversary with anal sex, so he was not to ask for it again for another ten years. He was never allowed to ask for a threesome or try to live out any of his other ridiculous fantasies involving bondage. They agreed to porn if the woman was in charge and didn't look like a babysitter.

Hotel nights were the best: no worries about the kids walking in or hearing them, no bed sheets to clean, and the allure of doing something naughty. They would return home by 10pm and make sure homework was done and that the kids were in their beds. The children had come to think of Howard Johnson as an uncle they had never met but whom their parents liked very much.

Lisa leaned into the table and pulled the gift cards close to her as if they were thousands of dollars in poker chips. "Rules are rules. You didn't specify that you had to have sex, you just said wear lingerie. And Meagan, why aren't you going to back-to-school night? That's bullshit."

"I don't expect you to understand," said Meagan. "Wait, no one got the bonus points this month?"

The girls all looked around the table relieved they were not alone in not even trying to earn the three bonus points.

"That's the second month in a row no one has earned bonus credit," said Allison. "We need to step it up, ladies."

"Screw that. No way am I stripping unless it's a celebration or I need a new car," said Lisa.

Allison choked on her latte. "Yeah, right," she blurted. "Like you need Gomez's approval to get a new car."

Lisa shot her a dirty look. "What's your excuse? With all of Tom's traveling, you should have filmed him a striptease or facetimed him in his hotel room."

"Yeah, yeah, yeah," said Allison. "We should have made that challenge for June. Just didn't feel like stripping after eating and drinking all summer."

"You always look beautiful." Rose smiled at Allison. "Meagan, I'll take notes for you."

Meagan was avoiding back-to-school night because she didn't want to see Mikey's father just yet. Plus, if he thought parenting was so easy, let him handle it all.

"It's my turn to pick this month," said Rose, jiggling in her chair.

Lisa faked a big yawn and shoved a croissant in her mouth to keep from talking.

Rose leaned back, folded her hands on her lap, and grinned widely. "I was thinking we could do expressing verbal appreciation or making them a healthy lunch to take to work."

Lisa spit her croissant into a napkin. "Rose, the contests are supposed to help us put excitement into our marriages, not send women back in history fifty fucking years."

Rose replied, "A strong marriage is an exciting marriage. Men need to feel appreciated. It all goes together."

"Okay, June Cleaver. Can't you come up with something that makes our orgasms bigger, better, longer, and stronger?"

Lisa wasn't even sure Rose had orgasms. Sure, she may fake them, but Lisa didn't think she experienced them. Although Rose seemed eager to be in the club, she shared very few details about her sex life no matter how hard Lisa pried.

Allison glared at Lisa to stop and then smiled at Rose. "I think it sounds like a great idea."

"Second time this morning I want to throw up, but whatever. It's Rose's month."

"And the bonus challenge is to give him a pedicure."

"Okay, I just threw up in my mouth. Are you fucking kidding me? Someone get a knife. I want to see if she bleeds."

"To get all the points, you must give him a truly romantic pedicure, like Robert Redford washing Meryl Streep's hair in Out of Africa." Rose pulled back her shoulders and straightened up. "Buff his heels and massage his calves."

"I'm not even going to try to compete this month," Lisa protested.

Meagan was not having it. "I did your sixty-nine month, and you know my ADD makes it hard for me to focus on two different things at once."

"You loved the sixty-nine month. You won it! Still, I'm out this month."

"Lisa, that's not fair." Allison felt the need to defend Rose, since she knew that Rose would not defend herself. "Rose didn't reject your women-on-top month, and we all know she gets a terrible infection every time she's on top."

It was about the only thing Rose had ever shared about her sex life— and not willingly. Lisa had interrogated her one morning when she was popping cranberries like M&Ms and constantly running to the bathroom. Why Rose had seemed horrified mystified Lisa, since Meagan had recently come clean about a yeast infection. Meagan had been unconsciously rubbing her genitals against the edge of her chair during breakfast at Allison's. "I ate too much garlic and got terrific gas," she had said. "It irritated my skin and gave me an infection."

"You think your farts gave you a yeast infection?" Lisa asked.

"Why not? If our ozone layer is affected by cow gas, why can't human gas give you a yeast infection?"

"Maybe you need underwear with a little ventilation? Do they make those?" asked Allison.

"I know they make flatulence-deodorizing pads to neutralize odor." Rose raised her eyebrows looking around the table. "It's a terribly embarrassing condition for some. Frank's cousin Sophia suffered horribly from gas, and the guys had to ask her not to eat Mexican food or corn cabbage for lunch anymore. She loved corn cabbage. They thought it was funny, but she was mortified—not that I blame her. Luckily, she found these pads to stick in her panties that absorbed the smell, and she felt much more confident with her bodily functions."

Lisa's brain hurt trying to comprehend what Rose was saying, so she turned back to Meagan. "Why don't you chill on the garlic and stop wearing those granny panties that trap your farts? I thought I bought you thongs for your birthday last year."

"They gave me a yeast infection too. And garlic is your liver's best friend."

"Not when you eat it like candy. I bet you didn't change out of your yoga pants after class, and that's why you're defiled Allison's chair."

Allison looked at Meagan rocking back and forth on the edge of her kitchen chair and wondered how she would clean it. Meagan said nothing. It wasn't her fault she had a million things to do after and didn't have a chance to shower after class.

So last month Meagan itched, but this month she was determined to win. She was planning a promising challenge for her month, but maybe she could persuade Rose to use it now.

"Wait, Rose," she said. "Think about it. Allison, the big kiss ass, does the verbal stuff all the time. We have no chance."

Allison couldn't deny it. She knew she would win this month hands down. Plus, she found the bonus sweet and very doable. She believed strongly in being her husband's greatest cheerleader. This made Meagan and Lisa want to kick Allison in the shins and confused the fuck out of them. Allison was a beautiful, educated woman whom any man would be thrilled to have. So why did she need to kiss Tom's ass? She frequently ran out on the girls or ended a conversation abruptly to pick up the house and pretty herself up before Tom got home. Allison didn't see it as ass kissing. It was no big deal to tidy up the house and throw on a comfortable dress. Tom worked hard for her and the kids, and it was nice for him to come home to a clean house and a wife who wasn't always in a pair of Lululemons.

Allison had never forgotten a very important lesson she had learned as a high school babysitter. Throughout her sophomore and junior years, she had babysat for the Wright family. The father was gorgeous and successful and always smelled of Old Spice. The mother was loud, talked with food in her mouth, and smelled like horse manure from the endless hours she spent in the garden. Her face resembled a distant relative whom Allison had only met once, at her Uncle Pete's funeral. She had never forgotten his face: the bump descending his nose and the strange way his eyes sat together. Mrs. Wright could have been his twin. Allison went over most days after school to keep an eye on the kids while Mrs. Wright tended her perennials. When her husband came home, this woman dropped everything and greeted him as if he had been gone for a month. Allison's mom and dad seemed more like brother and sister than husband and wife and didn't seem to notice each other's comings and goings. Allison's girlfriends drooled over Mr. Wright whenever they tagged along, but Allison knew he only had eyes for Mrs. Wright. He always asked about her day and listened so contently. He kissed her all over her face before turning his attention to the children.

One day, while Allison was helping Mrs. Wright carry a bag of peat moss from the garage to the garden, Mrs. Wright asked Allison if she wanted to be married someday. Allison answered, "But of course." Then Mrs. Wright let her in on her little secret gem. "Always remain his number one fan no matter what. It's a big, tough world out there, and people can be mean. Make sure you make him feel important and he always feels accepted by you. Men are fragile. Be gentle with them." She bent down to look Allison straight in the eye, then stood up straight and gestured towards the array of flowers in full bloom. "Just like my garden, I give it love and show it respect. And look what it gives me in return." Allison looked out at the abundance of beauty and never forgot these words of wisdom.

Rose looked at Meagan, then at Allison, then back at Meagan. "You're right."

Meagan leaned over, whispered in Rose's ear, and then smirked at Lisa and Allison.

Rose straightened up, excited with her pick as if no one had noticed that Meagan had just given it to her. "This month's challenge is to make out with your husband or partner." She turned to Meagan. "For at least ten full seconds. Kissing while having sex doesn't count."

"Like, make out on the couch as if we were teenagers?" Allison asked.

"Yep."

"Mouth-open, tongue kind of making out?" Lisa asked.

"Yep."

Lisa sat back, folded her arms, and nodded her head. "Damn, that's good."

# Chardonnay: Rose

"Be a good fuck and know how to make a great rigatoni."

Their voices played over and over in Rose's head. She had been Mrs. Frank Garden, as the priest referred to her, for less than four hours when Frank's mother and his two aunts had led her into the bathroom with promises of reapplying her lipstick and running a comb through her hair. However, once inside, they had locked the bathroom door and circled her like a band of coyotes moving in on Bambi.

"You can cook a good rigatoni, right?" Frank's mother got so close Rose could practically taste the Martini & Rossi Vermouth she had dribbled down her neck.

"I can cook spaghetti."

"Ah, Mother of God!" Aunt Teresa's hands rose to the sky, begging for mercy as if the Virgin Mary herself were a rigatoni expert.

"No, a rigatoni. It has to be rigatoni." Frank's mother clenched her teeth.

Rose, pressed up against the sink, could feel the cold stone through her silk white dress. She studied their faces, expressions, and gestures with the same perplexity she always felt when they spoke to her. Frank's family was all fair-skinned and freckled, with small physiques. They were all gorgeous, with tiny noses and bright blue eyes. The luck of the Irish was written all over them—yet every one of them spoke with a thick Italian accent. They were loud and dramatic, using hand gestures to accompany every word. The women all dyed their hair black, and the men smelled heavily of Armani cologne and stale cappuccino. The women were called Teresa, Francesca, and Sophia. The men were Vinnie, Mario, and Frank. Rose highly doubted these were their given names and she swore the black fuzz under Aunt Teresa's nose was the working of a black Maybelline brow pencil. When she had asked Frank about his family's Italian fixation, he had seemed offended and acted defensive. Rose had never brought it up again.

Aunt Sophia leaned in trying to comprehend what she was hearing. "You do know how to fuck, yes?"

The desperation on her face left Rose feeling flushed. She would have passed out right then and there if she hadn't been terrified of them kicking her once she hit the ground. She had never heard these women utter a swear word. Maybe an "oh gosh," "shucks," or "darn it." These were committed, church-going ladies who played Bingo on Monday nights and took turns making lasagna for Father Anthony on Thursday nights. Their skin never felt the sun, they were so covered up all the time. But now this. Rose just froze.

Aunt Teresa put one hand against the wall behind Rose's head and twisted Rose's beautiful yellow curls. She spoke with agonizing patience through clenched teeth. "Honey, are you telling us you never cooked a rigatoni or stuffed a sausage, if you know what I mean?"

The realization took the Irish wind from behind their backs and blew it right at Rose. Each tried to speak faster and louder than the other. Their Italian accents grew thicker and thicker as their Irish complexions grew redder and redder.

"Make sure you're always clean down there."

"It's all in the sauce."

"No, the noodles. You got to get the noodles just right."

"Move your hips like you're doing the hula hoop. You did the hula hoop when you were young, right?"

"Give a little moan here and there."

"But don't act like you like it too much. He'll think you're a floozy."

"Don't add your noodles unless the water is boiling rapidly, got it?"

"A rapid boil."

"Always close the bathroom door when you do your business. No man needs to see that."

Rose was not only a virgin who had never cooked a rigatoni, she had never cooked much at all. From the outside, the grand English Tudor where she had grown up, sitting high on a hill, looked like the perfect home for a child. But looks can be deceiving. Her mother had suffered from clinical depression and had required full-time nursing. Rose's father had sent Rose to boarding school at a young age, and when she was home, Ana's mother had taken care of everything. Rose had a lonely childhood. If it hadn't been for Ana, she would have had no one to play with growing up.

Frank came from a big, Irish, Italian-acting family with sisters and brothers and cousins all over the house. He was the love of her life, the only love of her life. He had told her the first time they met that he would marry her one day. He had believed their names were fate and had vowed not only to plant her a rose garden but to make her Mrs. Rose Garden.

It had happened on a warm Friday night at the end of Rose's senior year of high school, when she was just seventeen. Her best friend Suzie Burns had recently gotten braces and had to wear headgear in the evenings. Suzie was terrified of being spotted by anyone she knew, so she had begged her brother to pick her and Rose up from the mall. Frank was home from college visiting Suzie's brother and tagged along to get the girls.

Rose's heart began to pound the moment they pulled up. Frank was a young John F. Kennedy look-alike and just as charming as good- looking. They sat up all night talking, but Rose would not kiss him or date him for years. Frank had never met someone as kind and sweet as Rose. She was intelligent and wise, accepted to Yale and Princeton, yet so innocent and naïve. Frank also had never met a girl as beautiful as Rose, with her china-blue eyes, long fawn-like lashes, and golden locks of hair tumbling all the way down her back. But somehow he could always see pain hiding behind her smile and he yearned to make her happy. He was determined to work hard and give her a beautiful life. He was determined to fulfill his promises.

Rose had been overwhelmed with joy to marry into a big family. Over the years, she had learned how to cook all of Frank's favorite meals and made damn sure her rigatoni was as good as his mother's—though she knew better than to say that out loud. She did her best in the bedroom, reading Cosmopolitan and watching late-night HBO shows. She even joined Lisa's secret club.

Frank made good on his promise to plant her a beautiful rose garden—well, paid for the gardeners to plant it. Twelve different types of roses in every color of the rainbow bloomed every spring. He situated the garden in the back corner of their five acres and brought in benches and umbrellas so Rose would have a quiet place to go just for herself. Frank took good care of Rose and the girls. Never, in a million years, did Rose imagine Frank would become so successful. Nor did Rose need any of the things their money could buy. She only wanted the one thing from him—the one thing he had trouble giving her.

Rose had never heard any mention of sex from Frank's mother and aunts again, but their voices haunted her now, fifteen years later, as the pain ran through her hips and down her legs. "Be a good fuck and know how to make a great rigatoni."

She could feel her eyes start to water. *I can do this, I can do this. Just breathe. Think about other things. Do I have any eggs for the morning? I think there are wet clothes in the washer I need to move to the dryer. OMG, I don't think I can do this.*

Frank grunted familiar sounds from behind her as he thrusted faster and faster. She knew he was close to finishing, if only she could stay on all four a few moments longer. Why had she quit yoga? She slipped a corner of the sheet into her mouth and bit down hard. The bed began to squeak as he rapidly picked up pace moving back and forth, another familiar sound alerting her that he was close to finishing. Dandelion came face to face with Rose, wondering what had awoken her from her peaceful slumber at the foot of the bed.

"Go lie down," Rose tried to say through the sheet. The pain in her hips began to burn. *I just can't do it any longer. I have to move.*

Dandelion stared up at Rose, tilting her head from side to side. Rose avoided eye contact with the dog. "Frank, Frank Honey, I have to roll over. My legs are hurting."

Frank slowed his body before stopping completely and gave her room to move.

Carefully and painfully, she brought her knees together before rolling onto her back. "I'm sorry," she said, reaching out to him and pulling him close. He reentered her, trying to regain his pace. Dandelion was not sure what to do with herself and began running around in circles. Rose tried to ignore the dog. She moved her hands up and down Frank's back and squeezed his ass. His rhythm quickened as he glided over her body. Still eager, Dandelion jumped on Frank's back and stood on his shoulders, looking down at Rose. Dandelion fought to keep her balance, going up and down like a kid on a seesaw. Staring at Rose, her eyes asked, "What are we doing?" Her wagging tail said, "Wheeee!"

Frank slipped out of her, and Rose could feel what was once hard now lying sticky and soft against her thigh. She didn't move or say anything. If it had been a Saturday night, she would have tried to revive him, but it was late Tuesday night. Much had changed since that night in the bathroom with his mother and aunts. Now she had five daughters sleeping down the hall, all of whom had class in the morning. She could feel Frank's body heavy against hers, his strong arms and solid legs, his soft middle revealing his excess of food and alcohol over the past year. He was right beside her but seemed a million miles away. Rose silently questioned herself, *What have I done wrong?*

Frank shook off the dog, lifted himself off of Rose, and headed to the bathroom. "Fucking dog."

Rose said nothing as she tried to calm Dandelion.

"I have to work late tomorrow. I'm meeting my brother to go over some issues we're having with the staff."

"What about back-to-school night?" Rose asked. "I thought you were going to Dahlia's school. Fourth grade is a big year, Frank."

"I didn't say I was going out with the boys, Rose, but whatever. I'll try."

# Chardonnay: The Club

Back-to-school night was as uneventful as always. Over at the junior high, Lisa and Gomez split up, taking detailed notes for one another, while Rose and Allison did their best to get to as many teachers for as many kids as possible. All they saw of one another was a quick wave in the hall and a "Talk to you later" as they tried to make the bell. Frank made it to fourth grade but missed first, which Rose said was perfectly okay. She would email the teacher. Tom's plane was delayed, so he got to miss it all.

Afterwards, the girls headed home, settled in their children, and prepared to Zoom. This included selecting a comfortable outfit, a spot to rest their feet with a laptop, and a glass of wine. They had struggled for months to figure out how to sign in without bumping each other off, until one day Rose had walked into Jasmine's room while she was Zooming with Emma and Mary Jane. The teenagers had happily taught their mothers everything they needed to know and giggled with one another about old people and technology.

They also came to their mother's rescue with their Wednesday night closing ritual. At first, the girls took turns taking each other's outdated iPods home and adding a song to the group playlist. The idea was not to check what song was added, then on Wednesday night before saying goodnight while feeling good from the wine, putting on their headphones and dancing together. It was a great mid-week diversion and a ton of fun anticipating what music each other selected. The teenagers made this much easier for their mothers when they showed them how to create a shared playlist on Spotify. They also introduced them to AirPods, making it easier for them to freely dance around.

The younger kids were always in bed before the Wednesday night 9:00 Zoom, but the teenagers were still doing homework. They loved Zoom night, when their mothers were preoccupied and they could sneak in an extra show or Zoom themselves.

"Rose, did you get a chance to talk to Frank about tonight? What did I miss?" Allison rested her feet on her desk and sipped her wine.

Rose was lying on her bed, wrapped in a big, fuzzy robe petting Dandelion, who had felt abandoned while Rose had been at school. "The usual fourth-grade stuff. Book reports, field trips, and math, lots of math."

"What about the teacher? Henry says she looks like a bug with bulgy eyes but seemed nice."

"Kids. Dahlia said she was mean and called her a vampire. Frank said he didn't remember much about her when I asked."

"Men."

Lisa joined the Zoom call.

"Are you in the tub?" Allison asked.

"As a matter of fact, I am. Everyone on?" Lisa was soaking in a bubble bath.

"Meagan is running late. Romeo is over, so she'll join as soon as he leaves. And Lisa, hold your tongue."

"The hell I will. That's not being a good friend. Plus, she should have been at back-to-school night. Did you see her ex? He was on his fricking phone the whole time tonight."

"Can you turn your computer to the wall?"

"What, you never saw tits before?" Lisa lifted her chest and shook her breasts in the camera. "Did either of you two see Penny Mathews tonight with her gray hair?"

"I saw her passing by in the hall and thought she looked very pretty," said Rose.

"Fuck that with her stupid gray hair. What point is she trying to make, like she's all natural and shit? I hate these women that get all high on their horses aging naturally."

Allison swirled the wine in her glass, watching light shine through the crystal. "Some women choose to age gracefully. I think it's pretty cool."

"I think it's painful to look at and they should spare us all by getting some Botox and hair dye."

Meagan Zoomed in with a glass of wine in her hand and a smile the size of Texas across her face.

Rose's throat constricted over the confrontation she felt coming. "Meagan, honey, you look so happy."

"Did Mr. Romeo go home to his wife?"

"Go to hell, Lisa. Are you in the tub?"

Rose finished half a glass of wine in one gulp. "I just love the books the eighth graders have to read this year. I think we should all read them and discuss them with the kids, do a little book club of our own."

Tom walked up behind Allison and started rubbing her shoulders.

"Is that Tom? Hi Tom." Megan closed up her robe.

Lisa made no effort to cover up. "Tom, Gomez wanted me to confirm your tennis match next week if he's still alive."

Tom moved in closer to the screen. "Are you going to come and watch us play? Allison will be there."

Lisa tapped her temple with her index finger. "Uh, yeah. Let me think about that one."

"Goodnight, ladies." Tom kissed Allison's neck and turned to leave the room.

"Tom, wait," Allison called out as she jumped up in her seat and pulled h and passionately kissing him to the count of ten. Tom walked away shaking his head.

"Bitch! And gross," Lisa said sliding herself down under the water.

Allison laughed. "What did Gomez do now?"

"Sometimes he can be more of a pain in my ass than a hemorrhoid in a pair of thong panties. He's so goddamn color blind he uses my toothbrush all the time. I said to him, 'Why would you use the pink one when the green one is lying right here?' And why does Tom make you watch him play sports? What does he think he's Danny and you're Sandy? Do you sing and dance when he hits a winner?"

"He doesn't make her. She loves it, like a big kiss ass. Remember, she's his head cheerleader," said Megan. "Wait, Lisa. You have a pink toothbrush?"

"Yeah, why?" Lisa said climbing out of the tub and throwing on a nightshirt.

"I see you more like a red or black kind of toothbrush girl."

"They make black toothbrushes?" Lisa asked.

"Sorry to end early, girls, but I'm going to join my husband. So let's get the dance party going. "

"Wait," Lisa said grabbing her phone and bringing up the Spotify app. "Don't look, I'm adding this one for Meagan."

Allison, Rose and Megan all placed earbuds in their ears while Lisa remained loyal to her huge Sony headphones. They adjusted their camera screen, got their phones out and pressed play without looking at which song Lisa had just added to the list. In unison they all called out, "Kelly." Meagan gave Lisa the finger and then danced along with the other girls singing along to Kelly Clarkson, "Walk Away".

# Latte: Lisa

Lisa had barely reached the bathroom door when she smelled the stink coming from the shower. How hard could it be to urinate in the toilet like other modern day human beings and then walk six feet to the shower? She busted her ass keeping the house clean, and her shower smelled like the L platform in Union Station.

She picked up her pace, determined to catch Gomez in the act of peeing, but was more shocked by what she actually found. "Are you fucking kidding me?"

Gomez Pavlov was a tall, lanky man. His features were very pronounced, making his Ukrainian-born parents proud. He came from a large family in which everyone had a strong Ukrainian name like Viktor or Alexander, but to his misfortune, he was named after the Portuguese taxi driver who had safely transported his mother to the hospital just in time to deliver all ten pounds of him in the hospital lobby.

"You can't make this shit up," Lisa had told the girls. "The circus was in town, and apparently some elephant or tiger got loose and was terrorizing people. Traffic was stopped, but this crazy taxi driver from Portugal named Gomez drove the side roads and made it there just in time. His mother credited him for saving their lives. So, Gomez Pavlov it is."

Gomez, oblivious to everything except the sensation of water running down his face, was standing under the water rubbing a bar of Ivory soap between his ass cheeks. He was startled at the sound of Lisa's voice and moved the soap from his ass to his hairy armpits and then back again to his ass crevice.

"What?" he asked.

"What? I use that soap to wash my face. It's like I'm washing my face with your asshole!"

"Your stuff is all on that side." He pointed to a shower shelf. "How would I know you wash your face with my soap?"

Despite all the face products on the market, Lisa had been brainwashed as a child to wash her face with Ivory soap. After school, she would find her mother sitting on the couch watching her soap operas while sipping a Tab and smoking a True-Blue cigarette. Lisa loved watching her mother's expressions as characters would come home early, catch their lovers in bed with someone else, and accidentally shoot them after a passionate dialogue. This always seemed to happen in the last minutes of a Friday episode, leaving her mother agonizing all weekend.

The commercial breaks often included Ivory Soap ads, starring the most beautiful women with the most perfect skin—and all because they washed every day and night with Ivory soap. All her mother had kept in the house was Ivory soap and Ivory Snow detergent. Lisa had smelled like Ivory as a baby, and in puberty, she had washed away her pimples with it. She continued using it to this day. Her mother also kept only Ivory Snow detergent in the house, which also signified the purity of its brand by hiring a wholesome, beautiful young woman as their spokesperson. Her mother had sworn by Ivory Snow until that saintly girl on the box had become better known as Marilyn Chambers, one of the greatest porn stars of her generation. That may have explained why Lisa had found an empty container of detergent under her brother's bed.

"Why can't you put the soap on your hands and then wash your ass and pits? Or here's an idea: try using a washcloth." Lisa palmed the steam off the mirror so she could get a look at herself. "You know you're putting your ass germs under your armpit?"

Lisa was obsessed with real-life crime stories. She watched every episode of Forensic File, Dateline, and First 48 Hours. So she knew that if scientific research were done, evidence of Gomez's asshole would be found on that bar of soap. That bar of soap that she practically massaged into her pores.

"You know, if someone ever killed me, they'd find your DNA lodged into my eyebrows and think you did it."

She knew Gomez would never kill her. He wouldn't know where to find the light switch without her. Plus, he was obsessed with her. She was his feisty, bossy, pint-sized ball of love. Gomez continued enjoying the sensations of the water, opening his mouth, catching it, and then spitting it out. He did this again and again, lost in thought, ignoring everything Lisa was saying. She watched him for a moment, envious of his ability to become so lost in fantasy. He was a million miles away from any work worries, kids' homework, or shower etiquette. He was probably thinking about his new John Deere lawn mower that he couldn't wait to use that weekend or bringing his new beer cooler with wheels to Sunday's tailgate party.

Lisa turned back to the mirror and admired her new short haircut. She had started graying in her early thirties but didn't mind. She loved the glossy black hair color her stylist concocted for her. It made her feel powerful and tall. She blamed Gomez for being so tall, making her look shorter than 5'2". She demanded he sit in a shorter chair at dinner so the kids wouldn't subconsciously think he was dominating her during discussion time.

She twisted to get a good look at her ass, which now sat lower, with cellulite creeping in. "Not bad for a mother of two. Not bad at all."

"What?"

"Nothing. Just hurry. Rose's goddamn dog stole my sunglasses yesterday, and I have to run over there before I go to the office. I think I have a buyer for that house on Woodford." Lisa lifted her nighty to get a better look at her ass. "And that shower smells like pee."

Gomez started doing a little dance, thinking about the girls' meeting yesterday. "Ahaha, ahaha."

"What?"

"Nothing," Gomez quickly replied. "Sorry about the pee."

Lisa picked his dirty laundry off the floor as she headed out of the room. "I'll make you some eggs. You want scrambled or sunny side up?"

She headed to the kitchen to make some breakfast and start dinner. Her home was quaint, but it was all that she, Gomez, and the kids needed. For years, they had rented a condo. Now both Mary Jane and Adam had their own rooms, and she finally had a walk-in closet—a small walk-in closet, but a walk-in nevertheless, with places to store shoes and handbags. Lisa loved shoes and handbags. She was the queen of finding deals at TJ Max and Marshalls. Not so with eBay— she never knew which ones were fakes. Sure, they all looked, felt, and smelled the same—they were all probably from the same leather. But the real ones came from fancy factories, while the fakes came from ordinary factories. She knew it was all bullshit, but she loved her shoes and purses, so she ignored the materialistic nature of it all.

She threw some chicken, potatoes, and carrots into the crock-pot and set it to low. Lisa loved her crock-pot so much she swore if she were an appliance she would marry it. She also loved her Keurig latte maker. She thought it was ridiculous how much the other girls spent on lattes every day. *Shit, Allison probably spends more at fricking Starbucks in a month than what I paid for my Keurig machine.*

Sure, she was obsessed with winning Starbucks gift cards from the club but that had everything to do with her competitive nature and nothing to do with the prize. She kept a stack of her winnings in a kitchen drawer beside pens, paper scraps, and an array of sticky notes. They came in handy for teacher's gifts or when she was forced to meet the girls at a Starbucks; hence why she didn't demand a change in the rewards.

She woke her sleepy, grumpy monsters for school and quickly finished her morning chores. She and Gomez split the household responsibilities pretty evenly since they both worked hard outside the house. It was his turn to carpool the kids, so Lisa got an early start on her day. She was heading out the door when she remembered Rose's challenge.

"Ugh, fucking Rose," she said to herself. She headed back up the stairs. She could hear Gomez whistling "Whistle While You Work" as she reentered the bathroom. He was still wearing his towel, picking gray hairs out of his chest. Gomez did this consciously and subconsciously all the time, in private and in public. Lisa found it amusing, since he was covered in gray hair in all the places he could not see. But she refused to sit next to him at the pool if he did not get a grip on it.

"Hey," she said. "Kiss me goodbye," She walked towards him.

"Did you dent the car again pulling out of the drive?"

"No, you fool. I just thought a kiss goodbye would be nice."

Lisa began counting to herself as she tried to be passionate in her kissing. One, one hundred, two, two hundred...

"Well, aren't we feisty this morning? Yaba dabba do."

Lisa marched out of the bathroom, cursing Rose.

As she drove over the mountain heading into town, Lisa thought back to this time last year. The kids had been starting a new school year, the leaves had been turning beautiful shades, and her sex life had been in the ICU. She had driven this same road a year ago thinking,

"How could I have let this happen? Even stranger and borderline scarier, how could Gomez?" It had been two, maybe almost three weeks since they had last had sex. She had prided herself never to let it go past seven days. She knew it was possible for a bad marriage to have a good sex life, but a good marriage could not have a bad sex life. Ask any therapist. When the sex goes, so does the marriage.

She recalled the night that had changed her life or, should she say, saved her life. Keisha, her college roommate, had invited her home for Thanksgiving. Lisa had been in her final year at Howard University, miles away from her Connecticut home. Lisa was happy to leave the dorm and looked forward to finally meeting Keisha's sister after hearing about her for years. Keisha always talked about how rich and wonderful her sister's husband was and bragged that her sister was the luckiest woman in the world. Lisa thought Keisha was secretly in love with her brother-in-law but never brought it up.

When Lisa had arrived at the house, she was surprised that Keisha had failed to mention her sister and husband were incredibly beautiful. Lisa now understood why Keisha thought her sister was the luckiest woman in the world. Lisa thought so too, until they all stayed up late one night drinking Tequila Sunrises and talking about sex. Keisha's sister had blurted out that she never orgasmed with her husband, who seemed uninterested in pleasing her, but she didn't care because he was kind and gave her nice things. At that moment, looking at her high cheekbones, flawless face, big diamond, and fancy clothes, Lisa thought she was one of the unluckiest women in the world. She promised herself that she would only be with a man who wanted to please her.

This was not just because an orgasm was one of the greatest things in the world and anyone who disagreed just never had a good one, but because at her young age she understood the importance of sharing yourself, allowing yourself to be that vulnerable with another human being. She only wanted to be with a man who felt the same way. She promised herself that night that she would always have a good sex life when she was married.

There was also one of life's most basic facts, of which she periodically reminded herself and her female friends. Men fuck, plain and simple. They need to fuck just like a dog needs to sniff shit and a cat needs to bury it. If men don't fuck, their whole rhythm gets thrown off. They start banging into stuff and buying junk they don't need, like a six- foot body pillow or a twelve pack of Fix-a-Flat. They start making bad business deals and bitch about stupid shit, like why someone keeps using their hairbrush or why you have to hit the curb every time you park the car. Then there's the risk that they'll respond like a child who lives in a house with no sugar, finds donuts next door, and blames their bad behavior on you for depriving them.

The other girls thought Lisa was preoccupied with the male sex drive, and maybe she was. But that was not her fault. At the ripe age of twelve, when all the girls in class had been learning about female development from Judy's Blume's *Are You There God? It's Me, Margaret*, she was reading *Then Again, Maybe I Won't*, Judy's Blume's book on boy development and puberty from the boy's perspective. Her mother had explained to her that the bookstore was out of the girl version, but maybe she would enjoy the boys. Really? She sat for hours under the old oak tree in her backyard, chewing her fingernail cuticles while learning all about male masturbation and obsessive sexual thoughts. Shit, her friends were reading about menstruation and blossoming breasts, and she was getting a firsthand peek into the desires and fears of all the boys in math class.

It had felt so empowering, as if she had a two-way mirror to their locker room. Her curiosity about the male sex drive had continued to grow when she started babysitting for the Boyle boys down the street. She could still remember the first time she changed baby Griffin and he popped a boner. A full-fledged, ninety-degree boner. The little fucker couldn't figure out how to place one foot in front of the other, requiring Lisa to carry him around everywhere, yet he could get his pecker in a full salute.

Lisa didn't want to think about other men or desire sex with anyone but Gomez—not because she was a prude or overly devoted, but because she had bought and owned her marriage. She and Gomez had signed up for it and invested in it. They shared kids, joint bank accounts, and dining room furniture. It was more about the principle that you take responsibility for the commitments you make. So since they were in it to the end, why not make the best of it? It was also because Gomez was the greatest guy ever. Six feet and four inches of total mush and love, always nervous as a virgin on her wedding night.

His anxieties were adorable, except for when they screwed up Lisa's plans. Just last month, they had taken the kids to Hershey Park. They had rented a car at the train station, not realizing it had new technology that shut off the car and started it again each time you stopped. Gomez had nearly shit himself thinking he had stalled out during a traffic light. He had made them turn around and get a new car, completely throwing off Lisa's time schedule.

Reflecting back to last year, Lisa was proud of herself for making changes—while keeping it fun and, most importantly, secretive. It wasn't easy finding other interesting and interested women in her boring-ass town, where everyone protected their private lives like a catcher behind the plate protecting his nuts. No wonder half the people she knew were divorced, and another quarter wished they were. Every time she brought up sex in her town, she felt a breeze as all the women slammed their knees shut. What, did they think their coochies were going to start talking if they didn't close their legs? She had been invited to a book club to giggle over *Fifty Shades of Grey*, but that had just stirred her up more. Not that she wasn't into a little soft porn and titillating literature. But sitting around with a bunch of middle-aged moms creaming their jeans discussing the provocative sex life of a child barely legal to drink was of little interest to her. What was even more disturbing was that besides being aroused, these women were just as—or more— envious of the young woman's romantic life. Lisa wanted her own sex life to be worth reading about. She wanted to find romance in her home, not in a book. She knew what she needed to do and how to keep it fun. Thank God for Allison and Meagan. Oh yeah, and Rose. Sweet, gullible Rose.

# Latte: The Club

Life moved fast as everyone settled into the school year. Two weeks flew by with the girls barely speaking to one another. They had been too busy for Wednesday night calls, so they planned a Friday morning meeting at Starbucks after drop-off.

Allison parked her car and headed in, smiling at the group of men who started every day by meeting at Starbucks. She could not recall a single morning she had not seen this posse. The members switched up sometimes, but there were always the core five, nodding their heads hello to her like good neighbors. She liked these men, even though she had never had a real conversation with them or any words beyond "Good morning" or "Hello. Nice day, isn't it?" They offered a sense of warmth, like the sound of coffee grinding and the smell of espresso percolating.

Starbucks was a treat for Meagan and a dread for Lisa, but it was an addiction for Allison. Her eyes were barely open in the mornings when she had her first thought: *When do I get my latte?* These men were part of her morning ritual, as was "Mr. Mustache" or, as Lisa called him, "Creepy Mr. Mustache." He was another Starbucks regular. Unlike the other men, he was always trying to strike up conversation with Allison. They nicknamed him "Mr. Mustache" because of the thick black mustache that matched the thick black mound of hair sitting on his head. Lisa nicknamed him "Mr. Creepy

Mustache" because she hated the way he stared at Allison like he was an MRI machine scanning for a subdural hematoma. Allison defended him, saying he was just lonely, but she had to admit to herself that he was getting a bit creepy. Just yesterday he had caught her off guard while she was standing in line and asked her if thong underwear were comfortable. She did not share this with the girls to prevent Lisa from going berserk on him.

"Wake up, Meagan," said Lisa, sipping her perfectly made pumpkin spice latte. "The man never spends the night and will never meet you in public. Plus, he loves sex games. Do you wonder why he wants to play dirty pervert sex games?"

"Because it's fun." Meagan reached over and took a sip of Lisa's drink.

"No, because he respects his wife too much to ask her to dress up like Tinkerbell so he can roll his Peter in fairy dust before penetrating her. You know, that's why you end up getting so many damn yeast infections."

"Lisa, you don't know what the hell you're talking about. He's not married. I'm positive. And how in the hell can you drink this shit? It's so sweet!" Meagan pushed the drink back at Lisa. "For your information, he lives with his mother and cares for her. He goes home to check on her."

"Oh God. I'm going to masturbate right here." Lisa buried her face in her hands, then looked back at Meagan. "Really? Really?"

"Girls, be nice. We haven't even finished our coffee yet," said Rose. "Meagan, what's this about fairy dust?"

"It's dust candy. They sell it at the sex store. I think they have an idea what people are going to do with it." She glared in Lisa's direction. "I just need to do a better job keeping my adventures private if they're going to be judged by you boring-ass married women."

Lisa reached in her purse and pulled out a handful of lipsticks. "She has a point."

"Meagan, we're not trying to be judgmental," said Allison, "and obviously we all support a fun, healthy sex life in a relationship. We love you and just want to see you with a great guy. I don't care what games you play. I care that he takes you to dinner and introduces you to his family. I care that he talks about a future with you because I know that is what you want and deserve."

Rose sat quietly, never taking her cup away from her lips as she watched Lisa unbutton her shirt and stick the lipsticks one by one inside her bra.

Meagan grew weary. "Oh, it's so easy for you to say, sitting there with your perfect skin and Jennifer Lopez body. You all have husbands and Allison, you don't work."

Allison took a deep breath and counted to three before responding. "I may not bring home a paycheck, but my hours never start or stop."

Lisa straightened up, buttoned her shirt, and nudged Rose to come alive. "Flower, the shit's about to get real."

Rose mouthed, "What were you doing?"

Lisa turned to Rose and spoke quietly, wanting to hear Meagan and Allison. "I was picking a lip shade. I read that matching your nipple color is best. Shh, I want to hear this."

"I know that," said Meagan to Allison. "But your life is so much easier having a husband."

Allison took another deep breath. She looked away from the table, then back at Meagan. "It used to bother me that my single friends and working-mother friends thought I sat home all day doing my nails and lunching with acquaintances. I no longer need anyone to understand how hard I work to make my family function. Yes, having a husband is wonderful, and I love Tom very much, but you have a freedom that married women don't have. You don't have to think of anyone but you and Mikey. Husbands come with dry cleaning, laundry, food needs, work stress, and checking in with your whereabouts. But more importantly, they come with emotional commitment, obligation, and expectations. You're getting a taste of it with Mikey's dad showing up, but you don't know what it's like to want to teach your child one value system, but their father has a different opinion so you have to compromise." Allison leaned back and shook her head. "My job is to make sure everyone is on track. I have to take responsibility for every homework assignment not turned in, every messy room not cleaned up, every sleepover that goes bad, because that is my job. And my husband works his balls off so I can stay home and do it, but damn if he doesn't expect me to have it done right."

"But Allison, Tom is so good to you." Meagan sounded confused.

Lisa thought it was time to jump in, plus she was getting bored just listening. "Being good to her has nothing to do with him not having expectations of her. The grass is not always greener, just different."

Allison, Meagan, and Rose all looked at each other and smirked.

"What?" Lisa asked.

No one replied, but they all knew what they were all thinking. *Is Gomez allowed to have expectations?*

"Tom is wonderful to me, and I wouldn't want to spend a day not married to him. But know that when you meet Mr. Right, he will have expectations of you, and you will equally have expectations of him. Good relationships take work, a lot of work."

Meagan fiddled with her purse, uncomfortable with the confrontation, and a pamphlet fell from her bag. Lisa bent over to grab it, but Meagan pushed her hand away and seized it. Lisa immediately knew it was something worth fighting for and snatched it from Meagan's hands, reading the cover out loud.

"Vagina rejuvenation. Are you fucking kidding me?"

Meagan snapped back. "Sorry, Lisa. We don't all have almond-shaped vaginas, or even pecans for that matter. Mine looks more like a walnut, and I may just do something about it."

"What are you talking about?" Rose was shaken by the hostility at the table.

43

Lisa looked at Rose, then back at Meagan. "It's basically a facelift for your vagina."

Allison reached for Meagan's hand. "Are you serious about doing this?"

"There are many options—tightening the inside for better sex, labia reduction and some people even get work done on the clitoris."

Lisa leaned forward and spoke through her teeth. "Getting my boobs done was one of the best things I've ever done, and I'll lift my face when it falls. I have no problem with plastic surgery. But you cutting your vagina for some jerk-off who won't even have you over for dinner is too much for me."

Meagan just looked down at her latte, saying nothing. Trying desperately to find peace, Rose looked to Meagan. "How is work, honey? The commute okay on the days you have to go into the office?"

"The commute is fine, it's the job killing me right now. You will never guess the book I have been assigned to edit."

The girls all gave her their attention, yet no one spoke.

"Helmets and Hoses! A fucking children's book!"

"That's rough, going from a New York Times bestselling spiritual book to a children's book," Lisa said shaking her head. "What did you do wrong?"

Meagan reached over to Rose's plate and took one of her egg bites that she knew Rose would never eat. "Yeah well, I think Cersei Lannister got pissed because I skipped her stupid luncheon bridal shower. It's her fourth marriage for fuck sake."

Perplexed, Rose looked over to Allison. Allison mouthed, "Her new boss."

"Oh, oh, and the best part, guess what it is about?" Meagan continued.

Rose smiled as if she just finished the last word on a Sunday New York Crossword puzzle, "Firemen!"

"No, CIRCUMCISIONS!"

Lisa spit scone from her mouth, "You are editing a book about little boy's dicks! Am I the only one that finds it interesting that Meagan wants to cut her own genitalia while editing a book about it?"

"OMG, Lisa!," Allison said. "What is wrong with you, they are children, they have penises, or wieners."

Feed up, Lisa replied. "Whatever, weenie, wiener, schlong, dong."

Meagan reached over putting her hand across Lisa's mouth. "It's to help little boys understand the difference. You know, so they don't torment each other in the locker room."

"Well, I think that sounds like an important book and I am glad you get to edit it," Rose said.

Lisa grabbed Meagan's hand away from her mouth trying to bit it. "Gomez has a hose. I love it. It's the way nature wanted it. What does Mark have? A Maserati dick?"

They left Starbucks with an unease in the air. The girls hated to confront Meagan, but they also hated seeing her constantly waiting around for Mark. Meagan knew they were right. It was getting harder and harder to believe that he would come around anytime soon. Allison also felt an unrest in herself. The conversation had pushed a button in her, and it was time for her to make some changes— not because she had to prove a point, but because it was time for her to do something for herself. She yearned to have a place in her life to be Allison, just Allison, and not someone's mom or wife.

# Latte: Meagan

Meagan headed home to switch into her work clothes, pissed as hell because she knew the girls were right. *It's been almost a week since I've heard from Mark and I'm binge eating my feelings. I haven't been awake for more than two hours and I've already eaten my calories for the day. I wish I could puke, but I can't step over that line between serial dieter and someone who needs intervention. I could do a coffee enema, but I just did one Monday. I promised myself I'd only do them once a month for cleansing reasons. Why hasn't he called? Maybe he wants to break up with me. I think I flipped him out showing up at his office with cookies. Maybe I shouldn't have brought up commitment the last time we spoke.*

She parked the car, walked into the house, and went straight to the bathroom to step on the scale. *144, ugh.* She walked back into the kitchen and grabbed her third banana of the day. *Why did I throw away all the Oreos? Maybe I should just call him, but I texted him twice Saturday night and he still hasn't gotten back to me. I know he said his sister was visiting, but why should that stop him from contacting me? Why am I not meeting her, maybe he's ashamed of me? Maybe his sister is all gorgeous and perfect and he doesn't want her to see him with some fat redhead.* She grabbed a spoon from the drawer and added a spoonful of peanut butter to her banana. *You're not fat, Meagan. Remember what they say in yoga class: no negative self-talk. You are beautiful. A beautiful, full-figured woman.*

She picked up her phone and dialed. Before she could hang up, he answered.

"Hi babe. I was just thinking about you."

"Oh, that's nice. I thought you forgot about me."

"Megs, I told you my sister was visiting. I have been busting my ass doing boring tourist stuff."

"I thought it might be nice if I had met her."

"I can't do this right now. I'm at work, and I have a client waiting."

"There is never a time to do this, to talk about us."

"Meagan, you knew from the start that I was not looking for anything serious. We both agreed that a casual relationship was all we wanted. You can't just change the rules mid-game."

"Just tell me one thing, Mark. Will you ever want more than just sex from me?"

"Meagan, it's not just sex. I enjoy your company. But I don't want a relationship right now in my life with anyone. It's not you. It's me. Maybe in time."

"Have a nice life, Mark."

She didn't even think twice about it. She just walked over to her computer, brought up Yelp, and searched for Mark's firm. She gave him one star and left a simple message: "Service sucks." Then she sat down on the edge of her bed and cried. She cried hard and loud. He had told her he was not looking for a relationship, but she had thought that would change once they were together for a while. *Why am I so lonely?* She ached to love and be loved. She ached for a relationship.

# Chardonnay: Lisa

Today started like all of Lisa's other Howard Johnson Thursdays: wake up, make a latte with her Keurig machine, get the kids off to school, and show as many houses as she could before afternoon carpooling. After that, do laundry and straighten up the house while yelling at Mary Jane and Adam to pick up their messes and do their homework. Grocery shop, prepare something easy to serve the kids for supper, and put together a nice picnic dinner for herself and Gomez. She would stop by the liquor store and grab some chardonnay on her way to the hotel. After rightfully earning her night out, Lisa hollered to the kids to be good, and she was out the door.

She nodded hello to the young man behind the Howard Johnson counter. She and Gomez had been coming to this Howard Johnson for years. Dougy, the young man working tonight, was one of Lisa's favorites because he always had a compliment for her.

"Good evening, Mrs. Smith. Mr. Smith is waiting for you. Oh, and may I say you look divine tonight?"

Lisa entered the room. Gomez was on a bed paging through *Landscaping for Dummies*. She always asked for a room with two beds so they could have sex in one and then switch to a clean one to watch TV and sober up before driving home.

"Hi. You're late. Everything good at home?"

"All good, just a busy day." She stopped in her tracks. "Can you come here to the door and kiss me hello?"

Gomez didn't question her. He was enjoying the kissing kick while it lasted. He walked over and kissed her passionately. "Hey, I'm pretty sure I saw your girlfriend Rose parked in her car out front. She was just sitting there. I started to walk over to her, but she drove off."

"You're seeing things." Lisa counted in her head while kissing him again. Gomez's medicine bag sat on the edge of the bed. "What goodies did you bring us tonight?"

Gomez had purchased a portable DVD player from Amazon, (they really do have everything on there, don't they?) and he had become an expert at ordering just the right movies off the internet for Lisa. There could be no violence, female submission, or actors who looked like they were under twenty-five. They had to be professionally shot, with enough story to be interesting but not so much that it slowed down the sex. Of course, considering this and the fact that the DVD industry was becoming almost obsolete, it immensely limited Gomez's choices, however he always seemed to find one or two that worked. He had the movies shipped to his friend Donald's auto garage since Lisa would not allow porn in the house. Donald was cool with this and appreciated the beer Gomez brought him when he stopped by to pick up the DVDs. Most movies had already been opened, but Donald claimed he was doing Gomez a favor so he could watch for anything that may upset Lisa, *wink, wink*. Gomez had stopped trying to convince Donald years ago that he did not have a mistress.

Gomez jumped on the sex bed and opened his magical bag. "Well, I have *Housewives' Heaven* and *Dinner for Five*."

"Um, sounds interesting."

"And I have some eco-friendly, long-lasting lubricant with a lavender scent that also just happens to be vegan." Gomez held up the tube as if he were showcasing it on *The Price Is Right*. "Did you know your vagina is the most absorbent part of your body?"

Lisa, now naked, flopped on the bed beside him. "No, I didn't. Tell me more, Masters and Johnson."

"Well." He reached into his bag and paused. "Because as we both know, the couple that bangs together hangs together."

"And the couple that fucks together is happily stuck together."

"Yes, and because the couple that screws together is glued together. And making my woman happy is my life goal ... I bought these!" Gomez lifted up two silicone cups connected to a small electronic device.

"What!? You want me to pump breast milk?" Lisa tilted her head from side to side.

"No, no. They're nipple stimulators. We hook it up to your nipples, and while I'm working on your kitty downtown, the stimulator works on your puppies uptown."

Lisa wanted to hurt Gomez for his choice of speech for her body parts. Instead she reached over, took the toy from his hands, and held the cups to her breasts. "I likey. I likey."

Lisa poured each of them a glass of wine and made a cheese plate while Gomez undressed and set up the Bose speaker. They laid a towel on the bed because Lisa refused to sit naked on the comforter. The bed was comfortable enough and the room pleasantly appealing, with light yellow walls and stock art. Gomez was used to the drill of talking before sex and knew that if he rubbed Lisa's back while talking, they usually got to the sex quicker.

After futile conversation and great lovemaking, they moved over to the television-watching bed and flipped on reruns of *The Big Bang Theory*. They left the hotel together in their separate cars, feeling content and connected.

# Chardonnay: Rose

Rose was not sure when the night had ended and the morning had begun. After a long day of cleaning out every closet in the house to get ready for a big Goodwill run, she ran over to Frank's office to try to squeeze in a kiss. She had thought it would be romantic and he would love her spontaneity, but when she had arrived, Frank had been heading to a meeting and couldn't take a break. This month's kissing challenge was definitely a challenge for her. The month was coming to an end, and she had three lousy points. However, she happily reminded herself that she had earned the bonus by giving Frank a wonderful pedicure after work last Monday night, which he completely appreciated. Lisa was foolish not to embrace that one.

After picking up the girls from school and making sure homework was done, Rose hosted dinner for Frank's older brother, Leo, and Leo's newest fling. She had also invited his parents and younger sister and brother, but they had declined. His mother had not spoken to her oldest son in ten months—since he walked out on his wife and two children. His younger siblings always declined weekday dinners, knowing Frank and Leo would turn the night into a business meeting. The two were in business together manufacturing a line of high-end camping gear. The conversation always became heated and was pretty boring for everyone besides Frank and Leo.

After cleaning up, Rose found her glass of wine and made her way to the bath. She was not sure if she had dozed off or if the heat had just put her in a fog, but she was aroused by Frank yelling from the bedroom. "Rose, when are you coming to bed?"

"I'll be right there."

Rose wrapped herself in a towel and went to the bed without even brushing her teeth or putting on her nightly face cream. Frank was sitting up in bed with his head down, rubbing his temples. Dandelion slept in her new crate with heated blankets.

"Baby, what's wrong?" Rose asked, closing Dandelion's crate door.

"You know what's wrong. You heard my brother. No matter what I do, it's never good enough for him. The more I do, the more he wants from me. We are a partnership, and he acts like he owns the company. I just hate it, Rose. I hate it."

"Shh, relax. Lie down and let me rub your back."

"And what about that woman he brought? I couldn't understand a word she said. Where was she from? China or France or somewhere?"

"She was from New Jersey. I thought she was very nice."

"Well, if she has a brain, she'll run from that bastard." Frank turned onto his stomach and rested his head against his pillow.

Rose reached over, letting her towel fall from her body. Goosebumps rose on her soft, ivory curves as her damp skin met the air. "Frank, relax." She moved in closer and let her erect breast lean against the side of his body as she dug her thumb deep into his shoulder blade. She dug deeper, moving her thumb in circular movements, knowing right where his tension spot was.

"He has no idea how hard running sales is. How hard can production be? You just make the shit. But I have to make sure it gets sold."

Moving closer, Rose wrapped her leg around his body, letting the warmth of her vagina press against his ass. Frank lifted his head from the pillow. "What if he's right? What if I'm a loser and the company folds because of low sales? Do you know how many families rely on me to get it right?"

"Frank, you're thinking too much. The company is doing great. You're doing great. You know your brother always says those things just to get you going. I think he's jealous of you because you've always been so handsome and good at everything you do."

"What are you saying? You don't think Leo is good looking? He had all the girls in school growing up. He's not jealous of me."

Rose continued rubbing his back until she felt him relax. She rubbed his shoulders, arms, and then down his back. The deeper she dug, the more he relaxed. Slowly, she moved her fingers to his hard ass, which tightened under her control. Staying there for a moment, she then lowered her mouth to the back of his neck, breathing heavily into his ear. She moved her hands down between his thighs, feeling his testicles against the backs of her hands. Reaching over, she opened the drawer beside the bed and retrieved the Comfortably Numb spray. She squirted two large pumps to the back of her throat and went back to massaging Frank's balls. Slowly she lowered her face to his body and smothered his genitals with the moist warmth of her mouth. As she stroked his ass and moved her mouth up and down, Frank hardened and whispered, "What would I ever do without you?"

He came quickly, surprising Rose with a mouthful of unwanted semen that she dutifully swallowed, holding her breath. Frank pulled her up close to him. Rose went to kiss him, but he turned his face and kissed her on the cheek, avoiding contact with his own bodily fluids. Rose turned her body and curled into his. He held her close as they drifted off to sleep.

It was around 3am when Rose was awakened by what sounded like a baby crying. Confused and dazed, she realized it was Blossom, their Persian cat, accidentally locked in the basement and crying for freedom. Rose wandered down the stairs and granted Blossom's wish. She had stumbled back towards the bedroom before noticing that all the hall lights were on. One of the girls must have woken in the night and turned them all on. She walked down the hall, switching off lights while peeking into bedrooms to make sure everyone was covered. Climbing back into bed, she was almost asleep when she heard Frank moaning. "What's wrong?"

"My head is killing me. I shouldn't have had that last glass of wine."

"Hold on. I'll go get you some Tylenol." Rose grabbed for her robe and headed towards the bathroom.

"Can you get the Motrin instead? I know we have some on the kitchen shelf."

Rose headed back downstairs to get the Motrin and some water, then tried hard to fall back asleep. She had no idea how long she had been sleeping or when Frank had left for work when she was awakened by loud sounds down the hall.

"Shut up, Jasmine. Just shut up," Violet screamed.

"Oh, what? You can't handle the truth," Jasmine fired back.

"You're just a bulimic bitch."

Rose ran down the hall, tying her robe closed and wiping at her eyes. "Girls, girls, stop."

Lily yelled from her room. "Jasmine won't let Violet wear her jeans because she said Violet's ass is too fat."

Rose flung open Jasmine's door to find Jasmine and Violet standing across from one another, bellowing like two tomcats in a barn fight. These encounters were happening way too often as the girls got older. "What's the goddamn problem NOW!?"

Surprised by their mother's outburst, both girls backed away from one another. Jasmine grabbed her pants out of Violet's hands and jumped up on her bed. "These are my favorite jeans and she's not wearing them. She'll stretch them out and they'll never fit me again."

"Shut the fuck up, Jasmine," Violet yelled.

"Violet, what is wrong with you?" said Rose. "You can't talk that way in this house and you know it."

"She told me last night if I put away all the clothes on her floor I could wear anything of hers I wanted to school today."

"I didn't mean my favorite jeans."

"Jasmine, did you say that? Did you tell her she could wear anything of yours?" Rose asked.

"Yes, but she knows I never mean my jeans."

"Jasmine's a puker. She throws up, Mom. I heard her the other night."

Rose looked at Violet. "Calm down. Your sister had a bug the other night and I knew about it."

"Okay, well then she's anorexic. Do you ever see her eat anything?"

"Violet, go to your room," Rose demanded.

"This isn't fair. She promised."

"You're such a jerk. Just wear them, fat ass." Jasmine hurled her jeans at her sister's face.

Violet let the pants fall to the ground and hollered back as she left the room. "I don't want to wear any of your stupid clothes. They probably all smell like puke anyway."

Rose shook her head. "Jasmine, how many times have I asked you not to mention your sister's weight? She's very sensitive about it."

"Well, maybe she shouldn't eat so much."

"Can't you find it in your heart to be more understanding of her? Seventh grade is so tough."

"And like eighth grade isn't?"

"Get dressed. We aren't going to be late for carpool for this."

Rose walked over to Violet's door and knocked.

"Go away."

"Sweetheart, ten minutes, okay?"

Lily stepped into the hall. "You need to punish Jasmine. She told me she would give me her leftover Maybelline if I cleaned the cat box and she never did."

"Lily, you are too young to wear makeup, and I have told you before if you do your sister's chores, that is your problem. Learn to negotiate better."

When they had been little, having the three girls back to back had been a wonderful thing. They had played together all the time and rarely fought. But once the hormones had kicked in, it had become a never-ending drama-rama. Thank God the other two girls were spaced further apart.

Rose went to Dahlia and Daisy's room to see if they had slept through the morning chaos as Lily continued yelling at her. "Of course your perfect Jasmine can't do anything wrong. You favor her and you know it. And when are you going to stop treating me like I'm a baby? I'm in sixth grade. I wear a bra, Mother."

Rose ignored Lily's tantrum as she covered her sleeping angels with the blankets they had kicked off during the night. She loved how they wrapped their little legs together as they slept. She knew one day soon this would end. Dahlia was three years older than Daisy. Although she was a young soul, Dahlia's preteen years were upon them. For now, the two loved to be together, play together, and sleep together. Even though there were two twin beds in the room and every night Rose tucked them into their own beds, come morning she would find them together. Nine out of ten times it was Daisy in Dahlia's bed, since Dahlia's bed was next to the window and the girls liked to look up into the sky and wish on stars before falling asleep. They were convinced it was their wishing that had brought a local snowstorm and closed down the district for a week. Rose loved that they believed they had that much power—until their grandpa had experienced a fender bender on the icy roads and the girls had cried all night, thinking it was their fault.

Before Rose could return to her room, the beeping began. "Come on. We're going to be late."

Rose looked outside and saw Lisa sticking halfway out her window.

*Honk.* "Rose, let's go."

Rose ran down the steps, yelling back at the girls. "Let's go. Now!"

Jasmine and Lily came running down the stairs.

"Where's Violet?" asked Rose.

"She's not coming."

"What do you mean, she's not coming?"

*Honk.* Rose knew the phone would be next.

*Ring, ring.* Rose picked up the phone. "We're hurrying. I'm sorry."

"This is Mrs. Marcus, and I'm warning you that this is the last time, or I will call the authorities and report you. It is 7:30 in the morning, my husband is a retired police officer, and he deserves to sleep as late as he needs. You know how many lives he has protected and saved in this town. The mayor would be very upset to know he is bothered so much."

"I know, Mrs. Marcus. You have told me many times. I'm so very sorry. I will talk to my friend, I promise."

Call waiting buzzed in. "Thank you, Mrs. Marcus. Thank your husband for his service. Goodbye." *Click.* "Lisa, please. My neighbor is going to report me if you beep the horn one more time."

"I don't give a shit about your cranky-ass neighbor. I have a carload of kids and they can't be late because your girls are dilly-dallying. Where's Violet? Is she coming?"

"Just go without her. I'll take her myself."

"Suit yourself." And Lisa drove off in her SUV towards the junior high school.

Rose walked down the hall towards Violet's room. Daisy called out to her. "Is it morning?"

"No, honey. Go back to sleep for a bit."

Rose knocked on Violet's door, but she did not answer. "Violet. Violet, I'm coming in."

Rose opened the door and found Violet lying on her bed with the covers pulled over her head. Her body shook with soft sobs.

"Violet."

"GO AWAY."

"Violet, sweetheart, what's the matter?" Rose climbed onto the bed next to Violet and held her through the blankets. Violet cried even harder. Rose just held her until Violet spoke.

"Why are Jasmine and Lily so perfect and I'm fat and ugly?"

Rose's heart broke. "Violet, my beautiful girl, you are not fat or ugly. You are perfect just the way you are."

"That's what you say, Mom, but that's not what the other kids at school say. I heard a group of kids yesterday talking. They're in Jasmine's class and the one boy asked if I was part of the bouquet. You know they call us that at school, right, Mom? The bouquet. One of the girls said 'Yeah, but that sister is the weed,' and then another boy said I was the bud that had not blossomed. They all laughed and then the boy yelled out 'Hey, weed!'".

Violet removed the blankets from her head, buried her face in her mother's chest, and sobbed and sobbed. Rose just let her cry and get it out. She knew that whatever she said, Violet would not believe her. The other girls were much thinner than Violet and all had their mother's thick, golden hair, petite facial features, and beautiful blue eyes. Violet seemed to have the features of a distant relative, features that made for a very handsome man but were less flattering for a female. Yet Violet was beautiful in her own way. She had thick, wavy chocolate caramel hair that fell all the way down her back, saucer- round chestnut eyes with long lashes, and a freckle-covered face that made you smile every time you saw her. She was smart as a whip and had the best sense of humor. In fact, until this moment, Rose had always thought Violet had the confidence of a queen and could rule the world.

"Hey, you know what?" said Rose. "If anyone ever thinks you're a weed, dandelions are a weed, it's only because dandelions are the most special flower in the world. People blow on them to make wishes, which gives them hope and reasons to believe in their dreams. That's you, Violet. You are so very special. Always, since you were a baby girl, you gave people hope just by smiling. You have to believe me, baby, you are a very special flower, my flower."

After about a ten-minute good cry, Violet closed her eyes and fell back asleep. Rose slid from her grip and tiptoed down the hall. Her heart lay heavy in her chest as she thought about how hard junior high must be for Violet. She regretted her decision to have the girls so close in age, and for the first time in her life, she wished she had named them anything but flower names. *Why does the world have to be so tough? Why can't we all just be kind to one another?* Tears ran down Rose's face, partly from exhaustion and partly from sadness. She looked in at Dahlia and Daisy, who were still sleeping peacefully, wrapped in each other's arms. She walked over to the blinds and pulled them down to darken the room, then walked back to her bedroom, took off her robe, and climbed back into bed.

# Latte: Allison

He was a beautiful young man with slicked back dark hair framing his chiseled face and muscles so defined they flexed with each movement. She sat quietly on the lifeguard chair high above him, watching his every move. She wore a tiny crocheted white bikini. He wore nothing but a small cloth covering the gift God had blessed him with. His stride was deliberate as the ocean's tide fought him back. She parted her legs ever so slightly, enticing him to come closer. As he approached, she saw he was carrying a white, medium-sized paper coffee cup with a picture of a green, two-tailed mermaid on the front. Froth spilled over the sides and steam rose into the morning air as he lifted the cup towards her. She jumped down onto the sand, her body trembling as their fingers intertwined around the warm, moist cup. Their eyes met. As he placed his mouth on hers, the sound of a child's voice alarmed him—and he was gone.

"Mom! Mom!"

She felt a pang of desperation as she frantically scanned the beach in search of him and her latte, but he had disappeared into the morning sun.

"Mom! Mom!"

She woke suddenly. Her daughter Julia was shaking her. "Mom! Mom! I'm going to miss the bus again. And there's no milk and Boots brought a mouse into the house and Higgins is trying to get it."

Julia ran out of the bedroom, down the stairs, and out the front door. The cat, carrying a dead rodent in his mouth, ran into Allison's room and took refuge under the bed. The dog was right behind him, barking furiously. Allison held her breath and leaned over the side of the bed to get a good look at the cat who periodically brought her gifts. "Thank you, Boots." Half-awake, she sat up, covering her ears as the sound of crunching of rodent bones filled her room. On her nightstand, front and center, was a white, medium-sized cup with a green, two-tailed mermaid. Along the side in blue pen it read, "Good morning, my Mona Lisa." Tom called her his Mona Lisa when he was feeling especially loving. It was their thing, begun back when they were dating. She remembered that day well, lying on the hot sandy beach on the Cape with not a worry in the world, except whether to use SPF 5 or no sunscreen at all. They had their whole lives in front of them. Those were the days when she could slam a cheeseburger and fries while sucking back a Sam Adams and her stomach would remain flat as a board. She had never thought twice about it then, but now she wondered where all that good stuff had gone. Now on the few mornings she woke up with that same flat belly, the mere thought of food would bloat her.

But on that day, Allison had soaked up the sun, content as a baby after a good nursing, while Tom had doodled on the inside of a cardboard six pack holder, surprising Allison with a portrait of herself. The striking resemblance had taken Allison's breath away. Tom had drawn her often over the years, nicknaming her his Mona Lisa. She called him her Pablo even though she knew it was DaVinci who had painted the Mona Lisa. She had framed that first piece of cardboard and stowed the rest of his drawings in her vanity drawer. Of course, once adult life had taken over with careers and babies dominating their time, there was less time for drawings—but there was always time for nicknames. He had a few for her: Raquel because he thought of her to be just as sexy as Miss Welch, Florence because she and Carol Brady were the best homemakers ever, and Pavarotti because of her obsession with the opera. Tom loathed the opera, but she forced him to accompany her at least twice a year.

This morning he had gone to Starbucks for his Mona Lisa before heading to the office. It was his way of saying thank you. He had had trouble sleeping the night before. No problem falling asleep, but then waking up in the middle of the night with worries about his company's merger with a major competitor. Tom was very well respected at the biotech company where he was in charge of research and development. However, once the merger took place, he knew heads would roll. Allison tried to assure him that they would be fine no matter what happened, but Tom was a mess about it. He was the sole breadwinner in the family and felt an enormous responsibility to provide for his family. Allison had felt him stirring, so she had gotten up and given him a full body massage as she reassured him everything would be alright.

It was becoming a weekly occurrence. Of course his vulnerability and gratitude, combined with her massage expertise, led to passionate sex for the both of them. Allison cherished the lovemaking but she often struggled to fall asleep after a good orgasm. On the other hand, Tom was always out like a light after, leaving Allison wide awake to listen to him snore. Things were always pretty good between them, and sometimes things were great. Presently she felt like things were great, and she credited Rose for it. The kissing was really helping. The intimacy was awkward at first but then became comfortable and wonderful. She made a point of greeting Tom every day at the door when he came home from work. The kids hated the display of affection, but she didn't care. She knew she was owning this month's challenge and it was good for the kids to see their parents happy together, and the bonus was a no-brainer. She already gave Tom pedicures about every other month.

She took the latte in her hand, still warm enough to enjoy, and smiled, thinking he really should get her some jewelry. When they were young she had massaged him many times in the middle of the night, but now her energy levels were declining. She also remembered receiving flowers at work after most of those evenings, and now she got a latte. But she and Tom both knew that for Allison, waking up to a bedside latte was better than any flowers or jewelry.

Allison grabbed the silk cream teddy lying next to her and tried to cover up as she crawled out of bed, sore from yesterday's yoga class. She motioned to the dog to get out and shut the cat inside to prevent getting mouse guts all over the house.

Walking down the hall, she hoped to find all beds empty except Henry's. Henry was a sweet child, the youngest and only one who had yet to reach the obnoxious ages of preteen or teenager. In her day, teenagers had been unappreciative and self-indulged, but nowadays that behavior seemed to start at much earlier ages. Henry was nine years old but an emotionally young nine-year-old. His head was covered in thick golden brown curls, and his big honey brown eyes lit up a room. He never got tired of being held or covered in kisses and loved to sleep in his parents' bed whenever they would permit it— which was quite often. The other children continually complained that Allison babied him and that he was her favorite. She ignored them. She appreciated that all the children were different and needed to be raised differently. Henry needed a little more time growing up. He was a very sensitive child and worried way too much for a child so young. Plus, why wouldn't he be the favorite? The other children moaned and groaned, constantly asking for things, and the only thing Henry ever asked was, "Mommy, are you okay?"

She walked past Henry's room to check that the other children had left for school on time. Normally she would have been up helping everyone out the door, but she must have hit her snooze button one too many times. Hopefully, Tom had roused them when he had come back with her latte. She had set a goal for herself that the kids would never be tardy this school year and here it was still only September.

When she reached Emma's room she was pleased to find it empty, but not so pleased to find it such a mess. She turned to leave, then did a double take at the poster of the Jonas Brothers taped above Emma's bed. She shamefully acknowledged that the one in the middle must have snuck into her subconscious the night before when she was saying goodnight to Emma—and into her dream.

She poked her head into Tommy's room to find it also empty. Although covered in sports paraphernalia and dirty uniforms, it was pretty much cleaned up. She already knew Julia had made the bus, so she headed back to Henry's room.

"Sweetheart, wake up. The Sandman drank all the milk again but if we hurry, we can make it to the gas station and grab some breakfast."

Twenty minutes later, Henry had inhaled his Egg and Sausage Hot Pocket and ran through the school doors just as the bell rang. Allison caught a glimpse of her tired face in the rearview mirror and decided to drive to the Starbucks across town for a little caffeine top-off.

In the bittersweet reality of a small town, you know the Starbucks' regulars, and the barista is making your drink as soon as you arrive so you actually still enjoy popping in and ordering in person most often. However, on a morning like this, you just want to remain anonymous, order on the app, and quickly grab your latte already waiting for you on the "mobile-order only table". Clearly, today was not Allison's day. The app wasn't loading no matter how many times she hit refresh. She even turned her phone off and back on in sheer desperation, but no such luck.

Allison hustled in, happy to see only one woman ahead of her, which was strange for this hour. Lost in thought, it took her a moment to realize this woman was going nowhere quickly. "Well, are the pastries made fresh every day? I'll have a medium-sized drink, but I want it not so hot, so it doesn't burn me."

Allison wanted to die. First, everyone knows there is no such thing as a medium drink at Starbucks. You order a tall, grande, or venti. But everyone also knows the morning protocol. You go up to the counter, nod hello as you place your already-thought-out order and scan your app for those reward points, then you quickly move aside for the next poor soul. There is no talk of syrups or flavors or sizes, milk fat percentages or temperatures, foam or no foam, number of shots, pumps of this or adding that. If you aren't using the app, at least know your drink when you reach the counter, have your money ready, and move on. If you need a Starbucks' education, come back after 2:30pm when the high school kids crowd the place ordering Unicorn Frappuccinos, or whatever God awful drink is the latest trend.

Twenty minutes later, Allison was deep in thought while contently drinking her tall nonfat latte, driving down a tree-lined road and listening to Norah Jones. Her phone disturbed her, and the voice coming out of the speaker disturbed her more. Lisa.

"WTF? Where are you? I called you twice."

Lisa was the meanest, most devoted, wonderful friend anyone could ask for. It wasn't so much that Lisa was cruel as that she had zero filter. No thought ever stayed in her head for more than a split second, as if her brain entirely missed that check-engine-before-proceeding part. Sometimes her brutal honesty was refreshing, but sometimes it was outright hurtful. When confronted on the issue, Lisa had protested that if everyone spoke their truth as she did, she would be the nicest one of the bunch. Allison accepted that Lisa may have some competition, but she completely disagreed that Lisa would be the nicest one of the bunch.

"I'm having a tough morning. Nick Jonas ran away with my latte and I already had to clean up rodent guts." Of course, she left out the part where Tom had left a latte by her bed. Lisa would just call her spoiled and have no appreciation for how tired Allison had been after playing Jennifer Love Hewitt in *The Client List* at 3am.

She continued. "Save your two cents, but I'm heading over to the wax salon and applying for part-time work. Do you want to meet for coffee before I go home and try to get my face on?"

"You go, girl," said Lisa. "I'll meet, but only if we go to Dunkin' Donuts." Lisa was turning out of her neighborhood. The driver in front of her rolled down the window and threw out what was left of a McDonald's breakfast. "Are you fucking kidding me?"

"What? I already told Rose I would be at Starbucks. She's upset about her girls fighting."

"Yeah, she was rattled yesterday when I stopped by for carpool. You don't see that much. Hey, do you think if we cut off her head we would find wires like those Stepford wives? This making-out shit is killing me, and don't get me going on the pedicure."

"But Gomez loves it, right?"

"I don't care if he loves it. It gives him all the wrong ideas about me. Do you know he asked me to cut his toenails for him after I gave him that stupid pedicure? I told him bend over and cut your own goddamn toenails."

"Trimming toenails is kind of a big part of a pedicure. I don't think you're going to qualify for bonus points."

Lisa wasn't listening. She was fixated on the littering driver ahead of her. She drove up and collected the paper cups and egg sandwich wrappings lying in the middle of the road—obviously breakfast for two—and shoved it all in the paper bag also tossed out the window. *Probably kids on their way to the high school,* she thought as she followed closely behind the car. "I may be a few minutes late."

The blue sedan took a sharp right down a winding roadway before the high school turn, and Lisa saw two adults sitting in the front seats. Determined, she followed them across town and then across another town without losing sight of the car once. She had numerous pet peeves, but littering topped her list.

Finally, the little blue sedan turned into the driveway of a modest home that ironically had a huge American flag draped across the garage door. She waited for the middle-aged man and woman to get out of their car and approach the front door before exiting her car holding the bag of garbage.

"You left this back on the road," she said, walking across the lawn and spilling the trash smack in the middle of the front yard. The man and woman just stared, not knowing how to react. "Love your flag, real patriotic of you." She pointed towards the garage while standing over their garbage. "Thanks for keeping America beautiful." She wasn't sure if the couple was embarrassed or afraid, but they ran into the house, saying nothing. Lisa got back in her car and headed to Starbucks.

* * *

Allison, Rose, and Meagan were enjoying a quiet chat when Lisa entered Starbucks shouting on the phone. "She died. Yes, it is sad, very. She killed herself last month."

Lisa pulled out her chair and smiled at the girls as she continued her phone call. "Yeah, these Microsoft assholes wouldn't stop calling her about a computer virus, so she did herself in. Asshole!"

She clicked off her phone and started right in. "Okay, I'm going to talk about Kegels, but no one do one."

Rose, Allison, and Meagan all stared at Lisa, desperately trying not to squeeze their insides.

"You can't do it, can you? If I say 'Kegels,' you want to squeeze."

"Who invited her?" asked Allison.

Rose fiddled with the bakery bag in front of her. "I'm not doing it."

"Well, you should be! Kegel, Kegel, Kegel! We all need to be doing Kegels starting today. Fifty in the AM and fifty in the PM. I read an article in bed last night about women whose vaginas fall right out onto the floor."

"You're so full of shit," said Meagan.

"Okay, so I'm exaggerating. They don't hit the floor. But their vaginas did fall. I swear. It kind of looked like they had penises."

"And Kegels will keep our lady bits intact?" Meagan asked.

"First of all, Kegels are great for sex, so we should have included them as a permanent condition in the contract. But besides making your twat tighter for him and better orgasms for you, yes, they help keep your body parts right where they belong."

Lisa looked over at Rose. "Well, not so sure about our pretty flower. Five buds shooting out the Rose garden gate would have anyone peeing every time they sneezed."

"For your information, Lisa, I do Kegels regularly, so I'm not worried about anything falling out of me any time soon."

Allison eyed Lisa. "Didn't your so-called 'garden gate' get plenty of visitors in your college days, widening the entrance way?"

"Sweet Pea, newsflash: my sexual experimentation before settling down did not expand my vagina walls. It opened my mind to free thinking. However, you pushing four big heads out of your crotch versus me having two C-sections may be why you wear a feminine pad between your legs when you jog and I wear a thong."

Allison laughed. She had known it would come back to haunt her when she told the girls she peed herself when jumping on the kid's trampoline.

"Say what you want Lisa, but I wouldn't give up those vaginal births for the world. When I hear about women wanting to have C-sections so they don't stretch their crotch, I think it's the saddest thing ever. I'd ask for giving birth every Christmas if I could. I know that might sound crazy, but it's better than any pair of Jimmy Choo's or your freaking Prada bags. Only other time life gets that emotionally raw is at a funeral. Life and death."

Meagan apparently thought this was a perfect time to pitch her love for her squatty potty. "Any added strain to your vagina wall can cause internal problems, and that's why you should all be using a squatty potty."

Lisa covered her face with her hands. "Oh no. Here she goes again with the squatty potty."

Allison let out a laugh and lightly punched Lisa. Mr. Mustache walked by, smiling straight at Allison. "What brings you beautifully fine women here today?"

Lisa spoke before anyone could even open their mouths. "Well, it must be the fine gentlemen lining the place up and down. Obviously, the coffee. You do realize it's morning and we are at a coffee house drinking coffee, not sucking back shots at the tavern?"

Rose touched Lisa's arm. "So nice to see you. Enjoy your day."

Mr. Mustache cocked his head and glared at Lisa. "Good day, ladies." He walked away.

Allison spoke first. "Lisa, can you go a little easier on the guy? He's just trying to be nice."

"The hell with that! He gives me the creeps. And do you see the way he looks at you, Allison? I bet he has a few wet socks with your name on them lying on the floor by his bed."

A woman Meagan knew from yoga class walked by and said hello in an English accent. "Will I see you at class Saturday?"

"Yes, hopefully. Have a good day."

Lisa stared at her. "Why do you do that?"

"Do what?"

"Talk back to people with accents with an accent."

"I do that?"

"Yes." Lisa reached down into her oversized handbag. "I almost forgot. I bought us all something…"

Allison glanced at Rose and spoke before Lisa could finish her sentence. "Hey, you know how the girls all went to Jamie Hill's birthday party last Friday night?"

"Yeah." Lisa pulled four racerback T-shirts out of her bag and placed them on her lap.

"Well, Jasmine and Emma said Mary Jane was going in the closet with different boys. I guess they were playing seven minutes in heaven or something."

Every muscle in Lisa's body tensed. "I know my daughter, and it sounds like pure gossip to me." She stared at Allison and then Rose. She held up one of the T-shirts. It read, "*Life Is What Happens between the Latte and Chardonnay.*"

"Lisa, we didn't mean to upset you," said Rose. "We just thought maybe you would want to talk to Mary Jane."

"I need to get to the office. There's one here for each of you." Lisa rose from her chair and tossed the shirts in the middle of the table. She looked at Rose and repeated, "I know my daughter."

# Latte: Allison

A couple hours later, Allison did something she had not done in almost twenty years, she filled out an employment application. She handed it over to the child posing as an adult behind the counter. "Should I talk to the manager?" Allison asked.

"I'm the manager."

"Oh, I'm sorry. You just look so young."

"Yeah, I get that a lot. I guess it's all the good face products I use."

As the girl studied Allison's application, Allison studied her. She had six earrings in one ear and what looked like nine in the other. At least half her body was covered in tattoos, but Allison could not make out the pictures without staring.

The girl looked up from the application. "So you did waxing in college? About when was that?"

"Oh, it was a while ago. I'm sure things have changed. But I'm a quick learner and a hard worker."

The girl looked back at the application. "They tell a story." "Excuse me?"

"You're looking at my tattoos. They tell a story my grandmother wrote for me."

Allison felt embarrassed but at the same time very intrigued. "Can you show me?"

"Sure."

The girl placed Allison's application on the counter and removed her shirt in two seconds flat. She wore a tiny black lace bra no bigger than an AA cup, and her body was fully covered in ink. She spoke as if she were Michelangelo showing you the Sistine Chapel for the first time. Allison was blown away. She had never seen anything like it. It was a complete underwater world in a hundred shades of blue and green—sharks, mermaids, dolphins, and other ocean fish.

"My grandmother saved my life. Without her, I would be nothing. My parents were both druggies and she took me in, made sure I had a chance in life. She wrote me this poem." She turned around to display her back. There were more deep-sea scenes and a poem inked in black cursive down her spine. It was titled, "For You, I Wish the Sea."

Allison read the lines out loud so the young girl could hear them again. When she reached the end, the girl turned back around and pointed out which pictures went with each verse.

"And this one here," she said, pointing to a dolphin swimming through a wave on her right shoulder, "is because she always told me the world was mine and I could swim around it if I always remember to be kind and smart. Dolphins are kind and smart. I think whales are too." She pointed to a figure just beside her ocean landscape. "You need to look close at this one to get it."

Allison reached out without even realizing it and touched the face of the beautiful woman before her. She pulled back. "I'm sorry."

"No problem. You can touch."

The woman's eyes were startling, deep purple in color with an intensity that pierced straight through you. Her features were soft, her expression strong, a teardrop falling down the side of her face. She wore a bright red blouse cut down the middle, showing off her cleavage. In one hand, she held a bloody brick, and in the other she held a cross. Tattooed below her were the words "Mercy for All."

"My dad wasn't right from all the drugs. One time he came to visit me and wanted to take me away with him. I don't remember much, but my grandmother walked in on us and didn't like the way he was being with me. So she went around back and got a brick."

Allison stood frozen, unsure what to say.

The young girl continued. "Yeah, Nana gave it to him good. He didn't die or anything. Nana cried for days. We never saw my dad again after that."

"Your grandmother must be so proud of you."

"Yeah, she's proud alright." She pulled her shirt back over her head. "Enough about me. You seem pretty smart, like a quick learner and a nice lady. We can use someone around here on Mondays and Wednesdays to help. Those are our busy days when we run specials."

"Perfect."

"Be here Wednesday by 9:30? We open at 10. And by the way, I'm Elizabeth, but you can call me Izzy."

"Okay, Izzy. Thank you. I will see you tomorrow."

# Chardonnay: Allison

Allison lay in bed, unable to fall asleep. She was anxious about returning to work even if it was at a wax salon. And being pissed at Tom didn't help. Lisa had come into the house earlier to say hello when she was dropping off Emma after the girls' soccer practice.

"Anyone home?"

"In the kitchen."

"Wow. Do you always make such a mess cooking?"

"I'm making beef stew sauce from scratch."

"Looks like you're creating a crime scene." Lisa walked over to the counter, noticing a puddle on the floor by the back door. "Someone peed."

Ignoring her and the puddle, Allison added flour to the concoction on the stove.

Tom came flying in the door. "Hey Lisa. Babe, I'm late for tennis. I need white socks."

"Look in the basket at the top of the stairs."

Tom ran out of the room and up the stairs. Lisa walked over to Allison's pot and stuck in her finger for a taste.

"Allison!" Tom yelled from the top of the stairs. "There are no white socks in my drawer!"

"Tom," said Allison—but before she could finish her sentence he was flying through the kitchen.

"God damnit, I'm late," he snapped. "I'm wearing dirty socks." He slammed the back door.

"Asshole," Allison said loudly enough for Lisa to hear.

"Oh boy, I'm out of here. I have a family to feed."

Allison was humiliated that Tom would flip about clean socks but also that he had spoken to her like that in front of Lisa, of all people. She turned off the stove, headed up the stairs to the bucket of clean wash, and spilled it on the floor. There must have been fifteen pairs of white socks, which explained why there weren't any in his drawer. But she had told him to look in the basket. *How hard can that be?* After pairing the socks together, Allison carried them in her arms to their bedroom. She arranged the socks on the bed in a big heart shape, took the jar of Vaseline from the bathroom, and placed it smack in the center of the sock heart before heading downstairs to finish cooking her beef stew.

Tom came home and was delighted to see all his socks washed and folded. He thanked Allison, only making things worse.

"No problem, Honey," she had said, walking out of the bedroom. "Oh, and Tom, I left you the Vaseline to help you remove whatever is stuck in your ass."

He laughed, and the night proceeded like every other night. But now lying in bed, she felt uneasy. She had felt uneasy for a week, ever since watching the movie *Beaches* on Netflix. She had talked to Rose about it, but she didn't think Rose understood.

"Rose, do you remember the scene from *Beaches* when the pretty, dark-haired lady, the one who gets sick, do you remember her sitting in the kitchen in her robe and her husband buzzes through the kitchen on his way to work and asks her what her plans are for the day?"

"Yeah, kind of. It's been awhile."

"She tells him she's going to buy a screwdriver, and he asks why. She says, 'Because we don't have one.'" Allison paused. "I don't ever want to be that woman."

# Latte: Allison

The morning alarm seemed to ring more loudly than usual, but maybe everything sounds louder when you get up an hour earlier than you're used to.

Allison was showered and dressed before the kids woke. She went to the kitchen to start breakfast and was pleasantly surprised to see a Starbucks cup on the counter with a card resting against it. "Good luck on your first day of work. I love you, Tom."

Glancing at the clock, she decided the kids could do without eggs and bacon and get just as many vitamins out of a bowl of cereal if she threw some berries on top. With Higgins trailing behind her, she took her latte into the living room to sit in the quiet of the morning and sip her drink, feeling both grateful and silly. What was she trying to prove going to work now? Was it a mistake?

Outside the window, glorious colors were taking over the landscape. An empty bird's nest sat on a branch near the window. Allison contemplated the intricate creativity and dedication behind the mother bird's work in constructing this warm haven for her babies.

A robin flew up and perched herself close to the nest. Allison didn't know if the nest belonged to her or not but spoke to her anyway. "What about you? Do you get sick of sitting all day waiting for someone to need you?"

She could see Boots sitting on the front porch with a gift for her, a disgusting ritual she and the cat shared. Allison had come to respect the process and appreciated that she was the only one she knew without a rodent control service. Boots would bring her something he caught, Allison would say thank you, and within the next few hours she would find the remains. Boots always left the head, heart, and liver. *It's odd he would eat the tail and skin but skip the liver. Then again, I did get a C in Biology when we had to dissect the frog. Maybe it isn't the liver.*

Allison waited another ten minutes, then hollered up to the children. Julia and Tommy were the first ones in the kitchen.

"Where are you going? Why are you wearing makeup?" Tommy asked.

"What, I can't wear makeup?"

"No really, Mom. Why are you wearing so much makeup and dressed like...?" Julia grabbed the Cheerios box out of her brother's hand.

"Dressed like what?"

"Like you want to be Emma."

Emma came into the kitchen with music blaring out of her earbuds and went to the refrigerator. Allison walked up behind her and took the earbuds out of her ears. "Good morning, honey. Did you sleep okay?"

Emma turned around. "Wait, is that my shirt? Mom, you're stretching it out."

"No, this is not your shirt. I have owned this top for years. What's wrong with you kids? You act like you've never seen me in anything but sweatpants and a ponytail."

"You're a mom. That's what you're supposed to look like," said Julia.

"Whatever. Just eat."

"You just said 'whatever.' When I say that I get yelled at."

"Whatever."

Allison got the big kids off and then drove Henry to school. Driving back, she took a deep breath, preparing herself to belt along with Whitney Houston's "I Will Always Love You." The phone rang, cutting off the song, and Lisa's voice came over the speaker. "Can you hear me?"

"I can hear you."

"Wait. Rose, Meagan, are you on? We're trying to do a conference call."

"I'm here," said Rose.

"Me too."

"We called to say good luck today. Are you nervous?" Rose asked.

"Please. I'm going to wax eyebrows, not perform surgery."

"Oh, you're going to be waxing more than that." Lisa smirked.

"What?"

"Oh nothing, nothing at all."

"Ignore her." Meagan cut off Lisa from adding to Allison's first-day-on-the-job jitters. "We want to hear all about it. Are we all on for our Wednesday call?"

The girls all confirmed the evening's call and went on their ways.

Allison rechecked her hair and makeup in the rearview mirror and headed to the salon. She was surprised by the butterflies in her stomach. Upon entering the brick building with WAX IT AWAY in three-foot lettering on the front, Allison was greeted by a young man.

"Hey, you must be the new lady. Izzy said you were cooler than you look."

Allison suspected he was a handsome young man under all the piercings covering his face. His arms were covered with tattoos of crosses in every imaginable crucifix size, style, and color. Smack in the middle was a half-dressed woman. *Real nice, Jesus and a piece of ass.* But it was the holes in his ears that really threw Allison for a loop. She just couldn't help but ask. "Can you tell me about your ears?"

"Haha, that's funny. Izzy said you were all interested in her tattoos. These are my gauges. The ones I have in now are four-millimeter gauges. I'm working up to ten millimeters."

"Forgive me. I'm not being judgmental, just curious. But what about when you're older? Will you have these big holes in your head?"

"No man, it doesn't work like that. You gotta go slow, changing gauges only about once a month. If you do it that way, your ears go back to the way they were in about three months."

"You can actually stretch your ear out like that and it will return to normal?"

"Yeah, but my friend Charles, he got impatient. He skipped gauge sizes and changed them real fast. His ears were nasty after that and he needed surgery to fix them. Charles is stupid like that."

Izzy walked into the room looking like a beautiful young woman working in the accessories department at Saks Fifth Avenue. Her light pink blouse puffed at the shoulders and hugged her neck, giving her a Victorian look. Her black skirt hung straight to the ground. Her hair was pulled high in a bun, and she wore a little makeup and small pearl earrings. All of a sudden Allison felt ridiculous about the faded jeans and tie-dyed T-shirt she was wearing with two-and-a-half-inch hoop earrings.

"Oh, I'm sorry. I didn't know how to dress?"

"That's okay. But we dress pretty nice around here. I was doing inventory yesterday—that's why I was dressed down. I should have told you. We have a pretty fancy clientele here and we keep things nice. I'll give you something to throw over your outfit for today."

Izzy reached into the front closet and pulled out a full-length white jacket that looked like a surgeon's. "You're going to shadow Margie. She'll show you how we do things around here since things may have changed since you last waxed. Also, my brows are in need of a cleanup. I'll have you do them at the end of the day so I can see how you work. I should have asked you yesterday, but I got preoccupied."

Allison didn't know what to say and suddenly would have given anything to be at a school bake sale or helping out with a fourth grade science class.

"Babe, what time are you finished?" asked the young man.

"Allison, this is Andrew, my boyfriend."

"Yes, we spoke. But nice to meet you formally, Andrew."

"Yeah, likewise."

"Get out of here before a client comes in. Be back around six-ish. Or actually, I'll text you when I'm through."

"Tight," he responded, and out the door he went.

"You can help yourself to some coffee. Margie will be here any minute. I'll be in the office in the back catching up."

Allison looked over at the Mr. Maker coffee pot, half filled with thick black coffee with grains floating on the top. As much as she could use the boost, she wasn't feeling it for the pot sitting in front of her. Meagan told her repeatedly that she was foolish spending so much money at Starbucks and that the coffee Meagan made at home was much better than anything Allison could buy but Allison had her doubts.

The clock read 9:45. Allison sat on the sofa by the front door and leafed through the *Better Homes and Gardens* magazine she happily discovered on the table. It was a sweet waiting area with an array of items for sale: some sexy underwear, facial products, books with beauty tips, and cell phone cases. *Why cell phone cases?* she wondered.

Moments later, Allison heard a disturbance outside. It was hard to hear what was being said, but she could see an elderly woman engaged in conversation with two teenage girls holding cigarettes in their hands. Allison watched as the girls trailed behind the woman to a garbage can and threw in their cigarette packs. The older woman never stopped ranting at them as they scurried away, yelling something back at her. The elderly woman strode toward the salon and came in the door.

"Douche-bag kids they raise these days." She hung her coat in the front closet.

Izzy yelled out from the back. "Please, not already."

The woman turned toward Allison, "What do you need, honey? Eyebrows, mustache, a little help with your chin?"

"No, no, I'm Allison. I'm working here now."

"Yeah, I should have known better with you dressed like Madame Curie. What's wrong? You going through a divorce? Catch your old man dining on someone else's muffin?"

"Well, no. I just wanted a little something to do away from the home."

"Oh, you're going through that stage. What, you got a big birthday coming up? You going to be forty, fifty?"

"Nana, leave her alone for God's sake. Please just show her around. You're late, and we have a customer due any minute."

The woman looked at Allison. "'Mumble, mumble' is all I hear. That one has a mouth on her, but I like it. I taught her well never to take shit from no one, not even me. What did you say your name was, Dolly?"

Allison smiled and again said, "Allison."

"What? You have to speak up. I'm partly hard of hearing in this ear and can't hear at all with this one."

"Allison," said Allison more loudly.

"Oh, that won't work. I have an older sister named Allison. I haven't talked to her in years, ever since she played my ex-husband's skin flute. Rat bastard, he was. I'm going to call you Dolly. That's okay with you, Dolly?"

"Uh, sure. Why not? And I call you...?"

"My name is Margie, but you can call me Nana. Everyone around here calls me Nana, even the customers."

"Okay, well, nice to meet you, Nana." Allison reached out her hand to shake Nana's.

Nana was the smallest, biggest human being Allison had ever met, a cartoon character with lines in every direction on her face and short, curly gray hair. She could not have been an inch over four feet tall, with bright, cherry red lipstick and drawn-on eyebrows. She wore an emerald green, crushed velvet dress that looked like it was from the twenties and black, laced military boots. Once she had finished looking Allison up and down, she opened the top desk drawer, pulled out a rhinestone-studded tiara, and placed it on her own head.

"Okay Dolly, let's get started. Every morning when you come in— and make sure you're on time. We don't need to hear about period cramps or kids throwing up. You be here on time and always check your schedule for the day, that way you know if you have the right wax for the jobs you have ahead of you. Some jobs need a hard wax, like when you're doing the inside of someone's nose or ears."

"People wax the inside of their nose?"

"Dolly, if it shows, it goes. Actually, even if it doesn't show, it goes."

Nana looked over the schedule. "Pretty easy day. What time you in til?"

"Two o'clock. I have carpool."

"I don't need to know your business, Dolly, just need to know how much I can teach you in a day. Let's see. We have two legs, three eyebrows, and a nipple. A nose, two shoulders, and a back..."

Allison felt relief. She could handle all of that no problem by herself if she had to.

"And two lip sweaters."

Allison had no idea what she meant by that but let it go. She also wasn't so sure about the back and shoulders but thought it might be a man. How odd was that? A man in a waxing salon. In her day, you wouldn't have caught a man ten feet from the place.

"When they come in, make sure you have them fill out this form. We need their name, phone number, and signature, but also have them fill out the bottom part. It asks if they've been using fake tanners or if they have sensitive skin. Oh, and watch the young ones. They need a parent with them if they're under eighteen. These young girls nowadays want to remove the hair as soon as they're old enough to grow it. Damn, when I was young, we paraded that shit around the locker room, acting all nonchalant like we were just changing but really, we wanted everyone to see our full mound. I had red hair and a bush full of red pubes. I didn't care they called me fire crotch. I was proud. But nowadays, they act like something's wrong with having hair. I say if God gave it to you, leave it alone."

Izzy walked into the room. "I see you're getting to know Nana. I was going to warn you, but sometimes it's best to experience her on your own."

Allison gave Izzy a half-smile.

"Nana, Mrs. Romano called and asked if we could squeeze in her daughter this morning. Do you remember the young girl with the hair growing under her belly button? They're good customers."

"Oh, the Happy Trail family. Yeah, sure."

"Happy trail?" Allison questioned.

"That's an inappropriate way to discuss the hair that grows from the belly button down towards the genitals. We don't get many in here, but this family seems to have it running in the family. They also have nipple hair that we sometimes wax. Avoid tweezers altogether when doing their nipples, okay?"

Allison was beginning to feel like she had walked into another world, and she was loving every minute of it. The freedom, the honesty, the acceptance. It was all so bizarre and wonderful at the same time. The day flew by with tremendous speed, and Allison felt like she was walking on cloud nine. She trailed behind Nana and watched her wax this and wax that. At first, Allison was nervous, but by the end of the day she was intrigued by how very different and similar everyone's hair and bodies were. They had two walk-in bikini waxes and one Brazilian, but Allison stood off to the side to provide privacy. She was

102:g!. 

much more interested in the words coming out of Nana's mouth while waxing than in seeing the uniqueness of each vagina.

"Out with the hairy and in with the scary."

"You want some paper strips to go with your new fortune cookie?"

"Looks like you got a Persian sitting there sugar, what you want, a Burmese or Sphynx?"

And each time a customer would walk out the door Nana would mutter, "Fool, paying to look like a bald turkey."

# Chardonnay: The Club

Allison pulled into her driveway after work to find a beautiful bouquet of yellow roses in the doorway. The note read, "I am so proud of you. Love, Rose." Allison was touched and a bit embarrassed—it wasn't rocket science. Nevertheless, she called Rose to thank her.

"Rose, that was so sweet of you."

"I'm serious, Allison. I know you don't think it's a big deal because it's only waxing, but it takes courage to return to the work force. How long have you been out of it?"

"Oh gosh, I haven't worked since I was pregnant with Emma fifteen years ago. And I had only been out of grad school for two years. So sadly, my expensive education was useless."

"Do you love it, working?"

"I do."

Allison knew Rose understood the anxiety of going back to work. They had both been educated women with plans for big careers when motherhood had changed everything. Of course, they recognized it was a pure luxury to stay home with their children, but sacrifice and consequences came along with that choice too. Allison recalled a time when she had called Tom's office to say "Good morning," and she had overheard an impatient female colleague say to him, "Hurry up and give her the credit card number so we can get back to this."

Rose understood that as silly as it seemed to be nervous about working at a waxing house, it was also both exciting and liberating.

The euphoria wore off quickly when the chaos of carpooling began. *Bring me here. Can we stop there? I need this by tomorrow. What's for dinner? You forgot to pack me this or sign that. Are my pants washed? Did you order what I asked? Can I go here this weekend? Why can she do that but I can't? It's not my turn. You know I hate to eat that. Why, why, why...?*

After she had shopped for dinner, cooked, served, and cleaned up, Allison spent some time with Henry on spelling words and tested Julia on converting fractions to percentages. She sorted through the mail, checked messages on her home phone and cell, and returned some emails, apologizing for overdue library books, signing up for conferences, and explaining why medical forms were late for soccer and swimming, again. But the challenge was always figuring out Saturday schedules. She and Tom would split duties and somehow watch Emma and Tommy's soccer games at two different fields miles apart, drive Julia to dance class, attend a two-hour doggy training class with Higgins, and take Henry to a birthday party— remembering to buy a birthday gift first.

It was just 9pm, but she was beat. She had just poured herself a glass of Rombauer and headed up the stairs to climb into bed when the phone rang. Lisa's voice shouted over the receiver.

"Where the fuck are you? Why aren't you signing in? I've been waiting all day to hear about your job."

"Ugh. Give me a minute." Allison found her laptop and joined the Zoom call.

"Tell us. Tell us."

"Damn, you look like shit."

"Thanks, and yes, I had more close encounters with vaginas today than I did at that nude spa Lisa dragged us to."

"Whoa, hostile," Lisa said. "Mary Jane's softball coach raved about that place. How was I supposed to know you would get hit on all morning?"

Allison shook her head at Lisa's excuse. "I was just observing today—and actually, there were only three crotch waxes. I watch for two days and then next week, I'm on my own."

"Did you see any—" Meagan began, but Lisa cut her off. "Meagan, Allison is tired, no more questions."

"Lisa, you're an ass," said Meagan.

"I'm confused," said Rose.

"Don't mind Meagan, Allison," said Lisa. "We are proud of you and happy you have completed your first full day of work."

"She works every day," said Rose.

"Oh no, I'm not getting into this now," said Allison. "I need to disconnect. I'm exhausted. I just got on to say goodnight."

Meagan quickly jumped back in. "Wait. We just got on."

"Yeah, I have to go mix up Gomez's color-coordinated sock drawer. I keep catching him washing his ass with my face soap."

"I use Vagasil to wash my face," said Meagan.

Rose was perplexed. "Isn't that for your vagina?"

"Hey, if it's sensitive enough for my tender skin below, it's sensitive enough for my face, plus it's cheaper than a lot of face washes."

Allison replied "Sorry. I love you all, but no dancing for me tonight. Wishing you all beautiful dreams."

# Chardonnay: Meagan

Meagan did not tell the girls she had broken up with Mark. She needed time. It was just all too much, having Mikey staying over at his father's and now this. She missed Mark and didn't trust herself not to call him. It was a Friday night and she needed to get out of the house, so she decided to go pick up some dinner at White Horse Tavern.

An hour later, she found herself sitting on a barstool drinking her second glass of chardonnay as she watched him move behind the bar. His hands were so big, his fingers so long, as he squeezed the juice from a lemon. His chest muscles flexed under his Harley Davidson T-shirt as he carried a case of beer from the cooler. She felt dizzy, like a seventh-grade girl watching the football team doing drill practice. How had the night even come to this? All she had wanted was a meatball sandwich to go, but when she had walked into the bar, it had seemed like he had been expecting her and waiting all night for her arrival. He had asked her to join him, explaining he had an hour break and would love the company. He had chosen a table in the back, away from the light and noise. Her meatball sandwich had turned into a four-course meal of bacon-and-cream-cheese stuffed mushrooms, leek and potato soup, rosemary chicken, and pumpkin spice cheesecake. She had known his intentions were to take her home when he had held his wine glass over the candle flame and asked what her plans were for the evening. His espresso colored eyes, inquisitive and mysterious, held her gaze while the candlelight flickered. She was not offended. He did not make her feel cheap; he made her feel wanted and desired. She longed to feel his hands run down the sides of her waist, to feel his breath against her ear and feel his mouth caress her breast. She was not a girl who had sex on the first date, but tonight she was a woman, a woman in charge of her body, her future, her life. Now she sat at the end of the bar watching him finish his shift. Thoughts played loudly in her head as the wine warmed her body. *It's not like I just met the guy. I've been coming to this restaurant for the last five years, and I have spoken a hundred or more sentences to this man. I have watched him behind the bar smiling at customers, laughing and truly taking pride in his job as he stirred their drinks. I remember a woman puking all over his bar. He helped her find her friends to get her home safely. I have witnessed him break up fights between drunken assholes with the kindness of a mother separating her two sons, and I know his favorite football team. I know the way he smells, and I know that he rubs the skin beneath his nose when he's nervous. I want to have sex with him, so I'm doing it. He's kind and he bought me dinner.*

*Wait, would I still be having sex if he hadn't bought me dinner? Yes. Well, probably. But I don't feel obligated to have sex with him—I want to have sex. I'm dying to be held, to be touched, to be loved. I want to feel a man's arms around me. I want to feel sexy and vulnerable. And who knows? Maybe this could turn into something. Wait, shit, I haven't showered. What if I smell? Fuck, I haven't shaved either. Maybe I should leave. What does he want with me anyhow? Look how glorious he is. He could have anyone he wanted.*

Meagan looked around the bar and saw mostly men and a few women with dates. She headed to the bathroom and was discouraged to find a hand blower attached to the wall and about five sheets of one-ply toilet paper left on each roll. Although it was a three-stall bathroom, she locked the door. She took off her jeans and granny panties, which she tossed into her purse. Placing her hand over the sink drain, she concocted a vaginal wash using warm water, hand soap, and a splash of Nivea hand lotion she found in her purse. She splashed the mixture on the landing strip of pubic hair on her crotch. Then managing to foam up some good soapsuds, she washed between her legs, immediately feeling the burn. There was a knock at the door.

"Ouch, ouch. I'll be right out. Ouch."

She turned on the dryer and bent over, letting the hot air blow under her ass crack. She was impressed she could touch her toes. It felt good to stretch, and the warm air felt so good against her burning labia she forgot what she was doing until another knock on the door startled her.

"Sorry, sorry. Coming."

She threw on her jeans and looked back at the excess of soapy water under the sink. Walking out of the restroom, she glanced at the two irritated women waiting. "Be careful in there. Someone spilled something all over the floor."

As she reentered the bar, he signaled her to join him at the waitress station. She walked over, and before she could think, he put his hand on the small of her back, pulled her close, and kissed her with an open mouth. His lips were soft and wet. She felt the sting between her legs become a warm feeling that spread throughout her body.

"Do you want to get out of here?"

"Yes, I'd love to."

Holding hands, they walked across the parking lot and through an unkept field to his one-man apartment on top of Pete's Auto Shop. She ignored the voice in her head questioning her choice to be on the verge of fornicating with a grown man living above a car garage and remained focused on his soft touch. Once inside, things progressed quickly. He stopped her at the entrance and kissed her again, this time letting his lips wander down the sides of her neck and then back again to her lips. His hands moved over her jeans from her ass to the front zipper and back again.

"Come here." He led her to the couch. "Lean over."

She wasn't sure what he was asking but followed his direction and bent over the couch. He continued to caress her ass through her jeans, leaning his body against her. She ached for him to reach lower, unzip her pants, and touch her. Abruptly, he stopped and went into another room without saying a word. She waited a moment and then followed him.

He was lying on a bed in soft light, still and quiet. She walked over to the bed, turning off the lights, and lay next to him.

He spoke softly but clearly. "Touch me."

She placed her hand on his stomach and felt his muscles in her hand.

"Touch me," he said again. He took her hand and placed it on his jeans.

She took his direction and began to move her hand over his pants, feeling him hard beneath them. He moaned, reached over, and slipped his hand inside her pants, reaching to touch her pulsating flesh. His hand was soft and strong. For a moment she was in heaven as he stroked her, then plunged his fingers inside of her. Her back arched and toes curled, and then suddenly he took his hand out of her pants and pushed her hand off of him. He rubbed himself for a moment and then went still.

She was confused by what was happening. Had he gone soft? She stood up and slowly began to remove her clothes. She slowly lifted her shirt over her head and threw it to the floor. She reached back and unfastened her bra, letting it drop to the ground as she caressed her breast and pinched her nipples. She reached over him, letting her breast fall onto his face, and turned the light back on. His face was hard to read, but she continued with the show. Slowly, she unzipped her pants, reaching down inside for a moment before removing her jeans. Now completely naked, she moved her hips around and around, never taking her eyes off his. She knelt on the floor and ran her fingers slowly through her hair, lifting it from her shoulders. She spread her legs and let her hands slowly move down her body, caressing her breasts, circling her nipples, and stroking her stomach and hips before reaching down to the heat between her thighs. It felt so good, so erotic to finger herself under his watchful eyes. She let out a soft moan while slowly twirling her hips in a circle. He continued to lie quietly and watch every move she made. She got up from the floor and knelt over him, carefully unzipped his pants, and pulled them off. Slowly pulling his underwear down to his feet, she saw he had gone limp. She placed her mouth over his navel and slowly licked and kissed his body as she made her way down to take him into her mouth. She engulfed all of him and began to suck his cock softly while her hands massaged his balls. He remained flaccid. Determined, she moved her hand down to massage between his thighs. There she felt the sticky, wet come—he had ejaculated without her noticing. Every erotic nerve ending she had, once tingling, went numb. She was naked with a Mr. Softy in her mouth that she knew she had no chance of erecting.

*What the fuck! Wait until I tell the girls this one.*

# Latte: Meagan

After waking up hungover as shit, Meagan called an Uber to bring her to pick up her car that she had left at the tavern and then forced herself to go to yoga. As she drove from the bar to class, Christina Aguilera sang a sad song that made Meagan think about how much she missed Mikey. Then she started worrying that he might get hurt at his father's house. What if he died? What would she do? She imagined herself inconsolable at the funeral and the girls weeping with her. Real tears streamed down her face, making it difficult for her to see. She quickly shifted her stream of thoughts and safely drove to class.

As she walked into the yoga studio, she was relieved to see Jamie connecting her iPod to the studio speakers. Jamie taught a slow class, yet Meagan always left feeling refreshed and satisfied with the workout. Plus, she loved Jamie's music choices. Some of the stricter teachers played no music at all. Meagan understood yoga was supposed to be about mind, body, and spirit, but she was only there for her body. She searched the room for somewhere to place her mat, feeling angry with herself. *I can't believe what an idiot I am drinking so much wine on Friday night when I know I want to do class Saturday morning. Plus, think of all those calories I ate and drank for some jean-rubbing, prematurely ejaculating asshole.*

The room was pretty empty, suggesting she wasn't the only one who had indulged last night. She found a spot in the corner away from everyone and laid back on her mat. She had closed her eyes and was breathing deeply when an intense desire to go back to sleep came over her. *Maybe I should just leave. I could get out of here quickly and no one would notice. I'm doing it. Go, Meagan. Just roll up your mat and you can be back in the comfort of your bed in ten minutes.*

Meagan had quietly sat up and begun to roll up her mat when suddenly she was captured by the sight of a young woman walking in the door. She knew the woman was new to the studio because she was one of those people who you notice, who everyone notices. She was beautiful, strikingly beautiful. Statuesque with snow white, smooth skin and thick, long black hair which she had yet to pull back. Her eyes were so big, they took up half her face. Meagan could not tell if they were green or blue from the distance but saw they were a pale shade. The rest of her features were petite and perfectly placed, as if someone had painted them on her face. Her lips were full, but not too full. Meagan wondered what nationality she was. Russian? Italian? Maybe even Middle Eastern? There was something very exotic about her. She just may have been the most beautiful person Meagan had ever seen in person. *What is she doing here in this little town and taking a yoga class on a Saturday morning?* Meagan abandoned all plans to leave. She pretended she was just straightening out her mat and sat back onto it. As the woman came closer, Meagan figured she was probably in her late twenties or early thirties. She walked towards the corner and situated her mat right in front of Meagan's. Her tight yoga outfit showed off her amazing, bikini-ready body to go along with her face. *How does this happen to one person? Was she just born lucky as shit? I wonder if she is the happiest woman alive and has a hundred rich boyfriends. But wait, maybe she's miserable because she can only eat iceberg lettuce and drink tea that makes you poop. She's probably in town taking care of her dying mother who treated her like Cinderella her whole life. Or maybe she's a famous model from another country who's doing a photo shoot in town. They do that sometimes, bring models up from New York and photograph them in our woods.*

Class began and all was well until the teacher had them work through the pose of cat-cow. Cat-cow: down on all fours, rounding your back like a cat and then arching it like a cow. Any time a teacher led this stretch, Meagan purposely tried to lose the class rhythm because it felt too intimate, sticking out her ass in the face of the person behind her. Today she was good with only the wall behind her. She began the pose and *wham*, there it was, the Victoria's Secret ass sticking right in her face. *Oh My God. Every man I know would kill for the view I've got. Shit, look at that ass. Could it be more rounded? And the way she arches her back? I bet she's a high-priced stripper, one of those strippers who only works for one super-rich guy and travels the world.*

The teacher guided them through several more poses before finishing the class. Meagan was surprised by how sweaty she was and how much better she felt. She had rolled up her mat and was headed towards her shoes when she heard an unfamiliar voice behind her.

"Excuse me. Can you tell me where I can get a cup of tea around here? I'm new to the area and am still getting to know it."

Meagan turned around. The model was speaking to a group of women eager to grab their belongings and get out of there, so Meagan stepped in. "There's a coffee house right across the way— best lattes in town. I'm heading there now, if you'd like me to show you."

The woman smiled graciously and reached out her hand. "Jessica. Thank you."

*Of course, she's gracious, she's perfect. But, her voice is nothing special, kind of ordinary. I was expecting something deep and sexy or an intriguing accent.*

Meagan ordered a vanilla latte, while Jessica ordered an unsweetened green tea, making Meagan feel fat. She wanted to say she drank those all the time too but stopped herself. They made their way to a table in the back. Up close, Jessica was even more beautiful, with high cheekbones and dimples that lit up her face. Yet, she had a protruding mole on the side of her temple leaving Meagan to wonder why she had never had it removed. They shared idle information, more like the personal section of a new patient form at the doctor's office than the "About" section on Facebook. Meagan was floored to learn that Jessica had moved to town two months ago to teach fourth grade over at the elementary school. *Does she have any idea what she could have done with that face and body?*

"Oh my gosh! Two of my best friends have fourth graders—Henry O'Neil and Dahlia Garden."

Jessica paused for a moment and then replied. "Yes, yes. I have them both in class. Wonderful children. I met one of the dads but not the moms yet."

"I'll introduce you. You'll love them." Feeling more comfortable now, Meagan thought it was safe to get personal. "So, do you have a boyfriend?"

"I do. I actually do! I met him here. We've only been together for a short time obviously, but it feels like forever. Have you ever had that happen? When you meet someone and you know you were destined to be together?"

"Yeah," Meagan lied. *I can't believe I have lived in this town for ten years and can't find a decent man anywhere, and she's been here for two months and found her soulmate.* "How did you meet?"

"I met him this summer when I came to town to find housing. I was attracted to him the minute I saw him and could tell he was unhappy, but we didn't get together until I came back and started work."

"How wonderful and lucky for you to meet someone so quickly."

"Well, it's not that easy. He's in a bad situation, held hostage by the threats of some bitch who doesn't love him. She just wants his money." Jessica's expression changed, and for the first time she looked somewhat ordinary. She paused, looking down at the table and then back up at Meagan. "Can I tell you something and you won't think I'm crazy? Woman to woman?"

Meagan was totally intrigued just hearing the word "bitch" come out of Jessica's mouth, but now she was blown away. Two hours ago, she'd been hungover and wanting to go back to bed, and now she was sitting with Miss Universe about to get a girlfriend secret.

Jessica continued. "I manifested him. I know it sounds strange, but I one hundred percent manifested him and his love into my life. I was fed up with men and all their bullshit. I vowed to myself that if I took this job, I would find a great guy in the suburbs. I came across an online program called 'Manifest Love into Your Life in 28 Days.' I did everything the instructor suggested and wasn't even halfway through the program when I met him. I couldn't be happier—we couldn't be happier. I'm on a short-term lease, and we're already talking about living together once it's up."

"Shit, can I get that website address from you?"

# Chardonnay: The Club

That night Meagan was beyond excited to get into bed with a glass of wine and her laptop to explore the website. However, first she had a Zoom date with the girls. Rarely did they Zoom on a Saturday night, but Allison had sent out a text asking if anyone was game since Tom was meeting an old college buddy who was passing through town for dinner. It was a miserable, rainy night, and they all had the same idea to stay safe and sound at home.

There was no way Meagan could tell them about her love plan. Lisa would tear her apart, while Rose and Allison would tell her how wonderful she was and not to worry about Mr. Right. The girls were all online when Meagan joined in, and she could immediately tell it wasn't everyone's first chardonnay of the night that they were on. Rose giggled at everything, and Allison threw three F-bombs in the first five minutes. Then Lisa, wrapped in just a towel, started in. "Here's my thought. If your dick doesn't work, that's God's way of saying 'I don't want you spreading your seed any more. Your screwing allowance is used up.'"

"Yeah, I bet you won't be saying that when Gomez starts failing to launch," said Allison, filling up her glass for the third time.

"And what about women?" asked Rose. "We won't be fertile forever. Are we supposed to stop having intercourse?"

"Rose, for fuck sake, it's Saturday night. You can say screwing or banging!" Lisa said.

"Speaking of screwing, tomorrow is the end of the month," said Meagan, preoccupied. "Let's tally up now and just give Allison our cards when we see her because we all know the kiss ass won this month."

"True." Allison raised her fists to the sky. "Seventeen times for passionate make outs, and let me add that was only because Tom was traveling. Plus, of course, I got the simplest bonus ever. That puts me at twenty!"

Lisa choked, spitting wine back into her glass. "Those were the hardest bonus points ever! Anyway, I'm out."

Rose giggled. "Yeah, I'm out too."

Meagan had convinced Rose to pick making out, determined to win. Of course, at the time she had not known she would be breaking up with Mark. "I don't want to talk about it, but I broke up with Mark. But if I count Mr. Quickdraw, I get one for kissing in the bar."

No one said anything.

"Oh please, save the pity. I already have a new lover in mind, so watch out. And it's my turn to pick. I'm going full throttle ahead with dirty talk in bed as the challenge. And for the bonus, do something, anything, you have never done before, like having sex in an interesting place."

Rose shook her head. "Do you mean like our backsides?"

"No, Rose. She means like your ear or your nose." Lisa leaned towards the camera and stuck her knuckle up her nose.

Allison tried not to laugh. "Rose, honey, *interesting*, like the back of Frank's car or in your rose garden."

"Ohhhhh," Rose said looking so puzzled the other girls could not respond. "I don't think Frank would like it if I spoke dirty to him."

"Bullshit. They all love it," said Lisa. "I thought you Catholic girls had the Madonna-whore thing all worked out. You know, act all sweet and shit in public but then be a dirty girl in the bedroom."

Allison agreed with Lisa. "I think they do all love it. I just run out of things to say."

"Do you want me to google it?" Meagan asked.

Lisa leaned back in her chair as if getting ready to watch a great film.

"Sure, google it. Someone take notes."

"I will," Rose offered.

"I was kidding, Rose," said Lisa. "I think we'll remember when the time comes. Or when he comes. Get it?"

"Sometimes I think you're fifteen, Lisa. Okay, here's what it says." Meagan sat up straight and read the list of ideas to the girls. "Talking dirty to your partner increases sexual tension, making your relationship more passionate and fulfilling."

"What site are you on?" Allison asked.

"Bad Girl's Rule Book." She continued. "Holy shit. There's a video to learn how to give the best blowjob."

"Do you know they sell a spraying solution to numb your throat so you can give a better blowjob?" asked Allison.

"What the fuck? I bet not one married woman has ever bought that shit," said Lisa.

"Aren't we supposed to be committed to keeping the marriage exciting?" asked Rose not divulging any secrets.

"Tom is happier than a pig in shit with any blowjob."

"What makes you think pigs are happy in shit?" asked Meagan. "Pigs get a really bad deal."

"Keeping my marriage exciting is one thing. Choking on Gomez's wang is another. Get back to the dirty words."

Meagan skimmed through the site, concerned this may be a little too much for Rose. "Hold on. Let me see if I can come up with something else."

"Boring."

"Here are some tips from *Cosmo*. They suggest you whisper, moan, or scream any of these. 'I love the way you fill me up.' 'Put your mouth on my breast.' 'I want you.'"

"I'm dying over here of boredom." Lisa grabbed her iPhone and pulled up a different website. "This shit is by Jordan Gray, a relationship coach. He says, 'Before sex, say what you want. During sex, say what you like, and don't use too much profanity if that's a turnoff for your partner.' Well, what fun is that?"

"Just read!"

"Here are some ideas for beginners. Rose, listen up. 'Mmm… do you like that?' 'I'm getting so turned on/wet/hard.' 'Tell me what you like/if this is too hard/when you're about to come.' Here are some for intermediates. Ahem, Allison. 'I love sucking your cock so much.' 'Tell me how much you love it when I fuck you.' 'I want you to fuck me in front of the mirror.' 'You have such a perfect ass/cock.'" Lisa leaned toward the computer screen. "No one better be playing with themselves. All hands on deck. Let me see them."

Rose sat speechless while Allison contemplated. "If that's intermediate, I'm afraid to hear what's advanced."

Meagan felt restless, wanting to start her soulmate search. "I heard the sexiest thing a woman could ever say to a man was to let him know when she was coming. So Rose, when you feel an orgasm starting, just whisper in Frank's ear, 'I'm coming.' If he likes it, next time just say things that feel natural to you, like 'That feels so good! You make me so wet, I can feel you so hard inside of me.' It doesn't have to be super dirty to be sexy."

"Yeah, yeah, yeah," said Lisa. "But every guy loves to hear a woman say 'Fuck me' or something like 'Fuck me harder. Fuck me like that in the morning,' just like they all like their asshole rubbed. Why hasn't anyone challenged that? More nerve endings in an asshole than stars in the sky."

Then Meagan remembered. "I almost forgot to tell you. I met Henry and Dahlia's teacher today at yoga. She's the one who introduced me to my new guy."

Lisa's mouth dropped. "Buzzkill."

"Was she nice?" asked Rose. "She's cancelled on me twice for a meeting."

"Did she look like a vampire or a bug?"

"She's very sweet. I'll introduce you. And she hardly looks like a bug. She's gorgeous."

Rose giggled but was starting to feel a little too woozy from the wine. "I love you, my wonderful friends, but I need to check on the girls and Frank. You ready to dance? I added two new songs on the playlist when I heard we were sharing a Saturday night together. It's all about the girls tonight, whoo hoo!"

Thrilled by Rose's display of intoxication, Lisa dropped her towel and shimmied over to her full length mirror to watch herself dance, "Let's get this party started!"

Gwen Stefani started in with "Hollaback Girl." The girls sung every word together pounding their feet against the floor and pointing their fingers at one another and into the air. Mary Jane heard the thumping from down the hall and went to investigate, finding her naked mother, boobs flopping, jumping up and down wearing huge headphones while singing on the top of her lungs, "Let me hear you say, this shit is bananas, B-A-N-A-N-A-S! This shit is bananas, B-A-N-A-N-A-S."

"What the fuck?!"

And just when they couldn't get any louder, Van Morrison belted out "Brown Eyed Girl." Returning home, Tom also heard what seemed to be someone pounding on the floor above. He opened the bedroom door and watched Allison dance across the room always returning to her computer screen to do a little movement with her girls. He came up behind her and placed one of her earbuds in his ear. Enamored with his brown eyed girl, he pulled her close, placing his hands on her hips as they swayed together. He placed his head next to hers and serenaded along,

"In the misty morning fog with
Our hearts a thumpin' and you
My brown-eyed girl
You, my brown-eyed girl"

She felt him harden against her and then turned to him, placing her mouth on his, laughing, kissing, singing. She danced her way over to her computer screen blowing the girls a kiss good night and closed the cover.

* * *

Five minutes later, Meagan was rifling through her pajama drawer, where she found a sexy, pink teddy she had not worn in years. She threw on the lingerie, pleased with how well it still fit, and pulled her hair off her face. She gave herself a shot of perfume before heading to the kitchen to top off her wine glass. Then she settled herself under the covers to begin her journey of manifesting love into her life. For the first time, she felt control over her destiny. This time was for real. She was going to find the man of her dreams.

Butterflies fluttered in her stomach as she typed, "Wishingforlove. com." She was startled, moving back from the screen as a big bright, green, yellow, and red heart jumped out at her. Huge words with a 3-D feel appeared: "Are you lonely? Do you feel like the last one picked for the basketball team? The only one not going to the prom?"

"What bullshit," Meagan said out loud. Then she thought about Jessica and her soulmate. She thought about Mark and looked at the empty spot on the bed next to her. She clicked the link: "Let the universe know you're ready to find your soulmate."

The to-do list was long, but Meagan felt confident she could handle it all. *Create space. Buy him a coffee cup. Write him a love letter. Buy yourself some flowers and a ticket to a show you would like to see with him. Sleep on one side of the bed. Empty a drawer for his clothes.*

The idea was to let the universe know you were ready to find your soulmate by creating space in your life for him, by imagining he was already there. Meagan committed to starting every morning with a love mantra and then picturing her day with him in it. She wanted to seal the deal, bring it over the top like Kevin Costner in *Field of Dreams*. Since talking to Jessica, the phrase "If you build it, they will come" had been playing repeatedly in her head. *Kevin Costner didn't just think about the ball players and buy some gloves and water bottles. He built the whole field! Sure, it sounded crazy, but guess what? The players showed up. I'm doing this. I'm building the whole fucking field!*

She thought about her conversation with the girls and stopped herself from feeling badly about not telling the whole truth. *It wasn't like I lied to them. I just didn't tell the whole story. It's not like one of them asked if my boyfriend was real or fake. Stop, Meagan. Take the word "fake" out of your head. He is real. He is real in my head, so that makes him real. He needs a name. What should I call my beautiful soulmate?* She thought back to her first high school crush, her big brother's best friend who used to sneak into her room when her brother was preoccupied and talk to her. He had never once made her feel uncomfortable or threatened. She had known he liked her, but her brother would have disowned him if he had dared touch her. Josh Flannigan, not the cutest boy in school or the best in sports, just a great, normal guy. *Josh! My new lover, Josh!*

Meagan moved to the right side of the bed to give Josh room, then moved back to the middle and turned her back to his side of the bed. *Josh, I love that you love to cuddle. We have so much in common. Goodnight, my love.*

# Latte: Meagan

The morning sun beamed through Meagan's window, waking her to the sound of birds singing. Finding herself sprawled across the bed, she quickly rolled over to give Josh space.

"Good morning, my love. Should we lie in bed all day reading and making love? Yes, a perfect plan. However, we need to get you some belongings if you're going to be staying here. And we need to figure out some things about your life." She reached into the nightstand drawer and pulled out a pen and paper. Propping herself up against the pillows, she started a list. She felt that the more details she imagined, the more real Josh would be. She wrote about Josh's parents, siblings, friends, best friend, pets, hobbies, schooling, occupation, favorite music bands, where he had traveled, where he wanted to travel, and more.

After creating Josh's identity, Meagan headed to Target to buy him some toiletries and clothing items. She slid her day and night face creams to the right side of the sink, along with the little makeup she owned, giving Josh room for his razor and toothbrush. She placed his slippers in the closet under his three ties and hung his robe beside hers on the back of the bathroom door. Remembering that she had left groceries in the car trunk, she grabbed the bag and put Josh's beer in the refrigerator and his rack of spareribs in the freezer. She flipped through the channels and selected golf, but as she walked out of the room, she changed her mind and put on football. *Now what?* Remembering *Field of Dreams,* she sighed. "I wait."

# Latte: The Club

Everyone had a busy day ahead of them with fifteen minutes to spare between school drop-off and reality.

"Don't look now, but Sara Hopkins just walked in the door. She beats her children." Lisa picked a poppy seed from her teeth with her fingernail.

"What are you talking about?" Allison stirred half a raw sugar packet into her latte. "She couldn't be sweeter to her children."

"Exactly." Lisa leaned in and lowered her voice so only the girls could hear. "No one talks to their children that nicely in public unless they're beating them at home. And her husband's gay. Every time he shakes Gomez's hand I see him finger Gomez's palm with his index finger."

Meagan shook her head. "Wasn't it you calling the PTA moms judgmental fucks last week?"

"Those aren't judgements. They're observations."

"Actually, I think her husband has a condition," said Rose.

The men's club sat off to the side, chatting away with a hoot and holler every so often. They were fired up this morning, letting the whole café know that they differed on last night's referee calls. Mr. Mustache spotted Allison and made a beeline for the table. He did an about-face when he saw Lisa.

A young woman sat in the corner reading her iPhone screen while jiggling a baby on her lap. The baby dropped her teether and the mother simply picked it up off the floor and handed it back to the child without even a swipe across her pants. *I like that,* Lisa thought. But within moments the child started to fuss.

"What's wrong with people these days? Doesn't she hear her baby?"

The girls looked over at the mother, who was completely oblivious to her child's demands.

"I think when it's your own child, you don't hear them the same way other people do," said Rose.

"Fuck that. My babies never cried in public. But shit, I'll take an oblivious mother any day over one of those parents who thinks any of us cares how cute their kid is. I could give a shit if your baby can do sign language before talking or looks like a Gerber baby. He'll most likely still grow up to be an asshole."

The baby's moans turned to cries, alerting her mother it was time for a feeding. Without hesitation, the woman lifted her shirt. The baby curled up, reaching out with tiny fingers to grasp her mother's breast as she would a baby bottle. The woman continued reading her iPhone screen.

Meagan stared at the mother. "I know we all nursed our babies, but isn't it still freaky to watch?"

The girls looked at the beautiful sight of a nursing mother and then back at Meagan, puzzled.

"I mean, look behind you," said Meagan. "Gallons and gallons of milk being poured in all our lattes and cappuccinos, but that baby is sucking milk right out of another human being's body. You have to admit it's freaky."

"What's freaky is to think of the baby cow sucking milk from his mommy's titties and knowing we're all drinking the same milk." Lisa sipped her drink.

"You're ruining my latte," Allison protested.

"Doesn't bother me a bit," said Lisa. "Giving a blowjob to someone who hasn't showered—now that bothers me."

Allison reached into her pocket and pulled out a handful of one-dollar bills. She held them up high and did a little dance in her chair. "My first tip money. Whoo hoo."

"Yeah, congratulations," said Meagan. "What are you going to do with it?"

"Well, I think there's enough here that I can buy you all another round of lattes." Allison laughed, toppling over her cup and spilling a tiny puddle of latte on the table. "It just feels great to have earned my own money."

Lisa shot Allison a pathetic look. "Like you ever have to worry about money. Tom lets you spend whatever you want."

"That's the point right there: Tom lets me!" Allison walked to the counter to find some napkins. Mr. Mustache approached from behind and spoke right in her ear. "I must say, Allison, I love your outfit today and how it shows off your curves. Is it from Macy's or Nordstrom?"

Allison looked down at her T-shirt and yoga pants. "Walmart." She headed back to the table.

Rose adjusted the blanket on her lap, which was hiding Dandelion from the staff. She broke her pumpkin bread into equal parts and placed them in front of the girls. "Meagan, you look so pretty this morning." She corrected herself quickly. "I mean, you always look beautiful, but this morning you look especially pretty."

Meagan smiled at Rose. "Thank you, Rose. I have an appointment with my acupuncturist this morning."

Lisa perked up. "Do tell. Is he hot?"

"Yes, *she* is attractive."

"Wait. I thought you weren't open to eating sushi?"

Meagan ignored Lisa's vulgarity and directed her attention towards Rose and Allison. "At my last appointment, she said I looked pretty and young and then asked me all about my face products. Now I feel pressure to look good every time I go."

"Is there anything you don't overthink or analyze?" Lisa asked.

Rose put her hand on Meagan's shoulder. "I get it, and I think it's sweet."

Lisa twirled her finger in the air and then pointed at Rose and Meagan. "Table for two, cuckoo-for-cocoa-puffs, one and two."

Rose studied Lisa's expression, knowing something was bothering her, but remained silent. Lisa looked over at Rose watching her and then glanced at the dog. "Do you secretly wish you could nurse Dandelion?"

Rose smiled, rubbing Dandelion behind the ears. "This little girl weighs less than your purse, yet last night when Frank was gone and I heard a noise out front, she went running to protect us. She doesn't think about her size or that someone might have a gun. All she cares about is protecting us."

"She looks like one of those Hostess Marshmallow Snowballs. I want to pack her in Gomez's lunch with a bologna sandwich and a bag of Doritos."

Meagan looked puzzled. "You pack Gomez's lunch?"

"Hell, no! But if I did, I would pack Rose's dog in it."

Rose sensed something was up and took a chance. "Lisa, what's bothering you?"

"Nothing. What do you mean?"

"Whenever something is upsetting you, you tend to get a little, how do I say it, vulgar." This was quite an observation coming from Rose, who went out of her way never to say anything controversial or possibly offensive.

Allison laughed. "She's always vulgar."

"Maybe," said Rose. "But usually never before lunchtime."

For the first time, Lisa was truly furious with Rose, sweet, innocent wallflower Rose. Not because she had called Lisa out but because she was right. Lisa was upset this morning—very upset. But she was in no way interested in sharing her dirty business with anyone, not even her girls.

She had been picking up laundry off of Mary Jane's floor that morning when she had discovered a backpack under the bed filled with sexy underwear and small, empty vodka bottles. Lisa's heart had sunk at the thought of her daughter wearing such clothes at her age and drinking vodka. She was just fourteen. Lisa had an honest, communicative relationship with Mary Jane. Surely, she would tell her mother if something was going on. But how could these things have gotten under her bed? Maybe she was holding them for a girlfriend. Lisa had defended her daughter when Allison and Rose said they heard she was in the closet with different boys at the eighth grade party—and now this? Allison and Rose wouldn't understand. Their daughters looked like they could still play with dolls.

Poor Mary Jane had gotten her first period at the end of fourth grade and blossomed into a full-figured woman that summer. Lisa remembered bringing her to the community pool and watching a group of adolescent boys circle around her, grabbing at her hair clip and then playing keep-away. Mary Jane had jumped from one boy to the next, playing along as if they were her friends playing Marco Polo. But Lisa could see Mary Jane's freshly grown breasts bouncing up and down as she splashed around them and them loving it. It had sent Lisa into a hysteria. "You little shits! She's ten years old, for fuck sake!" Every mother and child had looked her way. Lisa and Mary Jane left shortly after that and were asked not to return.

But it hadn't ended there. Lisa had spent every day since protecting her sweet child from perverts, young and old, from mothers and teachers who treated her as if she were purposely wearing a low-cut shirt to attract sexual advances when she was wearing the same uniform as everyone else. When you're a tiny, cute fourteen-year-old, people treat you like you're an innocent child. When you're a fully developed fourteen-year-old, people treat you like you should know better and are too fast for your age. Yet Mary Jane was at exactly the same age and stage of emotional development as Rose's Jasmine and Allison's Emma.

Lisa would ask Mary Jane about the backpack after school even though she knew Mary Jane would go wild on Lisa for snooping. She wouldn't mention a thing to Gomez until she was positive there was a real problem. He would be no help at all, just add stress to her life. Shit, he had cried when she had told him Mary Jane had gotten her period, and he hadn't slept for a week when the child had been sent home from a playdate for looking at porn magazines. What hypocritical fucks those parents were. The dad had a stack of *Playboys* hidden under his bed, and the mom had gone berserk when she caught the girls going through them. Lisa had promised the mother that the girls were just reading the articles, but she had still called off the sleepover.

So yes, she was bitchy this morning. But what mother wouldn't be?

# Latte: Allison

Alison entered the salon feeling confident in her choice of attire: a white, button-down blouse with a tan, knee-length skirt and flat black candies. She had accented her outfit with some gold jewelry and pulled her hair into a soft bun. When she entered, Izzy was at the registrar looking as sweet as ever. Nana was standing behind her, but because of her tiny stature Allison could only see the top of her head. This morning she was not wearing a tiara but a white scarf that looked like a religious veil. "We got a doozer of a day today, Dolly. Do you have your big-girl panties on?"

"Let me have it," Allison replied. "I'm ready for anything."

"Our morning starts with one Brazilian and two Brozilian waxes, and then a leg and a brokini. And we have my favorite, the Boy Terminator. He's a bodybuilder, so he gets the works. Oh, how fun it gets around here when we run a Groupon ad."

"Brozilian? What is that?"

"A man's version of a Brazilian."

"What? Excuse me? Men wax their privates?"

"They sure do. Lots of them." Nana appeared from behind the counter in a full-length black dress with a thick, white collar. A cross hung from her neck.

"Is that a nun outfit?" Allison asked, unable to stay quiet.

"God, no. That would be sacrilegious. This here is a nun costume."

Tricia LaVoice

"Nana likes to wear it and mess with the clientele when we have a lot of men coming in on one day. I only allow it because they all love her around here and she threatens to quit if I don't let her have her fun."

"Yeah, and you're gonna help too, Dolly."

Allison wanted to faint. "Wait, I need to know more. I have not seen another man's privates in twenty years. Are you telling me they're going to be naked, and we're going to wax them?"

"A little difficult to reach the pubes through the sheet, don't you think?"

"Who are these men? Where do they come from?"

"Your house, honey. Get your head out of the oven. It's the twenty-first century. You never heard of manscaping before? The men do it as much as the girls these days."

"Young men?"

"No, mostly in their forties. Some late thirties and fifties. But we have some male clients in their sixties and seventies. Oldest one I ever waxed was eighty-two. Younger guys do it at home to save the money."

"These men in their forties—are they divorced? Back in the dating world with younger women?"

"No, not at all. A lot of them are married and some come in with their wives," Izzy said.

"What about you, Dolly? Your old man in need of a little hedge work? We can take some of it off, trim it all down, or wax the whole damn thing right down to a smoothy. What's your liking?" Nana spoke with great delight.

Allison remembered Lisa's excessive curiosity about her job duties, and it all started to make sense. *Oh, Lisa must be having a field day with this one, knowing that sooner or later I'll be exposed to the unexposed.*

"Here comes our first customer of the day," said Nana. "Dolly, you bring him into the room. Tell him to undress from the waist down, give him a towel to cover his junk, and tell him you'll be back in a

114

couple of minutes. He'll be expecting you—and then wait until you see his face when I walk in. That'll turn any chubber into flubber before I even start waxing."

"They have chubbers?"

Nana looked at Izzy. "Where did you get this one? The town library?"

Izzy shook her head. "Ignore her. About forty percent of them do, but don't worry. It's more embarrassing for them than it is for us, and they all disappear on the first wax strip."

Allison could feel the flush on her face, so she turned to the window to avoid Nana's mocking. A man with short sandy brown hair walked in wearing an Eagles jersey and jeans. He was average looking, probably early forties. *Now who would think he wanted a Brozilian? Do the people at work sitting next to him know he has no pubic hair on his genitals? What about when he's standing at the urinals? Does he hide it or flaunt it?* She was so confused.

Izzy caught Allison staring and let out a loud fake cough.

Startled, Allison turned to the man. "This way, please."

He smiled at her nervously, and she smiled back as her head raced. *I can't believe I'm going to see his penis in less than five minutes. I just thought it would be great to make a little side money and now I'm going to see a man's penis that's not my husband's. What will Tom think? I won't tell him. But I have to tell him. Fuck Lisa. I'm going to kill her. She knew exactly what I was walking into.*

They entered the waxing room, and Allison did her best to seem normal. "There's a hook on the back of the door for your clothes. Just get comfortable and the practitioner will be right in." She turned to leave, then remembered. "And here's a washcloth to cover yourself."

"Yes, I know the drill."

"Oh, you've been here before?"

"First time at this spa, but I've been getting waxed for years. Athlete, you know?"

"Yes, okay. Enjoy." She closed the door behind her. *Why did I say "Enjoy?" Shit.*

Nana came walking down the hall rubbing her hands together with a shit-eating grin as wide as the Grand Canyon. "Let's go, Dolly!" She flung open the door without even knocking. "Now what do we have here? You want it all off, sugar? Or you just looking for a little trim to the hedges?"

The poor guy instinctively grabbed at his washcloth and sat upright upon seeing Nana in her nun costume.

"Settle down, sugar. This here's just a little fun to keep my heart pumping. Wouldn't want to keel over on you halfway through a wax strip."

Allison remained in the doorway until Nana yelled at her. "You ain't going to learn anything standing over there. Get in here."

Nana turned back to the client, who had made it back to leaning on his elbows. "You don't care if she observes, right sugar?"

"No, no. Sure she can watch, I mean learn."

*Izzy was right,* Allison thought. *He seems much more uncomfortable than me. But what did I expect? He's the one with an old lady dressed like a nun standing over his genitals with a bowl of hot wax.*

Allison waited for Nana to put on the plastic gloves beside the wax, but she never did. She just dove right in, dipping her tongue stick into the bowl. "Okay, sugar. This is going to hurt like hell."

Allison kept her eyes on his face, which was getting redder by the minute.

"Get over here, Dolly. I told you last week, you ain't learning nothing from across the room."

*Okay, here I go. The moment of truth, when I see another man's penis live, in the flesh, a live penis that does not belong to a toddler.* Allison walked over to the table, and there it was, just lying there doing nothing like a beached sea lion. She wasn't sure if Nana had scared the woody out of him, but he was as flaccid as overcooked spaghetti.

No bigger than a few inches, all curled up and harmless. Actually, it looked pretty sad, like it knew it was about to be tortured.

Nana approached the table holding a wax-dripping tongue stick in one hand. She lifted his sleeping giant, or should she say sleeping midget. "You see this, Dolly? You got to move the wood out of the way. The gonads too. The new girls don't want to touch and so they have him move his own junk, but I'm telling you now, do yourself a favor and save the time. They don't bite." Nana pulled his family jewels to the side. "Brozilians are much easier and quicker than Brazilians. Women got a whole bunch of business going on down there with all those folds and holes. Don't they, sugar?" She nudged the guy with her forearm. "You know something about that, do you?"

Allison felt like she was having an out-of-body experience. An hour ago, she had been dropping kids off at school, and now she was watching Mother Superior manhandle a penis. She just couldn't tell if she was appalled or intrigued.

Nana thoroughly covered the hair above his member with wax and then pressed the cotton strips against his skin. "Who's your favorite ball team, sugar?"

"What?" he asked.

And *pow*. She yanked off a strip, pulling hundreds of pubic hairs out of his skin and onto the strip. He let out a soft "Fuck" but then did his best to relax into the experience. Nana yanked out hair again and again in the same area until he was red and raw. Allison wondered how much better hairless sex might be to make someone endure such pain. Again, Nana asked him who his favorite ball team was.

"I'm a Philadelphia Eagle's fan."

"*What?*" Nana squealed and began working at a much quicker pace. Wax, press, rip. Wax, press, rip. She tossed his junk from one side to the other and then pulled his ballsac up so fast he sat up. Allison could not believe what she was witnessing.

Bewildered, he looked around frantically and saw a picture of Tom Brady on the wall. "Well, I really like the Patriots too."

"You're damn right you like the Patriots." Nana moved to the foot of the table. "Okay sugar, let's get the old stink eye cleaned up. You know the drill. Pull up your legs and grab on to those knees for dear life."

He pulled up his legs, looking more like a Thanksgiving turkey than a man. Seeing Nana standing before him, Allison thought for a minute she looked like she might go fishing in there, searching for the giblets and neck. Or start changing his diaper. *How can this be happening in a little boutique in a little town in America?* Nana could not have seemed any less impressed.

Nana smeared wax all around his anus and then yanked that cotton strip again and again. Within minutes, it was all over. He was as clean as a whistle and didn't bother to wait for them to leave the room to dress. He threw on his pants, laid a bunch of twenties on the table, grabbed his shirt, and was out of there. Nana counted the cash, a tip bigger than the cost of the wax. She smiled at Allison while stuffing the bills into her bra. "Listen up Dolly, and listen good. It's that area around the scrotum that kills them the most. Go easy there."

*Scrotum? Why medical terms now?* Allison wasn't even sure exactly what part was the scrotum. *It must be the ballsac. Maybe it's the tip of the penis. But we didn't actually wax his penis.*

# Chardonnay: Meagan

Meagan had exactly twenty-two minutes to shop and drive home so she and Josh could watch the Thursday night lineup on NBC. She was pushing it, but she couldn't go another ten minutes without buying Monistat. She also needed some Ben and Jerry's and chips, but that was for Josh. Between his addiction to Chunky Monkey and Lay's, Meagan had put on five pounds since he had moved in. She stood in line, anxious to get out of there before anyone noticed her. Dressed in the oldest sweatpants she owned, her face was bare, her hair was in a ponytail, and there were slippers on her feet. She was handing the young woman behind the counter her credit card when she heard a familiar voice.

"Hey, stranger. How's the love life treating you?"

She turned around to see Jessica holding a bottle of Veuve Clicquot in her hands with a beaming smile on her face. Although Meagan thought it seemed impossible, she actually looked more beautiful under the Walgreens lighting than ever before. A tiny black Herve Leger dress hugged her perfect curves, silver Louboutin shoes lifted her legs four inches, and her makeup was flawless.

"Hey, hi." Meagan shifted to cover up the ice cream, chips, and yeast infection medicine. "How have you been? Are you adjusting to our quiet little town?"

"I'm loving it." She patted Meagan's hand and whispered, "How's the search for love going?"

The girl ringing up her stuff gave Meagan a smirk and slowly opened a plastic bag for her items. Meagan glared back before returning her attention to Jessica. "It's going well. I went to the website you gave me and I've been doing everything I'm supposed to. I actually feel really good about it."

"You see this dress, these shoes? No teacher's salary can afford this, but that's how much my man loves me. Stick it out. It will happen."

"So, you and your guy are still going strong?"

"Yes." Jessica held up the bottle of champagne.

"Are you still planning on moving in together?"

"Oh yeah, definitely. Look Meagan, at our age things don't always come all tidy. You need to be open to that and have patience. Me and my guy will be together, but of course, a man of his stature is going to have some things he needs to deal with before we can be together—I get it."

Meagan reached out and seized her bag from the girl behind the counter, who was having way too much fun eavesdropping on their conversation. "I don't know, Jessica. I mean, is your guy married? I don't think I can do that."

"His wife hasn't had sex with him in three years and treats him like he's invisible. Women change after becoming moms, and she has no one to blame but herself. I mean, what did she expect?"

Meagan didn't know how to respond. She loved having Josh in her life, and she understood that most men she would be dating would have a past, but dating a married man was out of the question for her. She turned back to Jessica before heading out the door. "Enjoy your evening."

# Chardonnay: Lisa

Lisa's day had been long, and she was hoping to unwind with more than her couple glasses of wine. She hopped into a taxi and rode to the Howard Johnson. When she walked into the bedroom, she was pleasantly surprised by Gomez's efforts to make the room look romantic with flowers and candles. It was his turn to get the wine and food, and he had done a great job. Flower petals lay in the shape of a heart on one bed, and a beautiful cheese platter lay on the other bed. Gomez came to the door to greet her and waited for her to finish her phone call.

"No, keep the money. I don't want it... Yes, I know you're trying to refund me—so nice of Microsoft—but I have enough money. You keep it... I have an idea. Buy yourself some *balls* to get a real job, you fucking asshole."

Gomez reached for her coat. "Microsoft again."

"Yeah. Now the scamming bastards want my credit card information so they can give me a refund for the money I paid them. Fuck, I can't believe I ever fell for that. Drives me nuts."

Gomez escorted her to the bed, motioned for her to sit, and took off her shoes. He pointed to the table. "Your pleasure, Madam?"

On the stand were a bottle of chardonnay chilling in a bucket of ice and some supplies from home to make a cocktail. Lisa pointed to the vodka and cranberry juice as she continued her rant. "You know what else drives me nuts? When assholes suddenly become considered mentally ill or addicts."

"What?"

"You know what I mean? Like that mailman who said stupid shit all the time and I got to call him an asshole. Then someone diagnoses him as bipolar and I become the asshole for cutting up someone with a mental disability. Same shit with addicts. My brother was such a dick growing up, only thought about himself. I always told him what an asshole he was, but the second he went to rehab my parents forced me to be all supportive and understanding. Just because you're mentally ill or a drug addict doesn't mean you can't be an asshole too."

Lisa sipped the cocktail Gomez had made, suddenly realizing it was merely water and cranberry juice. Mary Jane must have found their stash. When she had confronted Mary Jane about the backpack she had found under her bed, Mary Jane had assured her it was Chloe's backpack and the empty bottles were Chloe's big sister's. Lisa had believed Mary Jane as she had given details about how the sisters had mixed up their backpacks. The older sister was on her way to college, so Lisa had refrained from calling the mom.

Tonight, Lisa needed time for herself and time with Gomez, so she decided not to mention to him that the Grey Goose bottle was full of tap water until tomorrow. For her own mental health, she was going to pretend she just didn't realize she had a problem on her hands. A big problem. "You know what? I would much rather have wine." She walked to the bathroom and poured her drink down the drain.

Gomez let her vent as he slowly undressed her and then took off his own clothes. They sat on the sex bed longer than usual, talking about work and the kids even though both subjects were off-limits on Howard Johnson nights. Yet the conversation was supportive and intimate. Maybe they should talk naked more often, she thought.

Lisa loved him for so many reasons, but at this moment, it was his tenderness, his vulnerability and honesty as he opened up about his insecurities at work, that had her loving him for everything. She felt a tingle between her legs, leaned over, and kissed his mouth. He kissed her back and whispered, "I love you."

Lisa climbed on top of him. She remembered the dare of the month and smiled to herself thinking about Meagan. Allison always picked good ones, not too "Debbie Does Dallas" but not too "Little House on the Prairie" either. Fucking Rose killed her with her boring, ass-kissing husband shit, and Meagan usually tried to mess with their heads. But this month Meagan's pick was perfect. Dirty talk for the contest and something they had never done before as the bonus. Rose would probably massage Frank's balls for the first time and think she was going to hell.

In a twisted way, thinking about their contest turned her on. Sitting on top of Gomez, straddling his stomach, she moved back and forth so the warmth between her legs pressed hard against his flesh. Then she leaned over him, letting her breasts drape across his face as he rubbed his hands up and down her back. His hands felt big and strong, safe. He parted his lips as one of her nipples grazed his mouth. Gently sucking, he moved his tongue around and around each nipple as it hardened in the warmth of his mouth. His hands moved down her back to her ass, which he squeezed with just the right amount of tenderness and *I need to fuck you right now.* The wetness between her legs became a wave of heat running down her inner thighs and up the middle of her spine. She leaned down and whispered into his ear. "Do you want to fuck me?"

"Oh yeah."

"Then fuck me good. I want to feel your big cock deep inside me."

Gomez was hard and inside her in seconds. She could feel him deep in her as she grinded her body in slow movements. He moaned with pleasure, and she whispered again. "You make my pussy so wet. I love spreading my legs for your big hot cock."

The words came from her mouth so easily, surprising her. He moaned and groaned with delight, pulling her down harder against him, hitting her G-spot. She stayed there as long as she could, moving her hips to the rhythm of his. Her whispers turned to moans. "I'm coming."

Gomez raised his hips off the bed penetrating her deeper. She gasped with pleasure as her back arched and her toes curled. He then flipped her over and fucked her good just like she had asked. Now she could feel the wet between her legs dripping down the side of her ass. She wrapped her legs around him, letting her hot breath seep into his ear while moving her tongue from side to side. His body tightened, his thrusts quickened, and the expression on his face was pure ecstasy. She decided this was a great time to go in for bonus points. She would give up control—certainly something she had never done before. "Spank me. Spank my hot ass and tell me what a bad girl I've been."

He hesitated for a moment, then rolled her over on top again and spanked her ass.

"Harder. I've been a very bad girl. Spank me harder."

He spanked her again, this time harder. She felt a sharp sting shoot across her bottom.

"Oh, that feels so good," she lied. "I've been so naughty, I need to be spanked good."

"You have been a bad girl," he moaned, flipping her back over again and reentering her.

"Such a bad girl."

"Tell me what you've done."

"I covered my ass in baby oil and rubbed it real nice, and then I stuck my finger in my ass. It felt so good."

"Holy shit." He groaned, and Lisa could feel every single muscle in his body tighten. His eyebrows lifted and his eyeballs seemed to pop out of the sockets. Then he shuddered, his face so red that for a second, she thought he might be having a heart attack. But he gave her a faint smile and then collapsed on top of her. She could feel the pounding of his heart against her chest. He remained inside of her and kissed her face again and again. Then he rested, smothering his face in her hair before removing himself and rolling over to his side of the bed.

Lisa leaned over and kissed him. "I think we're ready for Cirque du Soleil."

"Wow, wow, wow!" he said.

Lisa went to the clean bed and turned on the television while Gomez headed for the shower. She could hear him singing: "I'll be coming around the mountain when she comes. I'll be coming around the mountain when she comes."

She got up, grabbed her underwear and T-shirt off the floor, and headed into the bathroom. There he was, her big hunk of fool using the Ivory soap to wash his asshole, singing the wrong words to a children's folk song.

"*She'll* be coming around the mountain, you big idiot."

"Well, I like it better my way. Plus, I *will* be coming around the mountain when she comes, you naughty girl." Gomez stuck his face outside the shower and grinned so big it looked like it hurt.

Lisa had the urge to reach in and twist his nipples, but he looked too cute. She felt so connected to him, as if they had a secret that was just theirs, a newfound bond. She decided she was going to keep this experience between them— no bonus points necessary. This one was just for Gomez.

"We should get back early tonight. I'm not feeling real good about Mary Jane being in charge," she said. "Hurry up. I'll meet you in the lobby. There's a magazine down there I want to take."

As Lisa headed to the elevator, she was already thinking about what she had to do when she got home. The doors to the lobby opened, and as she stepped out she was taken back to see the couple walking into the other elevator. She found her phone and called Allison.

"I just saw Frank at the Howard Johnson. He's about to tend to someone's garden and it ain't Rose's."

"I don't believe you. No offense, but he would never go to a Howard Johnson."

"Exactly." Lisa glanced at the front desk. "I'll be back in touch."

She approached the desk carefully. "Dougy, sweet child, do you know that couple that just got on the elevator?"

"Oh, Mr. Smith? He and Mrs. Smith usually come on Wednesday nights. Never seen him on a Thursday night before or this late in the evening."

"Mr. and Mrs. Smith?"

"Yes. We have several Smith couples in the area who visit us regularly."

"You don't say," Lisa said under her breath. "Tell me, does this Mr. Smith look very Irish but talk with a strong Italian accent?"

Dougy laughed. "Yeah. Me and the other guy who works the night shift always say what a douche he is."

"How long has he been coming?"

"Well, with this Mrs. Smith, not so long. Anyway, I could lose my job talking about another guest."

"Oh Dougy, drop the bullshit. I want to know the next time he has a reservation, capiche?" She handed him a twenty.

Dougy looked at the twenty and frowned. Lisa reached in her purse and handed him an additional ten. "Don't push it."

Gomez walked up. "What's going on?"

"Oh, nothing. Let's go. You drive."

As Gomez started the car, Lisa's gaze combed the parking lot for Frank's car. "Drive around back."

"Why?"

"Just do it."

There it was: his red Porsche conveniently parked between two service trucks. Lisa read the license plate, "LVMYBOK," and blew a gasket. "Fucking piece of shit loves his bouquet. Stop the car!" She jumped out and ran to Frank's car with her cell phone.

Gomez yelled after her. "Lisa, what are you doing? Mind your own business."

Lisa snapped a photo of the Porsche, making sure she captured some of the hotel in the background. She texted the picture to Allison with instructions: "Meet me after drop-off at Meagan's house."

# Latte: The Club

Lisa waited outside for Allison to arrive. It had been a dreadful morning with Lisa confronting Mary Jane at breakfast about the vodka and Gomez getting involved. Lisa had planned to meet Gomez for lunch and break the news to him calmly, but she had been so upset about Rose that when Mary Jane had walked into the kitchen dressed for school like an escort girl, Lisa had gone mad. There had been screaming and yelling and then Gomez's tears. It had ended with Mary Jane running out the door, promising never to return. Gomez had followed her, insisting she get in the car and put on the sweater Lisa had thrown his way before dropping her off at school. Lisa felt heartbroken. It seemed like Mary Jane had changed overnight, and for the first time, there was a distance between them.

Now Lisa sat waiting for Allison, worried for Rose's family and her own. She had warned Allison not to mention anything to Meagan before they spoke. She hadn't wanted to risk Meagan having any interaction with Rose before they had agreed on a plan. Meagan was the worst liar Lisa knew, riddled with guilt. If she had acted a bit strange and Rose had asked her why, it would have been unpredictable what she would say.

Once Allison arrived, the two of them said nothing as they walked to the door. They had to ring twice before Meagan, dressed in a bathrobe with her wet hair in a towel, answered the door. "What a surprise." Meagan grabbed at her robe tie and pulled it tighter.

"We were in town and thought we'd swing by to say good morning."

Lisa looked around, totally perplexed by what she was seeing.

Meagan was too panicked about all of Josh's belongings being scattered throughout the house to consider the oddity of Allison and Lisa showing up unannounced. She hurried around the room picking up his sneakers and jacket while shoving his car keys and *Men's Health* magazine into a drawer. He had left his cereal bowl out on the counter before leaving for work, but she didn't mind, he was so busy and working so hard. She grabbed it along with hers and both their coffee mugs and put them in the sink.

"Looks like you had company last night," said Allison, smiling.

"Looks like she's had company for quite a while."

Meagan was speechless but then surprised herself with how easy it was to talk about Josh. "I know it's so soon after Mark, but I really feel good about him. I was waiting to tell you guys about him until I felt more certain it was going to work out. You'll love him. He's sweet and kind and so good to me."

"Well, by the looks of this place, things seem to be working out just fine," Lisa replied. She noticed the toilet seat up and a folded newspaper on the floor next to the toilet as she walked around employing her investigative skills. She didn't like this guy already. It wasn't possible that they had been together that long and he was already making Meagan clean up after his shit. Lisa momentarily felt frustrated by Meagan's consistently bad boyfriend choices, then remembered why they were there and returned her focus to Rose.

"Meagan, we need to talk." Lisa sat down on the sofa, and Allison sat next to her. Meagan's heart began to pump hard in her chest. "It's about Rose."

Relieved and puzzled, Meagan sat across from them.

"Gomez and I were at Howard Johnson last night…"

"Did you score major points and hit your bonus?" Meagan interrupted.

Lisa smiled thinking back on her evening with Gomez. "No, we had a pretty mellow night. But I did see Frank Garden getting on the elevator with a ho, and I'm not talking about a garden tool."

"What?"

"He was pollinating someone else's flower."

"What she's trying to say is Frank was at the hotel with another woman, not Rose."

Meagan stared at Allison, feeling sick to her stomach. She thought of Rose and Frank as the perfect couple with a beautiful family, those people you read about who have everything. "Are you positive? Why would Frank go to a Howard Johnson?"

"Easy," said Lisa. She pulled up the photo of Frank's car and showed it to her.

Meagan stood up and began to pace the room. "What do we do?"

"We tell her," said Lisa. "Bust the bastard."

Allison had a different plan. "Not a chance. You don't go bursting into someone's marriage, risking a family breaking up, without thinking it through. Think about Rose. What will happen to her?"

"I don't know, but she can't be with that lying, cheating bastard."

"I agree with Allison," said Meagan. "It's a tough life being a single parent. She has five girls."

Lisa couldn't believe what she was hearing. "So you two want to let him just get away with it? Fuck his way all over town whenever he wants?"

Allison reached out to Meagan as she paced and touched her arm. "I just want us to take our time with it, figure out the best strategy. Right now, we're all freaking out and reacting." Meagan sat back down on the couch as Allison continued. "I can't believe I'm about to say this, but Rose may be better off never knowing. If they broke up, Frank would be remarried and starting a new family within a year and she'd be all alone with the five girls. How many men would get involved with a woman with five young girls?"

"This is such fucking bullshit," Lisa snapped. "There are a lot of men who would love to be with Rose. And who says she would even want to be with anyone?"

Meagan chewed at her nails. "She hasn't worked since the girls were born. How would she support herself?"

"Frank makes plenty of money," said Lisa. "She'd be fine."

Allison shook her head. "I don't know. You see it happen all the time, and it's always the same story. He says he's going to take care of you and his family, but time and time again, once a new woman is in his life everything changes. And the ex-wife is left raising the children and fighting for what's hers while the new wife and kids are living the happily-ever-after story. Rose can't handle that." Allison looked at Lisa. "I know it sounds strange. If it were you, I would tell you immediately, but not Rose."

Meagan started to cry. "So what do we do?"

"We wait," said Allison, gazing into Lisa's glaring eyes.

# Chardonnay: Allison

Allison could hear Tom yelling for her from the car to hurry up. He wouldn't admit it, but he was always nervous and full of anxiety when they had to go to Joe's home. Tom and Joe had started off together in business years ago, but luck and talent had gone Joe's way, and now Tom reported to him. Tom swore it didn't bother him. He said he really reported to Joe's boss, but often Allison heard him on the phone reporting to Joe.

Allison loved visiting Joe's over-the-top home, a beautiful, 10,000-square-foot English Tudor sitting on five acres. It sat on top of a mountain, with 360-degree views that went on forever. The only thing she found more interesting to look at than his extravagant decorating was the latest and greatest child bride hanging on his arm. She swore the last one hadn't looked a day over eighteen, and she had wanted to smash her own head or the girl's against the wall after just five minutes of conversation with her. She had told Tom that under no circumstances would she ever double-date with Joe again. She agreed to attend his work parties, but never again would she be subjected to his midlife-crisis disasters.

Allison took a second look in the mirror, felt happy with what she saw, and headed out the door. She had pulled out her big guns tonight, not for herself but for Tom. She was wearing his favorite Diane von Furstenberg little black dress, hanging just above her knees with the perfect slit right up the middle. The dress covered her shoulders but showed enough cleavage to attract appropriate attention. Her heels, strappy Jimmy Choo's, perfectly highlighted her crotchless fishnet stockings. But of course, no one would know they were crotchless but her. She had the perfect plan. Joe may have all the money in the world and hot women on his arm, but she would make Tom feel like the luckiest man at the party. He would be aching to devour her right then and there. She had to remember to thank Meagan later for the encouragement.

She hobbled out to the car while pulling up the straps on her shoes and pulling down her dress. Tom had brought out his baby tonight— the TR6 purred in the drive. She guessed it must feel empowering to drive it because no one would notice them pulling up. Plus, they both knew they would end up Ubering home, so why deal with getting the car in the morning? She wasn't going to fight it. She was determined to have a great night.

Tom was too distracted figuring out the gadgets on the dashboard to notice how sexy Allison was dressed tonight. "What took you so long?" he asked in a sharp tone.

She let him have this one too. "Sorry. I had a little trouble finding some things." She smiled. *Sorry. I was trying to look my best for your insecure ass, and I had to make sure your children were properly fed and clothed before locking up the house and setting the alarm since it's the first time we're letting Emma babysit.*

As they drove up the hill it felt like they were arriving at the governor's mansion, and Tom started his predictable moaning. Every light in the house shone, casting a glow in the sky. The valet took their car and they headed in, walking around a koi pond and avoiding being burnt by the sparklers that highlighted the drive. They could hear Elton John singing "Rocket Man" and laughter from inside. Joe, a tall, skinny man with sharp German features, greeted them at the door. Much to Allison's surprise, his mother was at his side. They exchanged hellos and left him to greet the next guests arriving.

Once inside, Allison became intrigued with the efforts Joe had put forth to make the night wonderful. She knew Tom would view it as pompous bragging, but Allison loved it and took mental notes while trying to sneak photos with her phone to share with the girls. Beautiful young servers dressed like different Hollywood stars walked around with hors d'oeuvres and cocktails. Allison took a mini crab cake from Audrey Hepburn, a stuffed mushroom from James Dean and a blood orange cosmopolitan from Marilyn Monroe. The food display was outrageous, with mounds of crab legs and lobster tails piled high next to shrimp cocktails. An oyster bar was spread across an ice sculpture of two dolphins splashing in the sea, and a six-foot ice sculpture of a martini glass was filled with olives and flowing with vodka.

Two masseuses worked on guests in massage chairs off to the side. Looking out back through the glass doors, Allison saw that every inch of every tree was covered with tiny lights, and silky white ribbons hung from the branches. Lavender spotlights turned the pool a beautiful shade of purple, showcasing a huge ball floating on the surface. Inside the ball was a well-defined, muscular man, dressed in what appeared to be a leather thong, doing some sort of acrobatics. Tom turned to Allison. "Is that a fucking human gerbil in his purple pool?"

The night proceeded with food and drink and then more food and drink. Allison spent most of the evening talking about the safe things that were okay to talk about at office parties: children, music bands, and the weather. One young woman took too much of her attention, pleading for advice on how to get her husband to have another baby. Allison could feel the party making that shift from proper and businesslike to out-and-out drunk. She looked over at Tom, who had been accosted by Joe's mother, who was now holding up the wall. Allison could tell by Tom's expression that she was probably talking about an ingrown toenail or gastritis. Allison thought it was a perfect time to execute her plan. She excused herself from the desperate want to be mother and was heading for the bathroom when Joe approached her.

"Allison, my love, do you have a minute?" He took her by the hand, uninterested in her answer, and led her to the privacy of the next room.

"I just wanted to say how beautiful you look tonight in your sexy fishnets." He leaned in for a kiss.

Allison put up her hand to stop him. "Joe, you're drunk."

"I wonder how Tom got a woman like you. He doesn't deserve you. I could give you so much more."

"Fuck you, Joe." She headed off to the bathroom.

Once in the bathroom, she reached down between her thighs. Her crotchless panties gave her full access, and she delved her fingers into the wet warmth of her body. She then curled back her fingers and walked through the crowd, searching for Tom. This time she spotted him speaking to a group of male employees—so much sexier than Joe's mother. She could feel her own body react to the excitement. The thought that her hard nipples were apparent to the crowd turned her on more than it concerned her. She walked straight through the circle of men talking to Tom with the secretion on her fingertips, leaned into him, and traced his lips with her fingers, not even caring if it seemed strange to the men around her. She stepped back and waited. Tom continued his conversation with the men, laughing, oblivious to anything else. Allison watched as he spontaneously licked his lips in response to the moisture on them. Then he shook his head and looked straight at her smiling back.

"Excuse me, gentlemen."

Allison took his hand and led him through the crowd to the back door. The cool night air felt refreshing on their alcohol-fueled bodies.

She led him past the pool and the human gerbil, down a winding, moss-covered path to the tennis courts. She knew anything having to do with tennis would only excite him more. She leaned against the linked fence, lifted her arms over her head, and secured her fingers in the links. The sounds of the shaking chains and the chill of the metal on her back made her feel like she was in a dream. Tom stood in front of her just staring, in his own dream.

"Lift my dress."

Tom lifted her dress above her hips and tucked it behind her. He studied her fishnets as if seeing them for the first time that night, then reached for the waistband to pull them down.

"They're crotchless."

He stepped back for a moment, then reached his hands between her thighs and felt her wet, warm, pulsating flesh between his fingers.

"What did I do to deserve you?"

"Everything. Now fuck me."

# Chardonnay: Rose

Rose had become such an expert at making rigatoni she could do it with her eyes closed. Although she worked hard at feeding her family gluten-free, organic meals that consisted mostly of protein and vegetables, on rigatoni night she served choices of garlic bread, parmesan bread, and toasted Italian bread with butter, lots of butter. It was the one night a week she could get Frank home on time and all the girls to sit for a full meal while giving Ana the night off. She happily sacrificed physical nutrition for emotional nutrition.

"Dinner!"

Daisy, Dahlia, and Lily ran in and started eating bread before Rose could put the pasta on the table. Jasmine and Violet soon followed.

"Girls, slow down."

Frank walked in and kissed Rose on top of the head. "Hey, babe. Everything looks great."

Forks flew, mouths were stuffed, and conversation filled the air.

"Okay, who's going first?" Frank asked.

"I will," Daisy answered. She sat up tall in her seat and folded her hands. "My thorn today was when Veronica Tucci cheated playing hopscotch and my rose was Mommy getting me Baskin Robbins after school."

"Nice," Frank said, smiling at Rose. "Lily, what rose and thorn did sixth grade bring you today?"

"Her rose was getting a training bra," Jasmine said.

"Shut up, Jasmine. We all know you put socks in your bra."

"I do not. You're such a liar."

"Girls," said Rose. "Go ahead, Lily. What was your rose and thorn for the day?"

"My rose was getting invited to Tommy Murphy's bowling party and my thorn was all the Spanish homework Miss Bernet gave us."

"Who's next? Jasmine, Violet, how was junior high today?"

"I'll go, I'll go," Violet said. "My rose was watching Jasmine get yelled at by Mr. Jocelyn because her shirt was unbuttoned down to her belly button."

"She's lying. I hate you, Violet. Accidentally, my shirt opened one button and Mr. Jocelyn kindly pointed it out." Jasmine gave her sister the finger.

"Violet, your thorn?" Frank asked, hoping to move the conversation along.

"My thorn was watching my poor, innocent big sister get yelled at by Mr. Jocelyn."

Frank put his hand up in the air. "Okay, okay. Jasmine, how was your day?"

"My thorn is having to sit here with my sisters."

"Jasmine!"

"Okay, my thorn was missing the bus and my rose was Mommy driving me to school."

"Oh, so interesting," Lily said.

"Dahlia, how was fourth grade today? Give us your roses and thorns," Frank said.

Dahlia sat up straight and grinned from ear to ear. "Well, my thorn is, it was raining at recess time so we had to stay in the classroom but my rose is, Miss Hall taught us how to hop like a bunny rabbit."

"Really?" Frank said with a look of concern on his face.

"Yeah, not all the kids wanted to try but I could hop from one side of the room to the other in five hops."

Lily shook her head. "Your teacher sounds creepy, Dahlia. You're in fourth grade, not kindergarten."

"She's the best teacher I ever had!"

Frank reached over and took Rose's hand. "Okay girls, quiet down. Mom, what was your rose and thorn for the day?"

Rose smiled a half-smile. He knew she didn't want him to call her Mom, but she let it go. "No thorns for today, just the rose of being here with all of you."

"I'll ditto that," Frank said. He got up from his chair and placed his palm on the middle of the table. Rose and the girls followed, stacking their hands on top of one another. Then in unison they all said, *"Thankful and grateful, forever family."*

The girls dutifully brought their dishes to the sink and scattered throughout the house. Frank walked over to Rose, who was standing in front of the sink finishing up. He wrapped his arms around her waist and kissed her neck. "Thank you for a wonderful meal, Mother Garden."

Rose turned around in Frank's arms so their eyes could meet. "Frank, you know what would make my rose for today?"

"What's that?"

"I feel like we've been off lately, disconnected. I miss us."

He pushed aside a strand of her hair that had fallen across her eyes. "How's this?" he said. "I'll get the girls settled while you pour us both a glass of wine and climb into something comfortable. I'll meet you in the bedroom."

Rose poured Frank a glass of merlot and herself a glass of chardonnay before hopping into the shower to give her lady bits a freshening up. She put on her new purple lace bra and matching underwear from Bloomingdale's that the girls had bought her for her birthday. She lit five rose-scented candles and placed them around the bedroom, connected her phone to the stereo system, and put on Simon and Garfunkel's greatest hits. Then she lay on the bed and pulled up her notes from the girls' conversation on dirty talk. She repeated a couple of phrases out loud and giggled thinking about saying them to Frank. Sipping her wine, she rubbed her hands over her bra, feeling the fine material between her fingers. Intrigued by how quickly her nipples hardened, she was eager to get the evening going and dared herself to send Frank a sex text. She typed out, "I am touching myself thinking of you" but resisted sending it.

*Do it, Rose. Do it! You know Allison would send it in a heartbeat and so would Lisa and Meagan. Come on. Just push send.* She looked down at Dandelion, loyal at her side, and asked, "Should I do it, girl?"

Dandelion gave a little growl back, prompting Rose to put her in her cage and cover her with a blanket.

Back on the bed, looking down at the text, her fingers hit the send button, and butterflies fluttered through her stomach. *Will he like it or will he think I'm weird? Desperate?*

A second later, Frank responded, "You are SO hot."

Rose leaned back on the bed, hugging her pillow and giggling to herself. Then Frank sent a second text: "I will call you when I'm free."

"What?" she said out loud. But before she could think much more about it, Frank was knocking on the bedroom door, which she had locked. "Delivery. Delivery for Mrs. Garden."

Rose hid behind the door as she opened it, wanting to surprise him with her new outfit, but he saw her immediately. "Is that new?" he asked.

"Yes. Do you like it?"

He hesitated for a moment. "Of course. You look great."

He leaned in to kiss her, but Rose stepped back. He studied her face as Art Garfunkel's smooth voice filled the room sweetly singing "For Emily." Frank reached for Rose, took her hand in his, and pulled her close. He placed his other hand on the small of her back and began moving to the music. He buried his face in her hair, smelling her and gently kissing her shoulders as they danced in the candlelit room.

"I want to feel your skin against mine," he said. He lifted his shirt over his head and then slowly reached for her bra straps, letting them fall to the side. Reaching behind her, he unfastened the clips and let her garment fall to the ground. He pulled her close, feeling her soft, smooth skin pressing against his. They slowly danced to "For Emily" and then "Kathy's Song."

As the song ended, Rose walked over to the window and stood in the moonlight. Frank followed, knelt down, and slowly pulled her panties to the floor. She stepped out of them as he removed the rest of his clothing. She walked over to the bed, trying to remember the sex verbiage she had rehearsed and considering the right time to use it. "Come," she said, reaching out to him.

Frank walked over, took the throw blanket from the foot of the bed, and pulled out a rose from the bouquet of flowers in the vase on the table. "I want to see you in the moonlight," he said, reaching once again for her hand.

Rose followed him back to the window, where he laid the blanket on the floor directly in the light. He signaled for her to lie down and then settled himself at her feet. Taking the flower in one hand, he slipped the other between her knees, parting her legs. He began running the rose up and down the inside of her thighs. Then, bending down, he kissed her right ankle and then her left. Slowing, inching his way up her body, he kissed her calves, her knees, and then the inside of her thighs, once, twice, three times. She forgot everything beyond their bedroom walls as she felt the warmth of his mouth gently licking then sucking her clitoris. His tongue caressed her labia, devouring all of her. He stayed there, making her feel alive and beautiful. Fighting off climaxing, she reached down to him. "Come inside me. I want to come with you."

He pulled himself up on top of her, once again taking the rose in his hand. She could feel him hard against her body as he took the bud of the flower, firm yet soft, and stroked it between her legs, teasing her at the point of entry. Then he released the rose and penetrated himself hard inside of her, thrusting against her swollen insides. She shuddered, no longer able to hold off her orgasm, and murmured "I'm coming."

With that he thrusted harder, burying his face in her neck until his moans signaled he too was climaxing. He breathed heavily, grunting his love for her while slowing his pace and then collapsing his body on top of hers. They lay in the moonlight, him still inside of her, their sweat mixing, kissing, when reality knocked at the door.

"Mom. Mom! Why is the door locked?" Lily screamed from the hallway, setting off Dandelion into unbearable yapping. "Mom, Jasmine took my curling iron and won't give it back. Mom, open the door."

# Chardonnay: Allison

Allison picked up Henry from school, then headed over to the salon, driving carefully in the rainy night. She never worked evenings, but Nana was sick with the flu and Izzy had begged—just this once. Tom was out of town and Allison thought it was good for the kids to have to fend for themselves and take care of one another. She noticed that the children of her working-mother friends were very self-sufficient and independent. She hoped her time at the salon would help loosen the cord.

When she walked into the salon, the lights were low and everything was quiet. All she could hear was the sound of rain on the rooftop.

No customers were in sight. She saw a room with the door closed and heard noises inside. Something didn't feel right. She called out to Izzy. "Hello? Izzy?"

Suddenly the door flew open and Izzy came barreling out, looking horrified. "You're early."

They both looked at the clock on the wall and saw that Allison was right on time. Seconds later, Andrew came waltzing out of the room buttoning his blue jeans, looking so proud Allison thought he was going to start pounding his chest. Izzy was mortified. "I'm so sorry. It's just Nana's been sick and we haven't had a chance to be alone. I swear it's the first time."

Allison looked puzzled, so Izzy clarified. "I mean, not the first time, but the first time here at the salon."

"I didn't see a thing," Allison said. She looked down at the logbook to see what was in store for the evening.

Izzy pushed Andrew out the door and quickly cleaned the room they had just occupied. When she returned to the lobby, she looked like her old business-oriented self. "I'm so behind on billing and have to get to it tonight before they shut the lights out on us. Do you think you can handle the front by yourself? I think the book is pretty light tonight."

From a glance, like most Mondays, the evening looked light—six customers in the course of three hours with an expected walk-in or two. Very doable for Allison. She was thrilled that Izzy trusted she was ready and was happy to prove her right.

Izzy put the Adele station on Pandora and disappeared while Allison turned up the lights and took a closer look at the evening.

*Brow … doable/boring.*
*Brow/lip … doable.*
*Ear and back … yuck but can't blame him.*
*Brozilian … oh, lovely.*
*Bikini/full leg … easy.*
*Brazilian … if I must.*
*Nipples … ouch.*

She then did a double-take at the name next to the Brazilian: Jessica Hall. *Jessica Hall, fuck. Please don't be the Jessica Hall who teaches my child.* Allison felt horrible that she had not yet made it up to the elementary school to introduce herself. She had planned to a couple of times but had never followed through. Ugh, and now she had to give the woman a Brazilian. She knew Rose had tried to catch up to the teacher a few times and had had no luck. She'd just pretend she had planned to tag along on those attempts. The last thing she wanted was for Henry's teacher to think he wasn't supported at home and not give him the same attention as the other kids in class.

The night progressed uneventfully. Both eyebrow waxes went quickly and painlessly, yielding good tips, which Allison purposely left out on the table for Izzy to see. Allison was checking the spa's phone messages when her Brozilian appointment walked in. He was a young man, tallish, red-haired and very freckled with milky white skin. *Ouch. This is going to hurt.* The fair-skinned customers always seemed to squirm and let out little sounds of discomfort.

"Um, hello, um."

"You must be Edward."

"Um, yes."

"Follow me, Edward. Is this your first time?" Allison led him down the hall to the room Nana used, since she hadn't had time to tidy up her own room after the previous client.

"Um, yes ma'am. It is."

*Ugh, he called me "ma'am." That will cost him a slow pull.*

Allison guided him into the waxing room, instructed him to remove everything from the waist down, and handed him a towel to cover himself.

"Even my underwear? You want me to take those off too?"

"You are here for a Brozilian, right?"

"Um, yes ma'am. I am."

"Well, I think it's best if you remove your underwear then." She smiled politely.

Allison walked out of the room thinking about the field day Nana would have had with this poor guy. She gave him an extra couple of minutes to settle himself before returning. She had already decided she was going to ask the customers to hold and move their own family jewels. She understood why Nana and Izzy both told her it was easier to do it yourself, but she just felt strange touching another man's penis and testicles. Tom had never asked for details about her waxing men and she never offered them. She wasn't sure how he would react at the thought of her alone in a room with a half-dressed man, but the reality of the situation couldn't be any less sexy.

"Knock, knock. Are you ready?" she asked, pausing at the door.

"Um, yeah. I guess so."

Allison walked into the room and let out a burst of laughter but quickly caught herself and turned it into a cough. Edward lay flat on the table with the little towel she had given him covering his face and one of his yellow, happy-faced sock draped over his full erection. It looked like the main character in a puppet show.

"Let's get started," she said. "I'm going to need you to help me out a little, so you may want to see what's going on."

He slowly pulled the towel down his beet-red face. "I'm so sorry, ma'am. The artwork just messes with my head."

Allison hadn't noticed the artwork before. She turned around to see a large Georgia O'Keefe painting of a red and pink iris that looked more like a vagina than most of the real vaginas she saw in the salon. "Oh, I'm sorry. One of our staff members has quite the sense of humor." Allison turned the painting around.

Like all the other erections she had witnessed in the waxing room, this one withered the second she pulled the first strip of wax. A few rips later, he relaxed and stopped calling her "ma'am." He did a good job holding his stuff out of the way so she could give him a good wax. The milky white flesh around his privates was smooth and red like an expensive cabernet, and he was out the door before Allison could thank him for visiting.

As she tidied up the salon, she could feel the anxiety in her stomach as 8:00 approached. Brazilians were different from bikini waxes and harder to do than Brozilians. There were so many tiny hairs hiding in and around all the folds and holes, the only way to do a good job was to jump right in there and wax your way out. The thought of meeting

Henry's teacher for the first time in this setting was unsettling. She imagined how the teacher was going to feel—she would be the one lying there spread-eagle in the breeze. Maybe Allison didn't need to tell her who she was. How would the teacher know she had read her name? And since they had never met in person... Well, it was the right thing to do even though she was dying to ask her questions about Meagan's boyfriend.

8:12pm and still no sign of the teacher. Allison was determined to leave the salon by 9:00 and she still had a nipple wax coming in after Ms. Hall. Izzy popped her head out from the back office to check on things. "You doing okay?"

"Yes. I love Nana's choice in art."

Izzy laughed. "I told her she had to take that down after a few laughs."

The bells on the door jingled, and a petite young girl walked in carrying an umbrella bigger than herself. "Hi. I'm early. Kristal." Allison looked down at her 8:30 appointment for Kristal: nipple wax. Allison wasn't sure if this girl was old enough to wax without a parent signature but ignored the thought. "I can take you now. This way, honey."

The amount and length of hair that surrounded the girl's nipples seemed unfair, and Allison was glad she had come in. It was quick and easy, and the bright smile on Kristal's face when she looked down made Allison feel good. She gave her some ice to hold on her nipples for a moment, then walked her to the lobby. Teacher Jessica sat waiting.

*Are you fucking kidding me?* She remembered Meagan saying the teacher was gorgeous, but Meagan thought everyone was gorgeous. This time Meagan had it right. She was the most beautiful woman Allison had ever seen, even with her rain-soaked hair.

"Hi. Sorry I'm late. Everyone forgets how to drive when it rains. I'm Jessica. I have an 8:00 appointment."

Allison opened the door for Kristal and turned to Jessica. "Wow, it's really picking up out there. Why don't we hang your coat here and I'll show you back to your room?"

As they walked down the hall, Allison had a realization. *How am I going to keep her from mentioning she's a teacher?* Talking to customers about their professional lives was the best distraction without getting too personal.

Allison showed her to the table, handed her the small cloth to cover herself, and gave her privacy to undress. While in the hall waiting, Allison did everything she could not to text the girls and tell them what was up. That would be divulging client information and Allison didn't want to do anything unethical. Strangely, she was loving her new job and didn't want to jeopardize it in any way.

She walked back into the room to see Jessica's statuesque body spread out across the table like a Botticelli painting. Jessica's ample breasts filled out her little black lace bra, and she wore nothing else. Her stomach was perfectly flat and toned, lying like a valley between her narrow hips. Her graceful legs stretched to the edge of the table, where the little washcloth Allison had given her lay bunched up. Allison was surprised to feel her heart begin to beat a little harder in her chest. She felt intimidated by Jessica's beauty and confidence. *What in the hell is she doing in our little town teaching fourth grade?*

"Are you cold? I usually use the towel to cover one side while I do the other to keep you warm."

"I'm hot-blooded and not shy." Jessica lifted her legs into frog position.

Allison prepped the sugar wax, dipped her popsicle stick, and turned back to Jessica's wide-open legs. She tried to make idle conversation without asking her why and what about her life. "Are you married? Children?" *Of course she doesn't have children. There isn't a stretch, scar, or droop anywhere on her body, and I'm looking at all of it.*

"Not yet, but my boyfriend and I are talking about it."

"That's exciting." Allison applied wax to the outside of her labia.

"I'm pretty hairy. Runs in my family. Can you make sure you get inside my lips and around my clitoris too?"

Allison was impressed by the beauty of her face and her nude body, but now, getting close and personal with her lady bits, Allison felt envious. How could a vagina be so perfect, so tightly packed and folded, like a professional tailor had hand-stitched it himself?

Allison carefully pulled back skin here and lifted there, waxing and tearing the strips off Jessica's most intimate body parts, amazed that Jessica never flinched. She just rested as if wanting to nap or as if Allison were massaging her.

"Will I still be red on Wednesday?" Jessica asked.

"You may be a little tender tomorrow, but you'll be fine by Wednesday." Allison finished up her vaginal area. "If you roll to one side and move your leg over, I can get the hairs in back."

Jessica flipped over, got up on her knees, and rested her chest against the table. "I know that's not the prettiest sight, but it's so much easier and quicker this way. My technician in Manhattan did it like this."

Allison walked around back. *Whoo, you ain't kidding.* Her backyard was so dirty Allison thought she was looking at a map of the backroads of Kansas.

Feeling somewhat redeemed by the reality of Jessica's backside and the mole she spotted on the side of her head, Allison was eager to finish up. She quickly stripped Jessica in and around and up and down.

"All finished. You can get dressed." Allison removed her gloves and began putting away the wax.

Jessica, still on all fours, lifted her chest. "Can you bleach my rectum?"

"Excuse me?"

Jessica reached up to her chest to straighten her bra. As she pulled at the lace, one of her plump breasts fell out of the cup, exposing a perfectly round, pretty pink nipple. "Last time I was here, a sweet little old lady dressed like Mary Poppins bleached them for me. She

was going to do my anus also, but she started talking about politics and slamming things around so I thought it was best to leave."

Allison's head spun as she looked at Jessica's bubblegum pink nipples and then down at her dark, chocolate brown hole. There was absolutely a design issue happening, but Allison wanted nothing to do with it.

Jessica continued talking. "I know it may sound strange that I'm confiding in you, but we may never see each other again and I don't know anyone in this godforsaken town, so I just have to share."

Allison continued to stand there blank-faced.

"For our two-month anniversary, I surprised him with a bunny getup, you know what I mean?" Jessica winked at Allison.

"No, I don't." Allison was confused.

"A bunny-tail butt plug and bunny ears. He loved it. Said I was his real-life Jessica Rabbit."

Allison remained blank-faced at the TMI.

"You know who Jessica Rabbit is, right? From *Who Framed Roger Rabbit*—the sexy bunny."

"Yes, we all know Jessica Rabbit. Why don't you get comfortable? I'll be right back." Allison left the room, went down the back steps, and barged into Izzy's office.

"Izzy, I'm sorry. I love my job but I'm not bleaching assholes, especially hers."

Izzy looked up from her stack of papers, apparently amused by Allison's hysteria. "Relax. Sell her a tube of bleaching cream and have her do it herself at home. It's on the shelf next to the musk oil perfume."

"We sell bleaching cream? I thought assholes were supposed to be brown." Allison walked back up the steps. "What the fuck!"

# Latte: Lisa

Lisa banged on Mary Jane's door for the tenth time. "Let's go, Mary Jane. We can't be late."

"Go away. I told you there's no way I'm talking to some fucked up psychologist."

"You don't have a choice. Let's go."

"You're the one who needs a therapist. You go."

"I'm not the one drinking alcohol in eighth grade."

Mary Jane opened the door with three times more eyeliner on than usual and flat-ironed hair, making her look much older than her fourteen years. "Now I get it. You're jealous of me. You weren't drinking alcohol in eighth grade because you didn't have any friends to drink with like you still don't have friends or at least any real ones."

"Okay. Whatever you say, but we're going."

"It's true, Mom. No one likes you. I don't even know why Emma and Jasmine's moms hang out with you, they're so much prettier and richer than you. They probably feel sorry for you or just need you to carpool their kids."

"What happened? Why are you so angry all of a sudden?"

Mary Jane stepped back and looked her mother up and down. "Yeah, I just don't see what they see in you." She paused. "Except that fat shit loser Meagan. I get why she hangs with you."

Lisa stepped into the room and pinned Mary Jane against the wall.

"You going to hit me?" Mary Jane asked. "Go right ahead and I'll call the police."

Lisa raised her hand, then let it drop. "Go ahead, you spoiled, ungrateful child. Call the police. I would love to show them the empty vodka bottles I found under your bed."

Mary Jane stared at her mother.

"Now wipe that shit off your face and get in the car."

# Chardonnay: The Club

Wednesday night came quickly, and as much as Allison had promised herself she would not talk about the teacher, one glass of wine down and she was a Chatty Cathy.

"First of all, can I just say if vaginas were queens, hers would rule the world. It was actually pretty."

"My vagina is pretty," Lisa said.

"So, wait." Meagan felt excited about inside—literally—information on Jessica. "What exactly was the problem?"

"There was a design issue coordinating the color of her lady parts, so she wanted me to bleach her."

"So, the donut hole was a few shades darker than her cupcakes?" Lisa asked.

"Oh, no. They were worlds apart," Allison shared. "Not even on the same color wheel."

"I don't get it," Rose cried. "Can someone please just talk normal?"

Delighted by Rose's frustration Lisa said, "Her asshole was one color and her nipples were another."

"How would anyone know or care what color their bottom was?" Rose asked.

"Mine match," Lisa said. "They're not bright pink, but they match."

Allison had never thought she would be having a conversation like this, but little surprised her lately. "You actually checked to see if your tits and ass matched?"

"Allison, just because you and sweet Rose over there live in a bubble... A lot of us have heard of bleaching before. I was curious, so I snapped a picture of both and got a good comparison. I bet Meagan has too."

"Guilty," Meagan responded. "So she's totally bare down there?"

"I left her bare as a baby."

"That's so messed up," Meagan said. "Can't you phrase it differently?"

Lisa sipped the smooth merlot from her glass. "Men get shit for liking a bare cooch, but it's not because they want us looking like we're eight years old. It's because they like seeing all your business, all the bits and parts. It's raw, primitive. Like men."

"Are you drinking red?" Allison asked.

"You know you sound like such a housewife when you ask questions like that? Hey, what do you guys call your puss?"

Allison sat back and smiled. "Juliet."

"Juliet! Who wants to fuck a pussy named Juliet? What do you think, Tom is going to get on his knees and start reciting poetry to your crotch? 'Oh, my beloved, how I plead for thee to part thy thighs, for my manhood wishes to enter the house of Juliet.'"

"Tom loves Juliet, but it wasn't Shakespeare who motivated me to name her that. It was my mean big sister. When I was in tenth grade, she wanted to name our dog Juliet. Who names a dog Juliet? I was adamant about calling her Buttons, so I told my sister I called my vagina Juliet."

"Did it work?" Meagan asked.

"Good old Buttons lived seventeen years."

Meagan raised her glass to toast Allison, then directed her attention at Lisa. "Lisa, what do you call yours? The Bermuda Triangle? Once you enter, you never come back."

"Haha. I call her Josie. You know, from Josie and the Pussycats."

Rose shook her head. "I know you guys think I can be naïve at times, but I can't believe the three of you have names for your lady parts."

Lisa spit out her wine. "Shit. My new pants."

Allison smirked, "Wouldn't have happened if you were drinking white."

"Rose needs a name for her lady garden." Lisa wiped at her pants with her T-shirt. "I say we call her Tulip. I bet she looks just like a little spring pink tulip down there. Rose, show it to us."

"What about Blossom?" Allison suggested.

"Oh, I like that but it's our cat's name," Rose replied, ignoring Lisa's request to view her vagina.

"Hey, a pussy is a pussy," Lisa said while removing her pants.

Allison laughed. "I think we all should wax ourselves bare. Lisa, it's your turn next month. Challenge us."

"I'll do it," said Meagan, excited as a school child on a field day.

Lisa laughed. "I thought you hated your meat curtains."

Rose tried to entertain Lisa's fondness of fifteen-year-old slang but again, just couldn't keep up after a glass of wine. "Lisa, could you pretend we're all adults or in medical school for just a moment so I can understand?"

"Well, Rose," Lisa explained, "Meagan has shared with me that her labia is a bit large resembling the drapes you would find in the Great Gasby. This makes her uncomfortable when in the presence of someone she would like to fornicate with, so she keeps the pubic hair on her vagina fully grown to mask her flaws."

"Ohhhhh."

"I'm over it. I love my messy bits. Josh says it's sexy as hell. So I'm into taking it all off. Who's with me?"

Allison was more familiar than any of them with the pain involved. "I'll do it, but I'm not waxing any of you. I'll get you appointments with Izzy. Rose, you in?"

Allison waited for a yes or a no, but they were all surprised by Rose's answer. "I'm already bare. I got lasered years ago so I don't have to deal with shaving."

"You're shitting us," Lisa said.

"Just because I don't talk details about sex doesn't mean I don't know what I'm doing. I'm just more private than the rest of you."

Lisa was impressed. "Any ideas for the bonus?"

"Well, if we're waxing our stuff, we should get the guys to do their stuff. Talk around the salon is the sex is great when both people are bare."

"So, you want me to send Gomez to sexy Izzy for a wax? Or can you get Nana to do it?"

"The hell with that. I'd kill Tom if he made some young girl lift his balls and wax him. We should get bonus points if we shave our men or at least get them to shave themselves."

"Do you really think sex could be that much better shaved?" Meagan asked.

"I don't know. I'm just telling you we get a lot, I mean *a lot,* of married couples in their forties and fifties coming in together for a full waxing."

"I feel lame," Meagan said.

"Wait, I didn't tell you guys the best part, but I swear if anyone ever found out I told you guys this, I would lose my job. And I love my job."

Lisa sipped what was left of her wine, "What, you think one of us is going to call the PTA and tell them one of their teachers have a bald beav?"

"She bragged about wearing a bunny-tail butt plug and ears for her guy and said he went crazy for it. Called her his real Jessica Rabbit."

"Men are so gross," Lisa said. "I can't believe they all fantasize about screwing a cartoon character."

"I'd screw Aladdin," Meagan said proudly.

"You'd screw the seven dwarfs," Lisa replied.

Rose remained quiet, thinking about Frank and Jessica Rabbit. "Frank's birthday is Friday night. Maybe I'll surprise him and see if he likes me as a rabbit."

They were all speechless, literally not knowing what or how to respond.

Rose laughed. "That'll earn me bonus points for the month!"

No one was in the mood to dance but faked their way through Allison's pick of David Bowie, "Modern Love."

Once the girls ended their call, Allison sat in the silence of her room. Seconds later the phone rang. "Hold on," Lisa said. "I'm conferencing in Meagan… Everyone on?"

Allison and Meagan groaned.

"I'm not waiting any longer," Lisa said. "I don't care if you guys are with me or not. I'm not sitting back knowing she's shoving bunny plugs up her ass for that jerk-off while he's plugging someone else. I'm texting Dougy tonight."

"Do you really think Rose is going to get a bunny plug and play Jessica Rabbit?" Allison asked.

"You guys in or out?"

Allison and Meagan both groaned grudgingly. "In."

# Chardonnay: Rose

Rose ran into the house and up the stairs. She locked herself in the bedroom bathroom and leaned against the wall, clutching the bag in her hand. She couldn't believe she had gone through with it—and all on her own. She had driven around the block four times, watching men and women go in and out of the sex shop, before summoning the courage to go inside. She had already decided that if she could not find the bunny plugs on her own, she was leaving. There was no way she was asking a sales girl for help. Surprisingly, she had no trouble finding them at all. They had been on the back wall next to the whips and blindfolds.

Rose had been shocked to see all the different colors and sizes they had, and after a minute she had found herself reading the backs of most of them, like trying to find the healthiest yogurt brand that still tasted good. She was mostly concerned with the plug, the part that went inside her body. Some were made of stainless steel, some were hypoallergenic, and some, stating that they were suitable for vegans, were silicone. The most expensive were made of glass and quite pretty. In fact, they were much prettier than she had expected, making her decision process that much more challenging. The tails were also made of different materials. A few were made of real bunny hair, but the majority consisted of fake fur or feathers.

After careful consideration, it had been a toss-up between the light purple fake fur and the ivory feathered one. But then she had ended up going with the midnight black fake bunny hair since it came with the cutest little rhinestone bunny ears. One thing she was sure of was size. It frightened her to see how large some of the plugs were, and she made sure she chose the smallest size they sold. Luckily, she had googled how to insert a butt plug before she had gone to the store, so she knew what lubricant to buy.

Now she hid in her bathroom, waiting for Ana to take the girls to the mall so she could bunny up. It was an expensive night, getting them all out of the house. If only she had had five boys! They probably would have been happy kicking a ball around a field at no expense.

She heard the door slam a hundred times and looked out the window to see Ana and the girls finally drive off. Once she had the house to herself, she ran downstairs and poured herself a glass of wine. Upon reconsideration, she poured in a little more. She put an R&B station on the sound system and collected as many candles from around the house as she could find. She knew Frank would enter through the garage door, so she lit candles all the way from the garage door up the stairs, and into the bedroom. She went back into the bathroom and arranged herself, leaving the butt plug for last. She pulled her hair back and pinned the ears to her head. She struggled but managed to apply false eyelashes to complement her made up face, then gave herself two squirts of her Chanel Gardenia perfume. She dropped her robe and stared at herself in the mirror. She was pleased with her naked body. She hadn't had much of an appetite lately and she was working her ass off at pilates. It showed. *Are you really going to go through with this, Rose?*

"Yes," she answered herself out loud. She took three deep breaths and removed the bunny plug from the box. She slathered the tip down to the neck with lubricant, then held onto the sink with one hand.

She took another deep breath and slowly inserted the plug with the other hand. *Ouuuuuuch.*

Surprisingly, once she got the hump in, it was actually comfortable, like getting a tight ring over your knuckle. "Oh, I look so cute," she said, twirling around in a circle and watching herself in the mirror. "I am one hot bunny."

"Rose! Rose, honey," Frank yelled from the bottom of the steps. "Where is everyone?"

Her heart pounded hard in her chest. Now looking back at herself in the mirror, she wasn't sure if this was a good idea. "Ana has them all at the mall," she called. "Pour yourself a glass of wine and come up here. I have something for you."

She was nervous as hell but remained committed to her plan to hop out of the bathroom. She finished her wine in three gulps while waiting for Frank to come upstairs. Moments later, she heard his voice just outside the bathroom door. "Rose, sweetheart. What's going on in there?"

"Go sit on the bed. I'll be right out."

She slowly turned the knob and let the door open wide. Standing in the doorway, she did a half-turn, showing off her new tail. Frank's mouth dropped.

"Who loves Jessica Rabbit?" she said. Her body was so toned and smooth, the ears and tail seemed natural. She hopped across the bedroom towards him.

"Rose, what are you doing? Stop! You look stupid as hell."

Rose stopped in her bunny tracks and glared at Frank before running back to the bathroom. She locked the bathroom door as Frank tried to apologize from the other side. "Rose, let me in. You just took me by surprise. I'm sorry, baby."

Rushing to get dressed and out of there, she did not flinch when pulling out the plug and ripping the bunny ears off her head. She called herself an Uber and pushed past Frank on her way out the door, leaving her bunny getup on his side of the closet.

"Where are you going?"

She had the Uber driver take her to the local movie theater, where she bought a large buttered popcorn, large Diet Coke, and huge box of M&Ms. She didn't care what they were playing. She wasn't even watching the movie. She just sat there.

# Chardonnay: The Club

Lisa had texted Dougy on Wednesday night after talking to Allison and Meagan, but Dougy didn't reply until Tuesday afternoon, when he texted that Mr. Smith had called to confirm his standing Wednesday night reservation. Dougy told her that Mr. Smith always liked to call ahead to pay with a Visa gift card and reassure Dougy there would be no incidentals. Lisa called Allison and Meagan to go over the plan. "So everyone knows the drill and what they're supposed to say?"

"I told you, I'm not saying anything," Meagan insisted. "I'm just there to be a united front for Rose."

"You're such a wimp."

"Lisa, you just do all the talking," Allison said.

"Whatever."

"Where should we park?" Meagan was worried about the details. "Do you want us to go around back?"

"No, I told you that's where the Gardener parks."

"Well, should we park in front then?" Meagan asked.

"No! I don't know. What, do you think I'm Nancy Drew or something?"

"Actually, I do," Allison said. "I think you're getting a sick kick out of this somehow."

"Go to hell. I'm doing this all for Rose. What, are you saying that I'm happy her husband is fucking the secretary so I can get my kicks off?"

"Hey, hey. Stop," said Meagan. "We're all upset for Rose and I think a little nervous, but we can't lose our cool on each other."

Lisa was offended and wanted to hang up. "I'll switch cars with Gomez and get the van. I'll pick you both up."

"Gomez," said Allison. "What does he think of all this?"

"I'm not stupid. I didn't tell him. What about you? Did you tell Tom?"

"I'm not stupid either. He would just tell me to mind my own business."

"I'm going to bed."

"Goodnight."

"Nite."

Lisa walked into the kitchen, grabbed a wine goblet, and filled it to the top with chardonnay. She walked into the living room, sat on the couch without turning on the lights, and looked out the window. Gomez heard her downstairs but felt worried when he didn't see any lights on. "Babe, everything okay?" he called to her.

"Yeah, sure," Lisa yelled back. "I just need a little time alone."

"Okay. Should I be waiting up for you?"

"No, go to sleep. And Gomez, thank you."

"Thank you for what?"

"Thank you for being such a great dad and husband."

"Lisa, are you sure you're alright?"

"Yes. Go to sleep."

\* \* \*

Two miles across town, Allison was walking into Tom's den in her maroon silk baby doll and robe with two glasses of wine. Handing him a wine glass she asked, "Do you have a lot to do?"

Immediately receiving her gesture as a mating call, Tom closed his laptop and smiled at her. "I can be done right now if you need me to be."

"I need you to be." She placed her hands on the arms of his chair and leaned over him. "Do you ever think about other women?"

"Of course not. You're the only woman I have eyes for."

"Tom, I'm serious. We've been married a long time. We've had our ups and downs like everyone else, and you're out there in the world. Are you telling me you never met someone you found attractive and wanted to sleep with them?"

"Allison, what is this about? I thought you came in here to be with me."

"I just want to know."

"Well, of course I see women who I find attractive, but I'm not looking to have sex with them. Why? Are you wanting to have sex with other men?"

"No, no. I was just asking. Let's change the subject. How was your day?"

"Pretty good until you put ideas in my head."

Allison walked over to the office door, locked it, and then double-checked the lock. She walked over to Tom sitting in his leather wingback chair and let her robe drop to the floor. The silk of her garment hugged her voluptuous body, outlining the same beautiful curves Tom remembered her having when they had first met. She lifted her baby doll up high on her thighs, stopping right before exposing all of herself. Then, she reached up and pulled the pin from her hair, letting it fall down her back. She walked to the desk, lifted herself onto it, and sat down in front of him. He smiled and sipped his wine, watching her.

Leaning back on her elbows, she slowly parted her legs to give him a glimpse of her world, then closed them, teasing him. He groaned, moved forward, and kissed the tops of her knees as he reached between her legs and pulled them apart. Carefully, he slid his hands down the inside of her thighs, caressing his way to the warmth and moisture of her flesh. She arched her back with pleasure, then abruptly closed her legs and pushed his hands away. He sat back, looking at her inquisitively. She climbed off the desk and straddled him in his chair, moving her hips around and around. Then lifting her lingerie over her head, she said, "Surprise."

She was completely bare, divulging all of herself to him. Tom moaned with delight while reaching to touch her freshly bare skin. He caressed her smooth, exposed clitoris with his fingertips while nuzzling his face in her hair and smelling her sweet skin. She shuddered at his touch. Spreading her legs wider, she held his head in her hands and kissed the top of it. Tom plunged forward, taking her into his arms and laying her down on the office floor. "I love you, Allison, and I want only you."

They made the best love they had made in years.

* * *

The next evening arrived much more quickly than the girls wished. As planned, Lisa waited for Gomez to come home, then took his van to pick up Meagan and then Allison. Allison heard her beeping in the driveway and yelled goodbye to the kids. At the van, she reached for the back door handle, but Lisa motioned for her to ride in front. Allison peered through the back window and saw Meagan sitting in the backseat in a tucked position, chewing on her fingers. Allison opened the front door, took one look at Lisa, and thought she would die. "You have to be fucking kidding me. You do think you're Nancy Drew."

Lisa was dressed head to toe in black with a black cap on her head covering half her face. She wore big Jackie O. sunglasses and black leather boots up to her knees. "You forget I frequent this place. People know me, and I don't want anyone pouncing on me before Mr. Romance shows up."

"Oh yeah, because no one will look at you dressed like that. You do realize the sun went down two hours ago?"

"Whatever." Lisa pulled the glasses off her face, letting them fall onto the console.

The girls said little on the drive over.

"Let's park over there," Meagan called from the backseat, pointing to a spot near the hotel restaurant entrance. The girls walked in the front door and sat down on the green, faux suede couch. Meagan looked around at the black and white diamond tile floor and white walls. "That man has more money than God, and this is where he picks to screw his flings."

"Hey, watch it. I'm a regular, remember?" Lisa replied, then gave it a second thought. "Yeah, you're right. If we had their money, we'd be banging it out at the Marriott."

Dougy walked in and took his place at the front desk. He had told Lisa that when the newest Mrs. Smith entered the building, he would wave at Lisa as if saying hello.

Moments later, a young woman wearing a full-length plaid skirt and a white blouse with a big bow walked in carrying a picnic basket in one hand and a portable speaker in the other. She put down her belongings and placed both hands on the counter as she spoke to Dougy.

"She doesn't look a day over eighteen," Meagan blurted. "And what's with the pigtails?"

"Calm down," Allison said. "Remember the plan."

Lisa watched Dougy, ready for a sign that this was the infamous Mrs. Smith. Dougy gave her an inquisitive look, but before Lisa could question him, a very manly looking woman walked in and kissed the childlike woman. The two of them disappeared into the elevator.

"Hey, do you think they were lovers?" Allison asked.

"Duh."

"What time is it?" Meagan felt like she was about to have diarrhea. "I have to go to the bathroom."

Lisa looked down at her watch. "You're not going anywhere. It's 7:00 on the dot. Dougy said Frank is always here at precisely 7:00 and in the elevator by 7:01. We have exactly one minute to confront him."

"What about letting them go up to the room and then knocking?" Allison suggested.

"No way. What if we lose them? And there's no way Dougy would give me his room number. He'd get fired in a minute for that."

"He'd get fired in a minute for any of this," said Allison.

"I don't feel good about this," Meagan said. "Let's go."

"Meagan, keep your shit together," said Lisa. "We'll simply look him in the face and tell him he has one week to tell Rose or we will. And then we'll simply turn and walk out."

"Holy fucking shit!" Meagan gasped.

"What's your problem?" Lisa snapped.

"Holy fucking shit," Meagan repeated. "It's Rose."

"Rose!" Lisa and Allison exclaimed in unison, turning to see Rose walking straight towards them. Her walk was fierce, but her demeanor was fiercer.

"I knew it would eventually come to this with Lisa screwing here." Rose spoke in a voice the girls didn't recognize.

Allison struggled to collect her thoughts. "Rose, what are you doing here?"

"Maybe I should be asking that same question." Rose stared straight at Allison. "The three of you calling off Zoom night. I called your house, and Henry said you were with your friends seeing Howard's garden. I knew immediately what you were up to. But if you're looking for my husband, he'll be a little late. I gave him an errand to run."

Dougy gestured at Lisa, but she missed his clue until his coughing became too loud for her to ignore. She looked over and saw him signaling toward the woman leaning against the wall by the elevator doors. "Ah," Lisa said. "Maybe we should go in the restaurant and talk."

Allison and Meagan sensed Lisa's urgency and turned towards the elevators. Meagan's mouth dropped. "Are you fucking kidding me?"

They turned back towards Rose, who now looked like a woman they had never known. "Stay the hell out of my marriage," she threatened through gritted teeth. She turned and walked straight out the door to where Ana was waiting for her.

"Wow, wow, wow," Lisa said. "What do we do now?"

Meagan bit down on her lip so hard she broke skin. She glared at the women. "I know what I'm going to do." She stormed across the hotel lobby with Lisa and Allison on her heels.

The young woman saw her and smiled with excitement. "Meagan, what are you doing here? My guy will be here any moment. I can finally introduce you."

"Your guy happens to be happily married with five daughters."

Jessica's smile collapsed. She squinted her eyes at Meagan in disbelief, then looked at Allison and Lisa. "My guy is *not* happily married. He's leaving his wife very soon. She's a bitch and he can't wait to get out of there."

Lisa lunged forward, but Allison pulled her back so Meagan could continue. "She happens to be one of the sweetest women in the world, and he loves her and the girls very much."

"Meagan, you know nothing. They don't even have sex, haven't in years, and he's almost positive she's sleeping with someone else."

Meagan wanted to hit her right in the face, but instead she moved in closer, pointing her finger right at Jessica. "You're so stupid it's pathetic."

"You're the pathetic one. You'll never find love."

Meagan stared at her and shook her head. "You teach her child, for God's sake. What is wrong with you?"

Jessica straightened herself and smirked. "You'll see. The truth will all come out very soon."

Lisa grabbed Meagan by the shirt and pulled her towards her. "Let's get out of here now before Frank shows up."

The two headed out the door, but Allison remained, looking Jessica up and down.

"What's your problem?" Jessica snarled.

Allison waited a moment, then spoke loudly enough so everyone in the lobby could hear. "You have a really ugly asshole."

She turned to leave and almost ran Frank over.

"Allison?" He looked shocked to see her. He looked at Jessica and then back to Allison.

"Fuck you," said Allison.

Allison closed the car door, buried her face in her hands, and cried. Lisa drove with one hand and rested the other on Allison's shoulder. Meagan sat in the back, feeling angry at Jessica and confused about Rose.

"I don't get it. Has Rose known all along? Why hasn't she ever come to us? She talks about Frank like he's the best man alive."

Allison lifted her face from her hands. "I feel awful. I knew it was wrong of us to get involved. What do we know about their situation, their marriage?"

"Okay, slow down." Lisa felt frustrated. "We were having Rose's back. How were we to know she knew?" She reached for the radio, blasted some music, and then turned it off. "Of course Miss Peace and Love, 'Everything is perfect,' would rather ignore an affair than have a confrontation. I have no respect for her at this moment at all. What is she teaching her girls, that it's okay for a man to shit on you as long as he pays the bills?"

"Lisa, we have no idea what the circumstances are," Allison said.

Meagan held her stomach in the backseat. "We should call her."

"No, we should go over to the house," Lisa replied.

"Oh, I don't know," Allison said. "I think we should give her space."

"Fuck space. We need to go to her." Lisa did a U-turn right in the middle of the road, missing the guardrail by inches, and headed for Rose's home. When they pulled up, the house was pitch-black.

"It's not even 8 o'clock. Where are the girls?"

"Rose knows us well enough to know we would head over here. Obviously she doesn't want to see us." Meagan laid down on the back seat. "Come on. Let's go."

"No way. I didn't drive all the way over here for nothing." Lisa threw the car in park. She opened her door and looked at Allison and Meagan. "Are you coming?"

"Not a chance," Meagan replied.

Lisa looked at Allison who seemed to be contemplating, "Sorry girlfriend, I'm with Meagan on this one."

Lisa walked up to the door and rang the bell. After minutes without an answer, she turned the knob, but the door was locked. Then she disappeared around the house. Meagan looked up and swore she saw a shadow in the window and the drapes moving. "Rose is watching us."

"We need to get out of here." Allison jumped into the driver's seat just as Lisa came sprinting around the corner.

Lisa jumped into the passenger's seat. "Drive. Drive."

Ana came running around the house carrying a broom yelling with Dandelion in tow, barking her head off.

It had been a long night, a long, bad night. Meagan was emotionally exhausted and so full of anxiety she had to go home and hide under the covers. *If I'm feeling this way, how must Rose be feeling right now?* The thought sickened her, and the thought that she and the other girls may have made it worse for Rose sickened her even more. Why had she listened to Lisa? She should have minded her own business and watched reruns of *Golden Girls* all night. This was why she loved Josh so much—there was no drama with him, and he always knew the right thing to say to her. She climbed under the covers and cried as he rubbed her back, reassuring her it would be alright. Oh, and the worst part was Jessica. How could she? Meagan had trusted her, believed her. Now she thought back on all the things Jessica had said about her boyfriend, all the secrets she'd shared with Meagan.

Now did she have to tell them to Rose!?

She knew Lisa would put it together soon that Jessica had confided in her about Frank, and Lisa would want to know everything. Meagan felt like her head was about to explode. She couldn't stop the memories of Jessica sitting across from her with her perfect nose, telling Meagan about the sweet messages her boyfriend left her each morning and how he loved the way she giggled when he tickled her belly button. Oh, and then all that stuff about his frigid, unappreciative, lazy wife. When Meagan had asked her how she felt about sleeping with someone else's husband, Jessica had said it was the wife's damn fault for not taking better care of a great man like him and that their marriage had been over for years. She had assured Meagan the wife had stopped having sex with him long ago and only stayed in the marriage for the money and her status in the community. Meagan had believed her and supported Jessica in the relationship. She had been happy for her, for them. Now Meagan was overcome with anxiety and guilt. She felt sick to her stomach and could do nothing but cry to Josh.

Allison and Lisa headed to Allison's house and killed two bottles of wine between them. Sure, Tom came in and helped a little, but he wanted no part of what had just happened and refused to comment. This infuriated Allison, but she was not getting into it with him tonight, not in front of Lisa. The kids knew something was up, but Allison assured them all was fine and gave them each an extra half-hour to stay up, so they happily went their own ways.

Lisa just raged all night, getting madder and madder. Allison couldn't tell who angered Lisa most: Rose, Frank, or the tramp, which Lisa proclaimed was the only name she would use for her. Finally around 10:30, Gomez called and said he was jogging over to drive her and the van home. She argued with him to give her more time, but he was at the front door twenty minutes later.

The moment Lisa saw him, she ran to him and cried in his arms. Allison didn't know what to say or do. She knew this brought up a lot of childhood memories for Lisa, bad memories, but Lisa never wanted to talk about it so Allison didn't pry. It was bittersweet to watch Gomez take care of her and only made her that much sadder about Rose.

# Latte: Lisa

Lisa opened her eyes and stared out the bedroom window. The sound of her mother screaming flooded her mind as she remembered all the fighting on the nights her father had come home late. There would always be doors slamming and her mother's sobbing throughout the night. And then there was the time Lisa had found a beautiful pair of earrings under her father's car seat. Oh, how she had loved to play in his car when she was young, but after that incident she had been forbidden. Lisa hadn't done anything wrong. She had just asked what had happened to the gold earrings when her mother had opened silver ones on Christmas morning. He had shunned her all Christmas day.

But no memory was as painful as remembering her father's hands running up and down her babysitter's back as they had groped each other on the front step after her mother had left for the night. Lisa had never told her mother about the babysitter, but somehow she must have found out because a month later, Lisa and her mother were living in the basement of her grandmother's house. And again, not even old enough to ride a rollercoaster, Lisa had spent her nights falling asleep to her mother's sobs.

Gomez walked into the bedroom and sat down next to her. "I brought you a latte. I made it all by myself with that fancy frothier of yours."

Lisa sat up and took the cup from Gomez's hands. "Sometimes, I don't think I deserve you."

"Hey, hey, hey. Don't get all soft on me."

Lisa smiled and sipped her latte, thinking about what she needed to do next.

* * *

Classes had begun and few children walked the halls. Lisa sat in the front office waiting to see the vice principal since the head principal was away at a seminar. *Yeah, right. Wasting taxpayers' money, I'm sure.*

"Mr. Newman will see you now," the assistant said, not hiding that Lisa was bothering her.

Lisa wondered why the woman was such a bitch. *Maybe her husband cheated on her and she was forced to go back to work. She may feel like she'll never be loved again. Well, it's not my fault, so she ought to be nicer. Maybe if she were nicer, her husband wouldn't have cheated, the lying bastard.*

"This way."

"You seem miserable. It must be hard working with all these snot-nosed kids."

The woman immediately straightened up and placed a smile on her face. "No, no. I love my job. But you have a nice day. He will be in in a minute."

Mr. Newman walked in and sat behind his desk. He was a young man who looked much older due to sun exposure and guilty pleasures. Lisa smelled stale cigarettes the moment he entered. He was taller than she remembered, with a crop of bristly, mousy brown hair above his plump face. He had a big, round belly and a complexion that screamed he needed blood pressure medication.

"Good morning, Mrs. Popov."

"Call me Lisa. I'm here because you have a home wrecking tramp working here and she needs to go."

"Excuse me. I don't understand."

"The new fourth grade teacher, the one with the buggy eyes. I think her name is Jessica Hall or Halls. She's a home wrecker, screwing one of the dads in her class, and I want her fired."

"Miss Hall is a great asset to our school, and what she does in her private time is none of the school's business. If, as you say, she really is involved with a married man—which I feel is unlikely—I do not have the authority to dismiss her over that."

Furious, Lisa stood up, walked to his desk, and leaned in as far as possible. "Listen here. Your 'Miss Innocent Teacher' Miss Hall is fucking a father she met at back-to-school night on school property, during a school event. His child is in her class. She threatens to tear apart this little girl's family and destroy all their lives, and she should not be near that child. Plus, she's cancelled every meeting the mother has scheduled to talk about her child's education."

Lisa turned to the door, then turned back around. "Interestingly, as I was waiting in the front office, a girl in a wheelchair came in complaining that it was the fifth day this school year that the elevator didn't work. Oh, and also, I heard a rumor that the teachers weren't giving homework for two weeks before standardized testing and some were even teaching to the test. Sure would suck if the local paper heard about that."

"Are you threatening me?"

She walked to the door and turned around one last time. "God, no. Just pointing out facts. And by the way, cigarettes kill. Good day."

Lisa stormed out of the building without looking at Miss Grouchy. She jumped into her car and drove away much faster than the school speed limit permitted as Rose watched her from her car.

Rose had driven up to the school as Lisa had been walking in and had waited for her to leave. She knew why Lisa was there. There was no mistaking her body language as Rose had watched her through Mr. Newman's office window. Rose wanted to be mad. *How dare she continue to be in my business?* But she wasn't. She was relieved.

She started her car and headed home.

# Chardonnay: Rose

Rose had been on the *Latte to Chardonnay* diet for over two weeks now and felt horrible. But she had no appetite for anything else. It was a vicious circle. She would swear every night she was just going to have one glass of wine and then end up having two or three. She'd wake up feeling bad and wind up going back to bed after carpool. She'd start her day with a latte, sometimes two, and feel sick at the thought of food. Around dinner, a nibble here and there just waiting for the clock to reach seven so she could have a glass of wine. She didn't want the kids seeing her drinking every night, so she kept a bottle next to her bed. *How pathetic to be drinking warm wine because your husband forgot his wedding vows. But I think I'm doing pretty well for someone whose life just got turned upside down. I could be living on Valium and not getting out of bed all day.*

She missed the girls but was not ready to talk to any of them. Allison sent love texts every morning, and Lisa periodically rang her doorbell. And poor sweet Meagan had written her many apology emails for having anything to do with Frank's mistress. Rose wanted to call Meagan and ask her what she knew, but she was afraid of what she might hear. She needed more time. If she decided a divorce was best, she could use Meagan's tell-all information as backup.

Rose forced herself out of the bedroom and curled up on a chair in the living room. She pretended to be reading a book as the girls came in and out with questions, wants, and demands. Dandelion sensed her sorrow and had not left her side since she had returned to the car on that awful night at the hotel.

She sat in the living room for hours, thinking. *God help me, I don't know what to do. I ache for Frank. I miss him and want to smell him and feel his arms around my body. I want everything to be like it was or how I thought it was. I wish I had never found out. Pitiful, but true. Now I have to deal with it. I'm not stupid. I know plenty of women look the other way. Lisa would die hearing this from me, but Lisa doesn't have five children asking every day when Daddy's coming home. She doesn't see the look in their eyes when they say how much they miss him. The thought of the girls going back and forth from one home to another - the holidays split between two houses - I'm not ready to throw away this family so quickly. I need time to think. And I need a glass of wine.*

She looked at the clock—6:15pm. The girls were spread all over the house, taking full advantage of her not checking homework. She had told them again tonight she was ordering pizza. No one dared ask why she didn't get the oven fixed. But then again, no one had asked why she had moved the answering machine from the kitchen to her bedroom, no one even left messages these days anyway. And no one asked why she'd been driving daddy's pride and joy, the classic 1990 Alfa Romeo C4, all around town when they knew Frank only took it out for a spin twice a year. Rose smiled. *And to think I couldn't drive a stick shift before last week.*

She walked out to the garage with Dandelion trailing right behind her to where she had stored a case of Rombauer behind the camping gear. She expected the bottle under her bed was close to finished. Looking at the clock again as she walked through the kitchen, she thought how ridiculous it was to wait until seven every night, but it was a rule she lived by that kept her from starting to drink at 2:00 on days like today. As she headed down the hall, a sign she had recently hung caught her eye: *"Home Is Wherever I Am with You."*

Frank had bought it for her last spring when the two of them had been downtown looking for a few shrubs to plant in the front yard. *What a liar he is. But I guess he didn't know her at the time he bought this sign. I know he didn't meet her until the school year began, right? Or maybe it was at the teacher meet-and-greet in July. Why didn't I go?* She wondered what had happened, what she had done over the summer that could have led him to have an affair. *Wasn't I attentive enough? She is so beautiful. I know I get caught up in the girls, and I was at the beach many nights. But still, I almost won July's Latte to Chardonnay challenge, and that wasn't easy finding different places in the house to have sex without the girls walking in. I have birthed five babies, his babies. Maybe my body seems ugly to him. I bet her tits stand perfectly, and every time I think of her perfectly bleached asshole I want to puke. I need wine. I don't care what time it is. I'm having a glass of wine.*

She walked down the hall and peeked in on the girls. Jasmine was showing Lily and Violet how to put on eyeshadow, and Daisy and Dahlia were laughing at animal videos on Dahlia's laptop. She walked into her bedroom, her sad, lonely bedroom, and started the tub. She added a little rosemary bath salt and lit three candles. All of the pictures of her and Frank were turned over. She tried to remain calm, but disturbing thoughts of Jessica's pretty pink nipples and asshole flooded her mind. She grabbed a picture on the shelf and turned it over to look at it. It was the one they had taken four summers ago on a family trip to Aruba. With all her might, she whacked it against the bathroom wall. It shattered, glass flying everywhere. Dandelion, confused and a bit scared, ran out of the bathroom and sought refuge on the bed. Moments later, there was a knock at the door. Rose slowly walked over and opened it just enough to peek her head out. Daisy, wide-eyed, asked, "You okay, Mommy?"

"Yes, baby. Silly Mommy tripped and knocked over a picture, but everything is just fine."

She walked back into the bathroom and took a sip of her wine. *I can't fall apart. If it were just me I could go live in a tent somewhere and never come out, but I have my girls. I must be strong for my girls… I should have known something was up sooner. He's been so distant and short with me. I just kept telling myself it was work stress. All those extra hours of work—now I know he was probably out fucking her. I hate him, and I really hate her. I want to call her parents and tell them what a shitty job they did raising a home wrecker.*

*I wonder if she and Frank are together right now. But I don't think so… I bet Frank told me what was wrong, what I did that made him cheat in one of the hundred voice messages he's left me. I'm not listening to a single one. I think he caught on that I'm not listening and that's why he's calling the house phone now, hoping one of the girls will pick up. He probably never thought I was smart enough to turn off the ringer and move the answering machine. And he probably doesn't think I have it in me to tell the florist I'm allergic to flowers and to send my deliveries over to the nursing home on Creeks Road, all seven of them. Poor delivery boy didn't even take the flowers out of the van on this last delivery. They keep getting bigger and bigger, and I keep turning them away.*

Rose climbed into the tub and let the warm water cradle her, taking ten deep breaths while thinking about her beautiful children. The wine began to do its job, softening her thoughts. Looking down at her body, she saw that it too was beautiful. *Rose, remember all the work you've done to love yourself and accept yourself. You are being challenged beyond belief right now, but you must stay strong… I want to call Allison, but I'm afraid the moment I let someone in I'll collapse and become weak. I think I should listen to Frank's messages. I'll do it. I'll find the courage and strength to listen to them once the girls are in bed.*

She finished her bath and took time tucking in all five of the girls one by one, amazed by how deeply she loved them with her broken heart. As they lay in their beds, she asked them to tell her about their days, and as they spoke to her, she realized that she was forever changed. *I see differently now. I am mystified by how utterly amazing each and every one of these girls is. These are my babies, my creations, my doing. I did this. Well, we did this. Why did he have to mess everything up for us? Why weren't we enough? Why wasn't I enough?*

She went back to her room to pour another glass of wine but decided against it and headed to the kitchen for some tea instead. *If I'm going to listen to these messages, I need my head on straight.*

She curled up on her bed holding Dandelion like a teddy bear and pushed play. "You have 37 new messages."

The first message was from the pharmacy, reminding her to pick up Violet's acne prescription that had been ready for over a week. The second message came on, and her stomach sank at the sound of Frank's voice. "Rose, pick up. I know you're there, Rose. Please pick up, Rose."

The third message: "Rose, I have tried your cell phone a million times. I don't want to upset the girls and come over without talking to you, but I am going to come over if you don't pick up. Pick up, Rose, please. Pick up."

The fourth and fifth and sixth messages were all the same. "Rose, please pick up. Rose." Messages seven, eight, nine and ten were pleading and desperate.

"Rose, I love you. I love you so much. I am so so sorry, Rose."

"You and the girls are my life. I can't live without you."

"Please, Rose. I want to come home. I'm sorry I hurt you."

"Rose, Rose, Rose. Please answer me, Rose."

Those messages had come the night after she had thrown him out. The rest that followed had arrived periodically over the last two weeks and were not as humble "Rose, this isn't fair. We need to talk."

*Fair? How dare he talk about fairness? I have been so dedicated to that man for the last seventeen years of my life. He screws the kid's teacher and he's talking about me not being fair.* She looked down at Dandelion, who gazed back at her with her big wide opened eyes.

Rose read her mind. "Yes, what an asshole." She played through the next few messages and heard a lot of the same from Frank. There were two from Lisa.

"Rose, I have called your cell a dozen times. Listen to me, Rose. I know you, and you'd better not be blaming yourself for one ounce of this. You did nothing wrong. This is all Frank's doing. You hear me, Rose? You did nothing wrong."

"Rose, it's me again. I just wanted to say I love you and I'm here for you. Anything you need, Rose, I'm here." It almost sounded like Lisa was crying. Rose rewound Lisa's messages and listened to them one more time.

The rest of the messages were Frank being Frank. She knew he was sorry but not sorry enough. "Rose, we need to talk. Rose, I said I was sorry. Rose, I love you."

Blah, blah, blah. She poured another glass of wine and searched her closet for the unopened vibrator Lisa had bought her for her birthday two years ago. Finding it hidden in an old shoe box on the top shelf, she put Dandelion in her carrying case out of sight and let the evening become hers. For the first time in fourteen days, three hours, and ten minutes, she felt a tad like herself.

* * *

The morning came more quickly than usual. It was not like Rose to hit the snooze button three times, but this morning she did, letting the rain outside her window lull her back to sleep. Violet came charging into the room. "Mom, what the fuck? I have a chemistry exam and we're going to be late."

"Violet, watch your mouth." Rose scrambled to get dressed and down the stairs.

"When is Dad coming home? He always gets me to school on time."

I'm doing my best, Violet."

"Well, your best isn't good enough. I'm riding with Sara," Violet hollered as she ran out the door.

"Violet, you know you're not allowed to ride with her."

But she was out the door and climbing into the teenage neighbor's car before Rose could grab her shoes and stop her. Lily and Jasmine came filing into the kitchen. "What's up Violet's ass this morning?" Jasmine asked.

"Jasmine, watch your mouth. What is happening around here?"

"When is Dad coming home? I need help with my American history paper."

"I can help you."

Jasmine tilted her head and gave her a sorry look. "Mom, no offense, but last time you helped me things didn't go so well."

"I graduated Wellesley College magna cum ..."

"... laude," Jasmine and Lily said in unison. "Yes, we know."

"When is Daddy coming home? It's not fair he has to work so hard."

After dropping off Lily and Jasmine at the junior high, Rose headed to the elementary school with knots in her stomach, like every other morning for the past two weeks.

"Do you like your new teacher?" Daisy asked Dahlia as they pulled up.

"Wait, Dahlia, you got a new teacher? Why didn't you tell me?" Rose felt like she was going to vomit.

"Yeah. Miss Hall has been sick lately, and they said she's not coming back to school. I'm not sad, though. She was being really mean before she left. Some of the kids said she has cancer, but Billy Bourman said his mother told him she was getting that ugly thing removed from the side of her face. Love you." And out the door she went.

Daisy sat smiling, waiting her turn to be dropped off around the back of the school. Rose smiled back and carefully pulled away, trying not to be seen by anyone, particularly Allison, who would be dropping off Henry. Rose wondered if the other girls knew that Jessica had left the school. She wondered if Lisa's meeting with Vice Principal Newman had anything to do with it. She should have felt pleased, some sort of relief, but she didn't. She just felt sadder. She slowly pulled around back, realizing they were later than she thought as she watched the carpool assistants walk into the school. She found a parking space and got Daisy out of the car.

Daisy shrieked. "Daddy! Daddy!"

Frank was standing at the door waiting for them. He looked like he had not slept or showered in two weeks. He had dark circles under his eyes, facial hair growing in different directions, and wrinkled sweatpants. *How do you wrinkle your sweatpants?* Rose wondered. She was happy to see him looking like crap and even happier she had taken a moment to run a comb through her hair before getting out of the car. Daisy ran, jumped into his arms, and smothered him with kisses. For Daisy's sake, Rose refrained from yelling at him to leave, although every cell in her body screamed at her to do so. Frank pitifully stared at her.

"Good morning. May I walk her in with you?"

Rose stood quietly but nodded towards the door. Frank walked inside to the front office, still holding Daisy while signing her in. Rose walked behind him, envisioning herself kicking him again and again. Then she imagined herself jumping on his back and biting him. First his shoulders, then the top of his head and both of his ears. He had ruined it for all of them. He had ruined it.

Once Daisy was signed in, she hugged her father goodbye. "Daddy, will you be home to tuck me in tonight?"

"Daddy has a lot going on at work right now, Pumpkin, but I'll do my best."

*He ruined everything.* Rose turned and headed out the door at lightning speed, amazed that she could walk that fast.

Frank had to jog a little to keep up. "Rose, will you please talk to me? Rose."

She kept her head down and waited until she had reached her car to face him. "What do you want to say, Frank? You didn't mean it. It just happened. Your dick has a mind of its own. What the fuck, Frank? You ruined everything."

"Rose, I know. I fucked up."

"Oh, you think so? And you think you can just show up here and apologize and everything will be okay? You are such a selfish, insecure man who is so used to getting his own way, you probably do believe it will be that easy."

"No, Rose. I don't think you'll forgive me that easily, but please give me a chance to make it up to you. I'll do whatever you want. Do you want to go to counseling? I will go."

"What I want is to know everything, Frank. Did you smell her hair? Rub her skin, thinking how soft and smooth it was?"

"Rose, stop."

She opened the car door, surprised by her ability to confront him. As she tried to close the door, Frank held it against her will. She stared back at him, hoping to kill with her gaze. "Is she softer than me, her skin smoother? I lie in bed at night and can't get the images out of my mind no matter how hard I try, Frank, of the two of you lying together, your flesh pressed against hers. I know the way you like to circle my nipples with your fingertips oh so lightly, and I think about you doing that to her. Or if I'm not wet enough for you, how you use your spit as lubricant, and I picture you doing that with her."

Rose continued. "I think about our trip to Bermuda when we stayed in that amazing villa and how romantic it was. I remember you putting your fingers so deeply inside of me and then tasting me, telling me how beautiful I was to you and how I tasted just like a flower. I wonder now if you do that to her. Everything that was you and me—I now think of you and her. And when I think of you inside her, your body inside her body, you humping up and down with that look you get on your face right before you come, that look that was only mine to see—when I think of you with her and her looking up at your face, I want to throw up. I have thrown up."

"Rose, it wasn't like that for me. I didn't think of her that way. She didn't mean anything to me. It's just you're so busy with the kids— and I love you for that. You are the best mom to our girls, but sometimes I get lonely. She was there, and I never thought you would know about it so it wouldn't hurt you. I made a huge mistake. I'm sorry, Rose."

"What did I do wrong, Frank? Why did you need another woman?"

"You did nothing wrong, but like I said, sometimes I need a little more attention, and I don't want to bother you."

"Well, maybe you should have gotten a puppy. And you told her those lies about me! Like not having sex. Like being a bitch."

He put his face in his hands and began to weep. "I fucked up real bad, Rose. What can I do? She meant nothing to me."

His tears did not impress Rose. "She meant nothing to you? Well, that's a real shame, Frank, because word has it she is crazy in love with you and you mean enough to her for her to bleach her asshole for you and shove a bunny tail in it. Really, Frank, that's what you want? A perfect pink asshole?"

Frank stood speechless as Rose grabbed the car door handle and looked right at him. "You're the perfect asshole, Frank."

Rose drove off, leaving Frank shell-shocked in the dust. Never had she called him a name in all the years they had been together, and he had rarely heard her curse. Rose felt so empowered, so strong. She slammed on the brake and put her car in reverse. Frank was still standing there with the same pathetic look on his face when she rolled down the window.

"As a matter of fact, Frank, you can come by the house. Be there tomorrow in the morning for carpool and plan to stay two nights.

I'll be going out of town, but I'm sure you can figure out where and when all your children need to be somewhere."

"Rose, I have work."

"That's not my problem. This is what divorce looks like, Frank, so I really hope your little affair was worth it. Be there by 7:15 and don't be late. I'll be gone by the time you get there, but Ana will have the girls dressed and fed."

# Chardonnay: Rose

"But Daddy doesn't know where any of my friends live," Lily moaned.

"He'll figure it out."

"How will we eat?"

"You'll figure it out."

Rose confirmed her reservation at Reflection Lake Resort and Spa, using a credit card that was only in her name so Frank couldn't track her down. She had applied for the card purely for the great points they were offering just for opening an account. She had never thought she would use the card or imagined the perfectly wonderful freedom it would provide.

Her bags and Dandelion's belongings were already in the trunk of her car, Frank's pride and joy, ready to go. She so wished she had a camera set up in the garage to see the look on his face when he discovered she had taken his stupid fricking car. It was not as comfortable as her SUV but much more fun to drive.

After saying good night to the girls, she headed off to bed. She noticed a text message from Allison and considered texting back but knew she needed more time on her own to figure out what to do next. No one who had not had a very similar experience could understand—it was too complicated. It was extremely over whelming to make such imperative decisions that affected her whole family. She and Frank had built a big life together, and there were five young lives to consider. Would she walk away from it without even considering forgiveness? Maybe.

She picked up her phone and read Allison's text: *"Goodnight, sweet, beautiful Rose. Please know I never stop thinking of you. I send you all the love, strength, and peace your kind soul needs. I love you."*

Rose half-smiled and went to sleep.

# Latte: Rose

Rose was dying for a latte, but the only Starbucks in the direction she was heading was the one she and the girls went to all the time. She knew they were probably all still sleeping, but the thought of running into one of them made her too anxious about stopping, so she ventured through the drive-thru at McDonald's and gave their latte a chance.

The drive was peaceful, as she had most of the roads to herself. She took as many backroads as possible to enjoy the beautiful countryside of Connecticut and then New York State while listening to Alanis Morissette. She had always considered her music to be angry and had struggled to listen to her in the past. However, Lisa had uploaded her "Jagged Little Pill" album to the group playlist five times and Rose knew it was for her.

Over the past two weeks, Rose had listened to every sad, heartbreaking song the Carpenters had ever written and all the sappy music Meagan had added to their Spotify list. Now, she needed music therapy. She listened to Alanis' album straight through a couple of times and then repeated "You Ought to Know" a dozen more before arriving at the hotel, and something inside of her changed. Instead of feeling sad and victimized, she felt empowered and embraced her angry feelings. She never allowed herself to get angry. She always looked at anger as a negative emotion stemming from some deep-seated, unresolved issue. However, in that moment, she was feeling pretty damn good about being angry. The other day when she had given Frank a piece of her mind, she had never raised her voice. *He must have been in shock to have his sweet Rose use a curse word in a fight. Just wait until he hears me yell.*

Rose walked Dandelion around the hotel until the room was ready, repeating in her head her new favorite verse: *And every time you speak her name, does she know how you told me you'd hold me until you died, 'til you died? But you're still alive.*

It was a beautiful resort on the edge of Reflection Lake in upstate New York. Very private, decorated with gorgeous antiques and countless amazing flower arrangements. She had read about the hotel in *The New York Times* and had always wanted to stay there, but it had been too expensive. Now she was treating herself and planned to get as many spa treatments as she wanted.

She found a little wooden bench on the edge of the water and sat down watching the ripples on the lake when a young man approached her. "Excuse me, Mrs. Gardener. Your room is ready."

Rose smiled. "It's Garden, Rose Garden." For the first time, she felt silly saying her name out loud and thought of Lisa.

"Oh, my apologies. Miss Garden, your room is ready."

They engaged in small talk as they found their way back to the hotel and to Rose's room with her bags. He was adorable. The biggest mahogany brown curls Rose had ever seen, with dreamy beautiful green eyes and dimples that dug deep into his cheeks. She thought how easily this boy must pick up girls but then came to learn he was not a boy at all. He said people always mistook him for a college kid, but actually he was turning twenty-seven in two days.

He had tried his best at acting in New York City and had just moved back upstate to work on his master's degree. Being a bellboy in New York City had been a great gig, but now he felt fortunate to have a job at this resort while in school. Rose asked him enough questions so he wouldn't ask her any. Normally, she didn't speak to strange men—Frank did all the talking. She was surprised how nice and freeing it felt.

Once inside, he asked her if she would like the bath drawn. She knew it was a routine hotel service, but it felt so intimate to be alone and have a man ask to draw you a bath. She summoned the courage to respond. "Yes, I would love you to draw me a bath, and bubbles would be wonderful."

She remained in the bedroom, looking at the beautiful art on the walls and admiring the comforter on the four-posted bed while he went into the bathroom. Everything was so romantic: the high ceilings, the chandelier, the soft drapes.

After the bellman left, Rose walked around the bathroom taking everything in. She had had no idea a bathroom could be so beautiful. The floors were heated, white marble veined with shades of gray. The walls were pure white with exquisite molding from top to bottom, and there were mirrors everywhere, framed in gold. A gorgeous crystal chandelier hung from the center of the ceiling right over the biggest, most amazing bathtub she had ever seen. A welcoming tray lay on the sink with fruits and cheeses, and a bottle of French champagne chilled in a bucket of ice. Obviously, the hotel was in the habit of entertaining happy couples, but she found it just perfect for a heartbroken, betrayed married woman.

She pulled a chair beside the tub and put the tray of food on it, poured herself a glass of champagne, and slipped out of her clothes. Dandelion slept peacefully in the bedroom, clearly unaware there was a tray of cheese nearby. Once submerged in bubbles and full of champagne, Rose considered facetiming the girls, knowing they would love to see this setup. Then that terrible feeling came back to her, and she knew she could no longer pretend life was as simple as a wall decorated with inspirational signs.

The night Gomez spotted her in the parking lot, she had been heartbroken to find that text on Frank's phone from Jessica saying she would be at the hotel by 7:00, but she had not been shocked. She had known something was up by the way Frank got short with her so easily and how he wasn't as interested in sex.

The late meetings and the sudden need to travel for work. Shit, no wonder Jessica had thought Frank was in love with her. From Rose's calculations, he was spending a lot of time with her. Rose should have confronted him but had chosen to act happy and pretend everything was fine. *Now look how fine everything is.*

She decided against calling the girls and instead cried into her champagne and bath bubbles until the water went cold. She joined Dandelion on the bed and fell asleep until about 4 AM, when she climbed under the covers and went back to sleep.

# Latte: Rose

Morning crept through the bedroom window. Rose felt sluggish and down, with a sore jaw from grinding her teeth. She called the front desk, ordered some food, and took all three spa treatments they had available without even asking the price. Twenty minutes later, room service knocked on her door with tea and toast. Rose was surprised to see her bellman friend pushing the breakfast cart.

"Bellman, room service," she said. "They have you working everywhere around here."

"We're a little short-staffed this week, so I happily offered to work a double today. Can I help you with anything else?"

"No, I'm good." She pulled her robe closed. "Hey, what did you say your name was?"

"Joey. My name is Joey."

As he walked out of the room, he hesitated and looked back at her as if wanting to say something else but excused himself. The look on his face was puzzling, not sad but concerned. Rose turned to the bed and saw used tissues all over the floor. She could feel her eyes were swollen from all the crying, but she really understood Joey's concern when she looked towards the bathroom and saw the red lipstick on the mirror. In big writing it read, "FRANK GARDEN IS A BIG UGLY COWARD." She vaguely remembered doing that after her last glass of champagne.

She soon forgot her embarrassment with the bellman and was deep into relaxation down at the spa. It felt wonderful to have human hands touch her so lovingly. She allowed it to feel good, knowing she would soon have to check her phone messages when she returned to the room. She was impressed she had held off checking this long, but she kept reminding herself that Frank was their father and if they separated, this would be the new normal.

She had messages from Violet, Daisy, and Dahlia all saying "I love you," "Goodnight," and "Daddy's doing a great job." She had asked them all to check in with her and was thankful some of them had listened. Then, a message from Frank.

"Rose, I don't know where you are, but I hope you're doing whatever you need to do for yourself right now. Rose, it feels so right to be home. The girls are doing great, they love me being here, they need me here, and I'm not saying that to guilt you, Rose." There was a long pause. "Rose, please, may I move home?"

She threw her cell phone across the room and looked at Dandelion who was, once again, stunned by her behavior. "Well, maybe he should have thought about his girls before he started fucking their teacher." It felt surprisingly great to say "fucking" out loud. *No wonder Lisa does it so much. I need a drink.*

* * *

She threw on a little red dress and tucked her hair up in a bun after applying a couple coats of mascara and lipstick. She planned to take herself out on a date and packed all the necessities. Dandelion paced the room, sensing she would be left behind soon. Rose gave her a doggy treat and assured her she would be back in an hour, then headed down to the bar.

Surprisingly, the place was much more crowded than it had been the previous night, and she had to take the only seat available at the bar. It was a beautiful room, with floor-to-ceiling windows highlighting the lake nestled among the trees outside. The thick oak bar was beautifully carved, antique oil paintings graced the walls, and grand vases of glorious floral arrangements were placed throughout. Rose smiled, thinking what the girls would say if they could see her now.

Most of what she knew about cocktails she had learned watching *Sex and the City*. Carrie always drank cosmopolitans, so she ordered a kale salad and a grapefruit cosmopolitan then nonchalantly scoped out the room while waiting for them. The room was buzzing with people chatting away with their lovers and friends. The bartender placed her drink on a coaster in front of her. After just a few sips, he sat a second one in front of her. "That's from the guy over there," he said with a sweet smile, pointing to a man standing near the windows.

She turned and saw a middle-aged man, his face ordinary yet gentle, wearing a gorgeous navy suit and smiling at her. He walked over and placed his hand on the bar next to hers. "Excuse me. I don't mean to be intrusive, but you looked all alone and I have a table over there. I would love some company."

Immediately, she felt for her wedding ring and was glad she had not removed it any of the hundred times that she had wanted to over the last two weeks. Yet, there was something so exciting about the thought of sitting with another man. She reminded herself that she was free to do whatever she wanted. Frank had broken the contract, their vows. If she wanted to talk or even flirt, she could. "I've been sitting here waiting for my husband's call, but I guess it's okay." She reached for her cocktail and made sure her wedding ring was front and center.

He politely picked up the drink he had ordered for her and gestured to the table. "Here, let me."

She signaled the bartender she was moving. He smiled back as she followed her new friend to a table for two in the corner of the room. It was nice to be out of the hectic bar area.

He seemed like a kind man, traveling through New York doing some business and heading to the city to see his daughter. He shared that his wife had passed away two years earlier, so he made every effort to visit his daughters when he could. Rose asked about the wedding ring he wore, and he replied that he didn't have the emotional ability to take it off. Rose sipped her drink, feeling sorry for him and guilty for the self-pity she had allowed herself.

It was odd how easy it was to talk to a complete stranger about personal things. She did not share what had happened with Frank but did share feelings of confusion and doubt. They moved on from family and talked about politics, real estate investments, and the legalization of marijuana. The conversation was easy, although she missed Frank more than ever. She tried to push thoughts of him out of her mind and excused herself to the bathroom, where she splashed some water on her face, not caring about her makeup. She felt the alcohol taking over her body and mind and knew it was time to go back to her room. As she headed back to the table, she saw a fresh drink waiting for her but was still prepared to excuse herself.

Then he looked up at her with what seemed to be tears in his eyes.

"I just got a phone call from my daughter. She found photos of my wife she's never seen before and is a mess. It kills me to hear her cry like that."

The pain his family had been through was written all over his face. Now thinking of Frank angered her. Here this man was, suffering over the loss of his wife, his family no longer all together, and Frank was breaking up their family willingly. Rose settled back down in her seat and gave him her full attention, sipping her drink while listening to story after story from his past.

The bartender stood behind the bar, relieved he could take a moment to wash up some glasses and wipe down the bar. Joey came up behind him. "Hey, man. I'm heading out. What are you doing after your shift tonight?"

"I may be here awhile. See that asshole over there? I swear he comes in every Thursday night and tries the same bullshit on some hotel guest."

Joey looked over and saw Rose half slumped over in her chair with a cocktail glass at her mouth. She was watching the man in front of her talking away.

Joey shook his head. "What are you talking about?"

Matt looked down, continuing to wash dirty beer glasses in the sink. "That dude, he's a local, golfs here, so he has bar and restaurant privileges. But I swear something isn't right with him. He's always up to the bar after a lady orders and says he wants to make that a double, and he always orders them fresher, stronger drinks once they go to the table."

Joey reached over and grabbed Matt by the shirt. "What the fuck, Matt? What's wrong with you?"

Matt held his hands up. "Hey, it's not my job to babysit everyone at the bar. He's a regular. I just pour the drinks."

Joey released his grip giving Matt a slight push. "Fuck you, Matt. Try pouring your sister's drinks next time and see how you feel."

He stormed off, but when he looked at Rose's table it was empty. He immediately felt sick to his stomach and frantically started searching the lobby for Rose. Susan from accounting was filling in at the front desk filing some papers.

"Hey, that pretty blonde woman, big smile, sad eyes, have you seen her?"

Susan continued filing never looking up. "Yeah. Her husband just came to the desk with her to get another door key. She seemed out of it."

"What did you fucking do?"

Susan looked up with her mouth wide opened. "Calm down, Joey. I gave him a new key."

Joey pulled at the curls on his head. "With the room number?"

"He forgot it, so yeah."

Joey slammed his hands on the desk, "FUCK."

Susan stepped back from the desk. "Joey, what is wrong with you?"

"Give me the master key now," Joey demanded holding his hand out towards her.

"I can't do that."

"Give it to me NOW!"

Susan handed Joey the master key and he ran off to the elevator, pushing the button again and again. The doors opened, and he made his way up to the eighth floor and to room 814. There was no sound coming from the room, so he knocked on the door. No response. Then he banged on the door, and a man spoke nervously from the other side. "We don't need anything. Go away."

"Open the door. Open the fucking door."

Again no response, so Joey used the master key and forced the door open. Rose was passed out on the bed, still fully dressed with Dandelion standing over her.

A man stood in the doorway of the bathroom in a robe. "We're just getting ready for bed. What's the problem?"

Joey lunged at him. He hit the man in the mouth, grabbed him by the throat, and jacked him up against the wall. "You are my fucking problem, you piece of shit. I should choke you right here."

He dropped the man to the ground, and the man ran towards the door, picking up his clothes. "You're fucking crazy. I didn't do a thing. She wanted me to come up here with her. You're fucking crazy and won't work here another day in your life!"

As he ran out the door, Joey went to Rose and covered her with the blanket. Dandelion growled at first but then seemed to sense safety.

"Don't go," Rose mumbled.

He could see how drunk she was, and flashbacks of his mother came into his head. He knew the drill, what to do so she would feel okay in the morning and so he wouldn't have to worry about her choking on her own vomit all night. He went into the bathroom and started the shower, lukewarm. He lifted Rose from the bed and sat her on the vanity chair in the bathroom, where he took off her shoes and sweater and unzipped her dress.

"Rose, step out of your dress and get in the shower."

"Oh, you are so sweet. What's your name again?" She giggled and rubbed his ear with her finger and then pulled at his hair. "Big curls, big curls."

He took her hand away from his face. "I'm Joey. Let's get you in the shower. I need you to step out of your dress. Rose, can you do that for me?"

"You're so cute." She let her dress drop to the floor.

He had been here a hundred times as a young boy helping his mother, whose drinking had been chronic. He could see Rose was in trouble, in some unknown territory. He could see she had come to the hotel that weekend to escape some kind of pain and had become the victim of some pig's malicious ploy. "Rose, listen to me. I want you to take off the rest of your clothes and get in the shower. Do you understand? Rose?"

"I understand." She giggled and tried to reach for his face as he pulled away.

Joey turned to avoid seeing her but stayed nearby to make sure she made it safely into the shower. Once he could see her silhouette behind the shower door, arms reaching towards the running water, he went to the minibar and grabbed some crackers and ginger ale.

Rose's phone rang again and again, and then there was the sound of a new text coming in. He knew it was wrong but read it as he moved her phone from the bed to the nightstand. "*Rose, being here at the house with the girls just clarifies what I already know. I don't want to be anywhere but with you and our family. How many times can I say I'm sorry? I screwed up, I know it. Please, Rose, give me a chance."*

Joey rolled his eyes. "Fucking idiot. Of course you're repenting, now you got caught." Joey set down Rose's phone, and his own phone started to fire off texts, all from Matt.

*"Where are you, man?"* Matt wrote. *"Shit is hitting the fan big time. Susan called the general manager and he was in the lobby asking about you. That guest says you beat him up. He wants to press charges against the hotel."* Matt texted again. *"Fuck, Joey, I can't lose my job. What did you do? Where are you?"*

Joey ignored the texts and went into the bathroom, retrieving a bathrobe from behind the door. "Come on now, Rose. Let's get you to bed."

He turned his face away from her as she stumbled from the shower and wrapped herself in the robe. He reached into the shower, turning off the water with one hand while supporting her with his other arm. In the bedroom, he tucked her into bed, propping her up a bit on two pillows. He dimmed the lights, took a pillow and blanket from the closet, and settled himself on the chair across from her.

He watched her sleep for some time, wondering about the complexity of her nature. She looked so beautiful and peaceful in one moment yet so troubled and sad in another. He had no idea why he felt the way he did, but he knew he would stay by her side and protect her no matter what the consequences were. Soon his thoughts faded and sleep overcame him.

# Latte: Rose

Rose woke to the morning sun shining through the window and Dandelion curled up next to her. She was startled to see Joey sleeping in the chair, but then blurry flashbacks of the evening raced through her head. She clearly remembered sitting with that poor fellow whose wife had died, and she remembered not feeling so good and telling him she was heading upstairs to bed. The last clear thought she had was of him telling her about how upset his daughter was, and then her memories were dim. *How did I get to my room? There was a fight, yelling. Was that Joey and the man? Why am I in a robe? The shower, I remember the shower, and someone was there. But it was okay. I was safe. It was Joey. He took care of me.*

He looked so sweet sleeping in the sunlight, still in his uniform from the night before. He opened his eyes as if her watching him had awoken him.

"Hey, Petals. How ya feeling?"

"Good, I feel good, but I feel like I owe you a huge apology. I just don't know what for."

"You don't owe me anything. It's that jerk you were sitting with who owes you an apology. He was feeding you alcohol without you knowing it so he could get you up here."

"But he was so sad about his wife."

"Lies, all lies. He's a regular here, a local golf member, so he has access to the facilities. Rumor has it, he uses that line often on our traveling guests."

"I'm confused. He made that all up?"

"Yup. Once I settled you in, I did a little research. His name is Donald Scarborough. Lives four miles down the road at 5 Lakeview Lane with his wife and two teenage boys. Been coming to the club for the last seven years. Somehow, he got Susan to give him a key to your room. She works the desk sometimes at night."

A wave of nausea passed over her as she considered what could have happened. *Why is life so ugly all of a sudden?* She needed time to process, and he gave it to her, sitting silently as she stared out the window.

Then she worried about Joey. "Won't you get in trouble for reading a member's file?"

"Oh, that ship has sailed. Old Donald didn't like the way I removed him from the room last night. He's pressing charges, I hear. Pretty confident I'll be looking for a new job soon, but I don't care. Tips aren't so great here anyway."

She felt horrible. He might have lost his job protecting her. "I'm so sorry, Joey."

"Petals, you did nothing but be your sweet self. He's the jerk."

Joey walked over to the coffee pot, prepared two cups, and broke a nutrition bar from the minibar in half.

As he walked back to the bed, he seemed older than twenty-six, and Rose remembered it was his birthday. He was now twenty-seven. Half of his curls were flattened from leaning against the chair all night and the other half were in disarray. His dimples managed to dig deeper into his rosy cheeks. Muscles she had not noticed before filled out his wrinkled shirt. His eyes seemed bigger in the morning light, his lashes every woman's dream. Something in Rose moved as he came closer to the bed. Her heart raced as her body flushed. "Happy Birthday."

He smiled back at her. "Here, let's get some nutrience in you." He sat down on the edge of the bed. "I read your text, from your husband. I'm sorry."

Rose looked into his kind emerald eyes and let his words comfort her before speaking. "It's been painful. You think you know someone, you trust them, build a family together. And then the betrayal hits you like a ton of bricks."

"I understand the feeling. My father left after he was caught. I think my mother would have forgiven him, but he never said he was sorry. It broke her."

"Do you wish he had come back?"

"We were a family. I wish they had tried harder. It wasn't easy growing up. Look, it's none of my business, but I think you should at least listen to what he has to say."

She stared at him. Where had this angel come from? She had just planned on a couple of nights away alone, and here she had this beautiful, insightful young man sitting on her bed. "Maybe I wanted to be there last night. Maybe I was rebelling against my husband to get back at him."

"I don't think so. Not at all."

"I've never been with another man, haven't even kissed one since Patrick Flanagan at a tenth-grade make out party. But Frank had sex with another woman. Who knows how many there have been?"

His expression changed, and he set down his coffee mug and reached for her hand. "Walk me to the door. I want to give you something before I leave."

She held her robe closed and took his hand, allowing him to direct her across the room. When they reached the door, he gently backed her up against the wall and gazed into her eyes. Her body began to tingle from head to toe and she could feel the wet between her legs as he reached behind her and touched her hair with his hand. He leaned in and teased her for a moment, holding his lips close to hers without touching them. Then, so lightly, he kissed only her upper lip, then her bottom lip with slight pressure. He moved to her neck and up behind her ear lobe, all the while grasping her hair. She felt every cell of her body come alive. She dropped her arms to her sides and let her robe fall open, exposing her erect breasts and body covered with goosebumps. He pulled back, taking a deep breath as he studied her like a piece of art. "You are so beautiful."

Rose tilted her face up to his, and he leaned in, placing his warm, open mouth against hers. So gently, he kissed her lips, and then tightening his grip on her hair, he pressed his tongue against hers as his hard body molded into her flesh. She could feel him erect against her and without hesitation, she dropped her robe to the floor and wrapped her arms around his neck, wanting him to carry her to the bed.

He pulled back and studied her once again, this time reaching for her chest and with his index finger tracing the outline of her curves. He circled his finger around her belly button and back up around the rims of her nipples, never touching them. She gasped at his touch.

Slowly, he bent down, his mouth grazing over her breast, her navel, her opened legs. He kissed the inside of her thighs once, twice, three times. Then he picked up her robe and stepped back, holding it out for her to take. Uncertain, she took it and held it against her as he moved back in and kissed her once again, this time so passionately her feet lifted off the ground.

He spoke in deep, breathy whispers as he lightly bit down on her bottom lip. The heat of his breath, the tenderness of his touch, and the hardness of his body told her one thing while his words struggled to tell her another.

"You have no idea how badly I want to make love to you right here against this wall and then take you to the bed and devour you all morning long. But you are hurt, you are raw, and I don't want you regretting anything you do. I must go." And before she could protest, the door shut behind him.

Rose remained up against the wall, frustrated, exhilarated, relieved, and disappointed as the sun slowly made its way up the morning sky. She could hear life beginning to move around outside her window. She knew there were two things she must do before heading home, so she packed her stuff and settled Dandelion in her carrier.

When she arrived in the lobby, only a few guests were up and about, sipping coffee and fiddling with their newspapers. The woman behind the desk looked rattled with her hair tousled, her eyes puffy and watering. Susan, she assumed. Rose approached quietly. "Excuse me. Is there a manager on site?"

Susan was taken aback and spoke harshly at first. "Is there something I can help you with?" She barely looked up from her computer monitor.

"Are you a manager?" Rose smiled.

"We've had a long night. The general manager is never here at this time, but he may still be in his office."

Rose sensed that Susan was oblivious to the words coming out of her mouth. All worries Rose had had about being recognized vanished. If she had been loud or embarrassing in the lobby the night before, Susan would be attending to her differently. If Susan had known it was Rose who had been the source of her long night, she would have responded differently.

Susan placed a ten-second call, struggling to secure the receiver back onto the hook. Rose stood patiently waiting until a small man, balding with wire-rimmed glasses, approached her. He also appeared very tired and expressionless. "Thank you, Susan." He turned to Rose and asked with frustration in his voice, "Can I help you?"

"Yes. One of your members, Donald Scarborough, drugged me with alcohol last night and was able to obtain a key to my room from your front desk." Rose glared at Susan. "Luckily for me, there are good men in this world who have the courage to stand up for what's right. I want Mr. Scarborough permanently banned from the property immediately and Joey reinstated to his position. Actually, Joey deserves a raise."

Dumbfounded, he and Susan stood with their mouths open as Rose continued. "I understand charges have been placed on the hotel and Joey. I will see to it they are dropped, but I will be pressing my own charges and contacting a lawyer if my requests are not met. Oh, and I assume you will have a talk with your bartender as well. Knowingly over-serving someone alcohol is assisting date rape.

Again, grant my request or you will hear from my lawyer and the police." She turned and headed out the door before they could collect their thoughts.

The valet had her car waiting. "Thank you for visiting. Can I help you with directions or get you anything else before you leave?"

"Yes, thank you. You can tell me which direction to head for 5 Lakeview Lane?"

The road was long, a beautiful drive of mostly large oak and willow trees. A house here and there, mostly ranchers and a few with some farmland attached to them. And then a glorious lake appeared, giving the street its namesake. Rose carefully watched the house numbers go down, surprised by how relaxed she felt. When they hit ten, she slowed so she wouldn't miss five. It was still early, 8am, and the street was quiet. She spotted a quaint yellow house on the right with a catcher's net and basketball hoop in the drive. A Corvette and a SUV were parked off to the side. Number five. She pulled right into the driveway, parked, and walked up the brick path to the front door. It took two rings and a lot of dog barking before a woman cracked the door just enough to speak to her. "Yes?"

"Good morning. Is this the home of Donald Scarborough?"

"Why yes, it is. What seems to be the problem?"

"I need to speak with him, please."

"He's sleeping. He was in an accident last night."

"No, he wasn't. I need to speak to him now."

Rose immediately recognized a deep voice coming from behind the woman. "Who is it, honey?"

The woman opened the door wider, and Rose could see she was much younger than him. She was slender with thick, ginger-spiced red hair all the way down her back, perfect freckles covering her pale, smooth face, and eyes that knew the morning was off to a bad start.

Donald came to the door already knowing it was Rose. Had the hotel called him? Or maybe he had seen her pull up. His bottom lip was cut and swollen and as Rose looked closer, she could see faint scratches and redness around his neck. "What are you doing here? What do you want from us?"

"Donald, do you know this woman?"

"I saw her last night at the club. She was very drunk, so I helped her get to her room safely." He turned to Rose. "I'm going to call the police if you don't leave immediately."

"Oh, please do call them. I would love to tell them what happened last night."

"Donald!"

"Kathleen, go to the kitchen."

"No, Kathleen. Don't bother. I'll be just a moment." Rose looked at her, woman to woman, then turned back to Donald. "Listen here, you piece of shit. I'll give you one hour to call the hotel and tell them you're not pressing charges, and while you're on the phone with them, make sure Joey has his job back and you cancel your membership. You're nothing short of a predator, a rapist, and I have evidence to prove it, so it's your choice. You can call the hotel, or if you want to call the police, I'm good with that too. I'll just wait out here."

Kathleen yelled, "What the fuck, Donald?" She ran up the stairs.

Donald glared at Rose as if she were the one at fault. Rose stared back, careful not to blink. "One hour."

Her heart beat slowly as she meandered back to her car. She headed back towards town and stopped at a little drive-thru coffee house for a latte. She felt ten feet taller and as peaceful as the smooth lake beside her. She sipped her latte a few times and then dialed the house. Frank answered on the first ring, sounding alert and surprised. "Rose."

"Frank, I'll be brief and to the point. I'm driving now and expect to be home by noon. I'd like you gone when I get there. However, you may move to the spare room in the basement tomorrow if you can come up with an excuse the girls will believe. At this point, we're not getting back together. But for the girls' sake, if you can find a good counselor, I'll be open to going with you. But Frank, I'm only willing to go because of the girls. Do you understand?"

"I understand. Rose, thank you."

Rose hung up without saying goodbye, clicked on the Alanis Morrissette playlist, and hit the gas pedal. She drove down the winding road, going over and over the moments she'd spent with Joey against the hotel wall feeling like a new woman.

# Latte: Allison

As Allison walked in through the spa door, a young girl blew past her so fast she almost knocked her over.

"Yeah, and do some jumping jacks next time too," Nana yelled as she walked out of her waxing room. "Good morning, Dolly."

"What was that all about?"

"Damn kids these days. She comes in here looking for a brazilian ten minutes after screwing. I ain't going near that."

"You can tell someone has had sex before coming in?"

"Hard to miss it. You go to the bank much?"

"What? Um, yes?"

"Yeah, and what do you do there? You put money in and you take money out. What goes in then comes out."

Allison had no idea where Nana was going with this, so she refrained from saying anything.

"They don't call vajajas sperm banks for nothing!"

"Okay, got it."

Allison had hung up her coat and walked over to the desk when she saw Rose through the window, stopped at the traffic light. Allison quickly ran over to the window to wave, but Rose didn't even look over. Allison's heart dropped.

"Did you come here to daydream or work?"

Allison turned around and saw Nana holding a big box towards her to take.

"Crack that baby open. We have some new merchandise to display."

Allison opened the box and looked inside at what appeared to be little bags of hair.

"That's right, Dolly. The bush is back."

"Are these what I think they are?"

"Yep. We now carry beav weaves."

Allison took one bag after another out of the box, in all different shapes and sizes. "I'm so confused. Isn't this bad for business?"

"Some men want to see a healthy bush, but the girls can't grow it. A good wax helps the glue stick better." Nana picked up a seventies-looking full red mound and placed it on her dress in front of her crotch. "Oh, I miss the good old days."

Allison shook her head and continued unloading. There were wigs in shades of blonde, brown, red, and black, in shapes of hearts, spades, and triangles. At the bottom of the box she found a few mustaches, arrows pointing down, and even one that spelled out "Headache."

The morning flew by with one eyebrow wax after another. Allison was getting really good at shaping the brow just right, sometimes taking years off her clients' appearances. She felt proud as customers were requesting her and booking appointments on days they knew she worked. Nana told her to make her lunch quick since it was only the two of them manning the ship. Allison grabbed a quick salad from the deli across the street and headed back to the spa.

"Got a customer waiting for you. Says they're a friend of yours and fancies your service."

Allison's heart leapt in her chest. "Rose!"

Nana reached for the new merchandise, picked a big, thick black mustache wig off the wall, and held it to her face. "No, Dolly. You got a Brozilian waiting for you. I put him in my room with the vagina flower art for kicks."

*You have to be kidding me. Mr. Mustache! Bastard, must be eavesdropping on our conversations.* "Nana, please do me a favor just this once and handle him."

Nana could see the disgrace on Allison's face and hated when a pervert abused the salon. "Let's have fun, Dolly. You go get the wax ready while I get my nun costume on."

Allison walked into the room to find Mr. Mustache lying on the table, covered from his chest to his toes in white hair with the hugest mound of pubic hair she had ever seen.

"Allison, I didn't know you worked here."

Allison was still upset about seeing Rose earlier and was not in the mood for anyone's crap. "Oh, I'm still in training. The technician will be in in a moment. You don't mind if I watch?"

He smiled, bent his elbows, and put his hands behind his head. "Not at all."

*What arrogance,* she thought, looking down to see what he was so proud of. But she saw nothing except a field of cotton. She walked closer to the table, pretending to be mixing wax to get a better look, and there it was: a tiny, skinny clump of flesh hiding in the field.

The door swung open, and Sister Nana walked in holding rosary beads in her hands, mumbling a prayer.

"Holy shit!" Mr. Mustache quickly sat up, cupping his hands over his tiny junk. "I'm sorry, Sister. I didn't mean to curse."

Nana stopped in her tracks and looked at his huge mound and black mustache. "Now that's what I call the carpet not matching the drapes."

Allison backed up and leaned against the wall, devouring every second.

"Whatcha hiding under there?" Nana moved closer.

"Maybe this is a bad idea," he said. "I don't know what I was thinking."

Nana pushed down on his shoulder, signaling him to lie back, and then pulled at his arm so she could get a look at his pecker. She paused for a minute, looked at Allison, then looked back at Mr. Mustache. "Don't tell me, sonny. You're a grower, not a show-er?"

Allison laughed the whole way home, thinking of him running out of there.

# Chardonnay: Meagan

It was a chilly Friday night. Meagan was tired from a long work week but yearned to get out of the house. She was missing Mikey terribly. It was her weekend to have him, but he had asked if he could go with his father on a hunting trip. Hunting, of all things. She hated hunting and judged hunters. She was sad he was not coming home for the weekend but had been shocked when he had not wanted to come home permanently. When he had asked to live with his father, she had agreed, thinking it would last about two weeks.

She and Mikey had a great relationship with few rules needed. Meagan knew from listening to Big Mike in teacher conferences that he would be a strict parent. She had intended to give him a heads-up to go easy on Mikey when he moved in, explain how Mikey excelled when feeling independent and responded best to positive reinforcement, but she had conveniently forgotten.

Amy Schumer's latest movie was playing down the street. Meagan worried it would be too much of a chick flick for Josh, but he happily agreed to go along. Before leaving for the show, they spent time on the couch stalking Meagan's friends on Facebook. She hesitated to show him Jessica's profile in fear he would fall in love with her beauty, but he was unimpressed. He said he found most beautiful women boring and all about their looks but of course, not Meagan. Plus, Jessica was a home wrecker, and he wanted nothing to do with that, ever.

At the theater, Meagan ordered them a large unbuttered popcorn to share and two waters. Josh gave her that look: *It's Friday night. Let's live a little.* So Meagan changed the order to buttered popcorn and added a box of Jujubes.

The movie theater was packed, but they still managed to find great middle seats ten rows in. Meagan placed her coat on the back of Josh's seat so he had something comfortable to lean against. She tried not to get frustrated when repeatedly asked, "Is this seat taken?" She ignored the dirty looks when the movie started and Josh's seat appeared to remain vacant to the other patrons.

They both loved the film and laughed the whole way home reminiscing about their favorite parts. It was a great night that only got better when Josh praised Amy Schumer's sex appeal, her confidence, and her curves. Concerned, he explained he was not trying to be disrespectful talking about another woman sexually, but he thought it was important to their relationship that Meagan understood how he felt rather than assume. He shared with her that for him, nothing was sexier in a woman than high self-esteem, a woman who knew and liked herself on the inside. Then smiling, he reached over, tickled her stomach, and guaranteed her that the allure of a voluptuous woman was intoxicating. He enlightened her, saying most of his guy friends agreed they would much rather be with a self-assured curvy woman than someone checking the mirror all the time obsessed with taking selfies.

While lying in bed, Meagan shared with him her sadness about Mikey. He assured her that Mikey would return home at the right time and reminded her of what a great mother she was for her selflessness in letting him move out in the first place. He understood she was thrilled for Mikey to have his father in his life, yet acknowledged the challenges for her now to co-parent.

That night when they made love, Josh asked her to leave the lights on so he could watch her beautiful body as she moved. He was so tender with her, so loving, whispering in her ear his desire for her. She decided she wanted to do something special for him, so she planned to sneak out in the morning while he was still asleep and bring him home a gift. It would be a great gift, and she could even collect bonus points. A sure win-win.

# Latte: Meagan

"I need a favor."

"What?"

"Don't laugh, and I'll bring you a latte if you do it. I'll even go to Dunkin Donuts for you. I just need an hour of your time."

Lisa had an early flight to Seattle the next day and a million things to do before leaving, but Meagan seemed desperate. "Just tell me what it is."

Meagan took a deep breath. "I want you to paint my body."

Lisa stayed quiet. Even on the hottest pool days of summer, Meagan wore a full-length cover-up over her one-piece swimsuit, and now she was asking to be painted? *Maybe her hands and feet,* Lisa thought.

"Can you draw?"

"I'm not Picasso, but I'm pretty good at basic stuff. You saw the ballerinas I painted on Mary Jane's wall."

"Do you think you can handle a snake?"

"Easy."

"Do you think you could paint one down my stomach? Have his tail start at my breast and his tongue spit out down my happy valley?"

"Well, if by 'happy valley' you mean your labia, sure. No big deal." Lisa couldn't believe her ears. "Did it for a friend once before. You two must have read the same book," she lied.

Twenty minutes later, Meagan rang Lisa's doorbell holding two lattes and a supply of body paints and brushes. Mary Jane opened the door and barely looked at Meagan as she stormed off. "If you're looking for the Wicked Witch of the West, she's in her bedroom probably sacrificing our cat to some evil spirit."

Meagan had no idea how to respond, but even if she had, Mary Jane had slammed the door to her room before she could utter a word. She walked up the stairs to Lisa's room feeling anxious and excited. When she opened the door, Lisa was holding the family cat high in the air over her head. Meagan's mouth dropped.

"Ah, I'm just fucking with you. I heard Mary Jane so sweetly greet you."

"What's going on? You two are so close and never fight."

"She hates me, but I don't want to talk about it." Lisa tossed the cat out of the room. "Let me see your paints."

Lisa took the paints from Meagan and considered how to make this happen without Meagan changing her mind. She knew Meagan must be dying inside, but Lisa was so happy Meagan was feeling this comfortable with her body. "There's a robe on the back of the bathroom door. Why don't you put it on and come lie on my bed? I'll put down some towels and we can work in there."

"Where's Gomez?"

"In the bathroom waiting for you." Lisa just couldn't help herself. "Kidding. He took Adam to a friend's house."

Lisa covered her bed with dark blue towels, put some Norah Jones on the sound system, and lit a few candles around the room, trying to create a relaxing atmosphere. She waited for Meagan to emerge from the bathroom before opening the paints. Meagan entered, wrapped in a towel. "I don't want to get your robe messy."

Lisa gave Meagan privacy, turning towards the window as Meagan climbed onto the bed and opened the towel. Nonchalantly, she walked over to Meagan, taken aback by her beautiful, pale body. This poor child had persecuted herself with bad body image her whole life, and all Lisa could see was beauty, full-figured, soft white beauty. She casually looked down, acting unimpressed at Meagan's recently waxed Brazilian. "Nice beav. Did Nana give you that?"

"No. I did it myself."

"Too bad Rose dumped us, you could of gotten points for that."

"She'll be back, and I expect points for the wax and the snake."

Lisa studied Meagan's body. "My thoughts are to start the tail right at your nipple and head south with a few twists and turns and then put his head about here." She poked Meagan's pubic bone with the tip of the paintbrush. "You good?"

"Sounds great," Meagan said, careful not to make eye contact.

They did not speak as Lisa concentrated on doing the finest artistic job she could. She was honored that Meagan felt this comfortable with her and she wanted to make it the best experience she could for Meagan. She started painting the tip of the tail at the center of Meagan's full, rounded breast, meandering her way down Meagan's soft belly, painting the serpent's body. As Lisa worked closely, creating details in the snake's skin, she could see faded marks on Meagan's abdomen that looked like scars from all the strings that had once held her tight, reminding Meagan she had eaten enough for the day. Lisa wanted to hurl at the sight of it but remained calm. Meagan was there now celebrating her body and the scars looked somewhat old. Lisa finished painting the snake's head smack on top of her bare vagina. "Girl, you look hot! You ready for the tongue?"

Meagan sat up on her elbows and looked down at her newly painted physique. "Holy shit, I am hot!"

Lisa fought back tears, struggling to sound normal. "Josh is going to flip."

"Do it. Just paint the tongue right down the middle. It's okay. The stuff is vegan."

Lisa painted a long red tongue right over her sweet friend's clitoris and split it down the sides of her labia. "Beautiful," she said, stepping back and looking at her work of art. "I need to go do a few things. But I'll be back soon to check on you."

Lisa turned to walk away, but Meagan reached out, clutched her hand, and pulled her closer. "Thank you." She kissed the top of Lisa's hand. Lisa smiled down at her and then went to pack, giving Meagan time to dry while she fantasized about Josh seeing her erotic body.

# Chardonnay: The Club

"How was your trip?" Allison asked Lisa. "Are you ready to come home?"

"The trip was fabulous—beautiful wedding, and Seattle is such a great city. But time to come home. My liver and crotch need a break." Lisa put the last of her things in her suitcase to get ready for her morning flight.

"You sound like Meagan."

"Oh, and the best part of Seattle … I bought us all joints! Even Rose."

"Are you out of your mind, flying with those? That's a federal crime!" Allison said.

"Oh please, Miss Neurotic, now you sound like Meagan. I've tossed them in my Seattle's Best ground coffee bags, and I'll put them through baggage. TSA isn't interested in some middle-aged mother wanting to relive her youth." Lisa zipped up her bag and set it by the door. "Wouldn't you kill to see Rose high?"

Allison paused, then said quietly, "At this point, I'd kill just to see Rose again."

"Yeah, me too," Lisa said. "I'll bring the pot to our Friday coffee unless I'm in jail."

Allison hung up and thought how much she missed Rose and her beautiful outlook on life. Allison had had a fight with Tom the night before and knew Rose would have understood and made her feel better.

Tom had walked through the door with the energy of a pent-up rodeo bull. Allison knew it well, as would Rose: his work mode. From time to time, he forgot to leave it at the office after a bad day. He headed towards his den without seeming to acknowledge any of the two-legged or four-legged creatures around him.

"Well, hello to you," Allison said.

"Hello. I have a conference call I need to prepare for and someone peed by the garage door."

"Higgins, who else?" Allison said, frustrated with the dog's use of her house as a toilet.

Tom turned back to Allison, face reddening, hand clutched, voice seven decimals higher. "I don't know who did it. I'm not fighting with you!"

"Are you fucking kidding me? Who do you think did it, one of the kids? Take your work energy and shove it up your ass." Allison had stormed out of the room and back to the kitchen to finish making dinner when she stepped on something that made a very loud crunch. Her first thought was a snail, a large snail. She lifted her foot to find the remains of a crushed mouse head. It was the last straw to a bad day, which had started when she had tried to pay her phone bill. The young shit customer service girl wouldn't take her credit card information because she was not the primary account holder.

"I'm trying to give you money," she had said to the girl.

"Yes, I know, but I would need to talk to Mr. O'Neil to get his okay to speak with you about the account. Is he available?"

Time passed, and Tom appeared with his hands folded together and raised to his mouth. He found a seat at the table and sat quietly. Allison continued chopping the last of the vegetables. "We need to talk," he said.

*Shit. Please don't have been fired.*

"We can't be cursing at one another. The other night you called me an asshole right before I was going to sleep. Not cool. We need to be able to argue without cursing."

"Oh, no we don't. You use subtle put-downs, degrading little comments that make me feel stupid, and cursing is my weapon. You degrade me without even knowing it. I don't go to an office every day and have people complimenting me and appreciating me. I don't get a paycheck that represents all my hard work here at home.

I spent the last two hours before you came home organizing your closet, which sounds pathetic because it is, but someone has to do it so you're organized to go out in the world. I make sure the house is picked up and I remind the kids to give you some time to unwind. I purposely changed out of my yoga pants and was making you something healthy for dinner when you barged in here and lost it because I got frustrated that I had to clean up dog pee yet again!"

She moved in a step closer and lowered her voice. "And Tom, how many times have I told you I can't pay the bills around here if you don't make me a primary on the accounts? I couldn't even pay the fucking cable bill this morning."

"That's not fair. You know you can get onto all our accounts. Banking and everything."

"Yeah, well, giving me access to view accounts is different from access to change them." She chopped louder and louder. Then she put the knife down on the cutting board and looked straight at Tom.

"Sometimes, cursing is all I got."

He let her have this one. He went back to his den, and Allison went back to chopping.

# Latte: The Club

"Ugh, fucking preschoolers. Don't these moms have a better place to meet, like their living rooms?" Lisa shot a dirty look at a bunch of mothers chatting away in the corner as their children chased one another around the table.

"Jet-lagged?" Allison asked. "Not that you need to be jet-lagged to be your charming self."

Lisa gave Allison the finger, and Allison puckered her lips in a kiss back at her. Meagan was still over at the counter waiting on her drink.

"These fucking moms at the wedding had toddlers and were talking about watching the clock every night to turn five so they could have their wine."

"We drink wine all the time."

"Yeah, after duties are done."

"Maybe they're just having one glass while cooking dinner."

"One glass my ass. There's no such thing as one glass of wine." Lisa broke off a piece of Allison's muffin and stuffed it in her mouth. "If we had to read *Goodnight Moon* a million times sober, so do they."

"What did I miss? Who's sober?" Meagan asked, joining the girls.

"Nothing. Lisa is just being judgmental even though she swears by the golden rule to never judge another mother."

Lisa gave Allison the finger for the second time that morning. "To think I risked jail time for you. With an ass like mine I would be someone's bitch the first weekend I was in."

"Please. You wouldn't be anybody's bitch. You would have a bitch."

"Really?"

Allison and Meagan responded simultaneously: "Really!"

Lisa thought for a minute, "I would get so frustrated not having a guy to have sex with."

"Oh, I'm sure you'd find something in there to use," Allison said.

Meagan went into deep concentration. "I hear lesbians are supposed to have the best sex."

"Who said lesbians have the best sex? They say lesbians have the best relationships but not the best sex," Lisa clarified.

"What's the difference?" Meagan asked.

"Are you kidding me? Think what it would be like to be the male catcher in anal sex. My money is on gay men having the best sex."

Allison braced herself. "Catcher?"

Lisa shook her head. "Do I have to teach you kids everything? There's a pitcher and a catcher, one giving it and one getting it!"

Meagan looked around to make sure no one could hear Lisa over the yelling toddlers. Allison stayed engaged. "When two gay men meet at a bar and go home together, how do they know which one is the pitcher and which one is the catcher? What if they get in bed and both want to pitch?"

"Why? Do they only pitch or catch? They don't take turns?" Meagan asked.

"They just know!" Lisa said. "Geez, you two need to get out some more."

"Oh, how I wish Rose were here for this conversation. Her commentary would be priceless," Meagan said.

They all sat quietly for a moment and then Lisa remembered her little gifts. "Oh, before I forget, I have your presents."

"I'm going to try it this afternoon while the kids are at school. I have so much cleaning to do before Tom gets home tonight."

"I don't feel sorry for you living in that big house and refusing to get help."

"I have help once a week. I don't need more than that, but that house is a germ pit since Tommy was sick and the damn dog pissed all over my kitchen floor this morning," Allison said. "I thought I would put on some old tunes, take a puff, and clean away."

"It's called a hit, you dork. A hit, not a puff. And you should so get rid of that dog." Lisa reached down into her bag and pulled out two Seattle's Best coffee bags. There are two joints in each bag . One for energy and one for your love machine." Lisa took a big swig of her latte. "I learned all about it. I got us one called Jack Herer. It's a sativa, which makes you energetic and creative. I thought it would be good for housecleaning."

"What's sativa and who is Jack Herer?" Meagan was puzzled.

"Sativa is a head high, and Jack Herer wrote '*The King Has No Clothes.*'"

"*The Emperor Wears No Clothes!*" Allison corrected as she accidentally knocked over her drink. She jumped up to grab napkins from the bar.

"Yeah, yeah. And I brought home … wait for it, wait for it. I got us each a Berry White!"

"Barry White, the singer with that deep voice that makes you want to have sex?" Meagan asked.

"Exactly. They call it Berry White for Barry White because this shit supposedly makes you hornier than a shepherd in a field of sheep."

"How can that be?" Meagan sat up in her chair while Allison wiped up her spilt latte.

"I don't know. It's a body-high strain, indica. Maybe the pot goes right to your vagina like when you take those pain pills for a bladder infection and they know to go to your crotch. Weed in the bush, get it?"

Lisa was heading out of Starbucks when she heard a young man's voice. "Hey, Momma Janie. What's hanging?"

She turned around to see a teenage boy on the sidewalk smoking a cigarette, leaning against the outside wall of the building.

"Excuse me?"

"Aren't you Janie's mom? I've seen you with her in there before."

Lisa walked up, crossing through the comfort zones of two strangers.

"Do you mean Mary Jane?"

"Yeah, yeah. She likes it when we call her Janie, Zany Janie."

"And who is 'we'?"

"Me and my boys. Most of us are on the varsity lacrosse team over at the high school. I just got accepted to Notre Dame to play next year."

Lisa looked at his cigarette and then back at him and pointed her finger right in his face. "Listen here, you little prick. I don't care if you got accepted into the NFL to play quarterback. And I don't know what your buddies told you, but my daughter is in eighth grade. I'll see to it that none of you go anywhere next year if you go anywhere near her again."

The boy turned white. Lost for words, he dropped his cigarette and leaned harder into the wall for support. Allison and Meagan came out the door, and Lisa joined them as they walked into the parking lot. Allison could sense something was not right. "Everything okay?"

"Yeah, yeah. Just some kid I'm thinking of hiring to help Adam with his science."

Allison and Meagan got into their cars, but Lisa remained in the parking lot until they drove off. She turned back to see the young man still leaning against the wall, scared as shit. As she walked back over to him, he began to plead. "Look, I'm sorry, ma'am. Janie, I mean Mary Jane told us she was in tenth grade, sixteen."

"Don't worry about it."

"I can't lose my scholarship. I mean, my parents can't afford a university and they were thrilled when I got in. Please, I can't lose my scholarship."

"I'm sorry. I overreacted." Lisa reached out and touched the boy on his shoulder. "I'm just so concerned about my daughter. I'm sure she told you she was older and I promise you I'm not going to say a word to anyone."

"Wow, thank you." He put his hands in prayer position and bowed slightly towards Lisa.

"Why aren't you in school, and what's with that disgusting cigarette?"

"I had a dentist appointment earlier and I promise, that was my last cigarette."

"Hmm, sure." Lisa turned to walk back to her car.

"Ma'am, um …"

Lisa turned back.

"I just want you to know your daughter hasn't done anything. I mean with the guys. They call her Plain Jane behind her back because all she'll do is kiss. I promise. I only saw her drinking one time, and she threw up. She's pretty tame."

Lisa looked at the young man, thinking about how much life he had in front of him and how proud his parents must be about his scholarship. She smiled. "Thank you. Thank you very much for that."

* * *

Allison returned home and came up with the perfect plan. She'd take a puff or a hit and clean until the kids got off the bus. As she remembered from college, the buzz lasted about an hour or two, so she would be perfectly fine by the time the kids were home.

She reached into the coffee bag and pulled out a little plastic tube holding a perfectly rolled joint. It read "Berry White" along the outside of the tube. She hadn't followed Lisa very well this morning when she had explained the marijuana types, but she did remember that the cleaning joint was a man's name.

It was fun to feel so naughty, home alone in her house searching for a match and looking out the window as if the police were tipped off to a housewife armed with dope. She went to her bathroom, closed the door behind her, and lit the tip of the joint. At first, she didn't feel like she got much, so she lit it again and took a big, deep drag. She coughed and coughed and coughed some more.

Once she had calmed herself down, she pulled up Alicia Keys on her Sonos App, turning up the sound louder than it had ever played in the home. *Oh, this is fun, but I don't feel anything yet. Where should I start?* She went to the closet and took out the broom and Old English furniture polish. *Maybe I should take another hit. In college, we would take like four or five hits.* She headed back up to her bathroom and coughed her head off for another five minutes.

As she walked down the stairs, things began to get weird. *Whooo... Now I feel it. Okay, what was I doing?*

*You are cleaning, Allison. Clean the house, Allison.*

*Damn, this stuff is a lot stronger than when I was in college.*

*What were you just thinking? Clean the house.*

*What if the school calls? What if one of the kids gets sick or falls off the jungle gym or punches someone?*

*Clean! Clean! Clean!*

*But I don't feel like cleaning. I don't want to clean. I want to lie in the sun and feel the sun on my body.*

"You are cleaning, Allison," she said out loud.

"Oh, shit. Was that my mother's voice? My mother is taking over my head." She giggled.

"No, it was Sister Mary Lou and you're in big trouble, young lady." Allison burst out laughing at the sound of her own voice and the thought of Sister Mary Lou in her habit. She was the meanest nun of all at St. Francis's, where Allison had gone to high school.

*Okay, I'm cleaning, I'm cleaning.* Allison walked to the dining room table and squirted the oil onto the table. "That's right. Rub it real nice. Get deep into those crevices. Oh, that is so smooth." She squirted the table again and again. Old English now saturated half the table, but she just laughed at the sight of it. "You're in trouble now. Wait until Sister Mary Lou sees this." She began to rub the table again, but her cloth became so wet with product it soaked straight through to her hands. "I will get a bath towel to soak this up," she whispered to herself.

She turned, her hands coated in oil, and grabbed the broomstick as she left the room. She was not even halfway to the stairs when the broomstick slipped from her wet hands. Higher than a kite, she bent over and lifted it in front of her. Up and down she rubbed her hands, violating the broomstick while Alicia Keys moaned the lyrics to "If I Ain't Got You." The urge to reach down and stimulate herself was unbearable.

*No, Allison. You will get an infection.*

*What was I just thinking?*

*Shit. I am high, too high. Wait, get your vibrator.*

*You lost the charger, idiot! Order a new charger!*

*Wait, what?*

*Find something that vibrates.*

She dropped the broomstick and headed to the kitchen, where she pulled all sorts of appliances from the cupboard. *I could try the blender—no. Where's my handheld cake mixer? I know: the dryer. I saw it on Mad Men.*

She ran up the stairs giggling like a schoolgirl. In the laundry room, she turned on the dryer and pressed her body hard against the side. *I don't feel anything. Wait, maybe it was the washer. Yes, the washer, but on what speed? The spin cycle, idiot. But how do I get to the spin cycle?* Her body tingled from head to toe, and everything she touched felt sensual and beautiful. But modern-day appliances just didn't move like they did in the sixties. *This won't work.*

She ran into Tommy's bathroom, the closest to her, and grabbed his electric toothbrush. The Old English still moist in her hand made holding the toothbrush more arousing than she could handle. She looked at its long rubber handle and reached one of her hands into her shirt to caress her already very hard nipple.

*No, Allison. That's Tommy's toothbrush, for fuck's sake. He's just a little boy.*

*Yes, you are right.*

She left his room and was headed for her own when a mess on her daughter's floor caught her eye. Not knowing why, she climbed over it and headed into Emma's bathroom. There on the sink lay the child's face scrub and YES, her Clarisonic. Perfectly round and soft with two speeds of vibration. She put the cap on the face wash and headed back downstairs before that voice spoke again. *It's all wrong, Allison. Wrong.*

Then, a faint sound in the background. A ringing. *Is someone at the door? No, it's the phone. Oh shit, what if it's the school? I'm not answering. What if it's Mom? Don't answer it. Allison, what if it is the school?* She walked quickly down the hall, not knowing what to feel or think. "Yes, hello. O'Neil resident."

"What the fuck? Who are you? How's the cleaning going?" Lisa's voice seemed to echo through the wires.

"I don't feel like cleaning. I feel like sleeping. What is in this shit you gave me?"

"Which one did you smoke?"

The one you told me. The man who wrote the book, Berry White."

"Oh shit, this is so great! I'm going to piss myself. That's the sex one, you fool! Are you telling me you never screwed to Barry White?

"I hate you." And with that, Allison hung up while Lisa rolled laughing, holding her crotch not to pee.

Allison went into her bathroom, searching high and low for something else that jiggled. *Not perfect, but good enough.* She removed the blade from Tom's electric razor, and down the stairs she went, carrying her daughter's face machine as a backup and her husband's shaver. She held the banister tight in her hands, feeling the waxed wood press hard against her flesh. She entered the kitchen and saw the mess she had created, but her mind and body were so fixated on getting to the back patio she did not care. Her desire to feel the sun hot against her flesh and the soft afternoon breeze while she touched herself was all that mattered.

She found her spot on the lounge chair and searched for Barry White on her phone. Moments later, a deep, sultry, shockingly sexy voice of a man radiated throughout the house telling her everything he wanted to do to her and just how provocatively he was going to do it. Away he took her to her beautiful man on the beach while her hands took her to utopia.

"Are you kidding me? Oh my god." The tingles, the sensation, it was mind boggling. *"Holy shit, Sister Mary Lou!"* And with that she collapsed and passed out with exhaustion.

* * *

"Mom, Mom, what happened to the house!?"

Allison opened her eyes and tried to collect her thoughts while Emma stood over her.

"Mom, what is this music and why is my Clarisonic on the floor!?"

# Chardonnay: Meagan

Meagan sat at her dining room table sipping a glass of chardonnay and looking over at Josh. "It's Saturday night. What fun thing should we do?" she asked the empty chair.

"A walk sounds wonderful."

She grabbed a light jacket from the hall closet and double-checked the oven was off before heading out.

"After you."

"Well, thank you." She loved dating a gentleman. Most of the men these days wouldn't even think to open the door for her. Josh was different that way. He treated her like a lady and the equal person she was. He was not threatened by a woman in control of her life with big dreams and ambition. He loved Meagan's spirit. Of course, one day he was hoping she would slow down and let him take over the bills while she made a glorious home and pursued her dream of writing.

"Just look at that sky," Meagan said out loud, pointing to a sky full of stars and a big, beautiful moon. Just then she felt a pang of excitement in her stomach. "You know what we should do? We should go find a perfect spot under the moon and make love."

"Oh, yes." Meagan twirled in circles, thinking *He is so wonderful and romantic.*

"Where should we go?" she asked herself.

"I know the perfect place. The trail where I walk is not too far from here and there are many beautiful spots to lie down."

They walked quietly, so comfortable with one another, holding hands and enjoying the night sounds. When they turned around the bend, the moon lit the opening of the trail and a small dirt area for hikers to park their cars.

"There, beyond those trees is a patch of grass where I sit to stretch before my walks. It's perfect!"

*I love the way Josh makes it so comfortable for me,* Meagan thought as she took off her jacket and spread it across the grass.

At first, they just laid on their backs looking up at the stars, giggling about silly wishes and trying to find the Big and Little Dippers. And then Josh, so very gently, started to kiss her. First on her lips, then over to her ears and then from one side of her neck to the other. His hand slipped under her shirt, and he continued to kiss her neck while he caressed her breasts, squeezing them just so perfectly. He moved his mouth to hers as his hand slowly moved from her breast to her underwear. He teased her, caressing the fabric up and down. Then his fingers slid beneath the lace and every cell in her body screamed in joy.

Meagan was so caught up in her lovemaking, lying under the night's moon with her hands in her pants, that she did not notice the car pull up or hear the footsteps until they were almost upon her. She shot up like a mortar on the Fourth of July, pulling up her pants and yanking down her shirt. The police officer looked just as startled to see her as she was to see him.

"Ma'am, what are you doing out here all alone?"

Meagan had to stop herself from saying *I'm not alone.* "Um, the moon is so beautiful. I was just enjoying it."

"Okay, but it's not safe for you to be out here alone. You just never know. Can I take you somewhere?"

"No, no. I'll be fine. I live just around the corner."

Meagan couldn't walk fast enough. She knew the officer would stay nearby until she made it home. When she got inside the door she fell to the floor, her heart still pounding. She looked up at the dining room table set for two. She looked at Josh's shoes lying in the middle of the floor, his work folders spread across the kitchen table, and his empty beer bottles sitting on the countertop. The sound of the house phone ringing startled her. No one called the house phone but solicitors, so she let it ring as she looked around at the mess Josh had created.

The ancient answering machine went off and she heard the sweet sounds of Mikey's voice. "Mom, Mom, are you there? Mom, can I come home? Mom, I'm sorry. I didn't mean to hurt you. Dad's nice and all, but I miss you. I want to come home. Can I, Mom?"

Meagan ran to the phone and grabbed it before he could hang up. "Baby, I'm here. Of course you can come home. I'll get you in the morning."

"Can you come now, Mom?"

Scanning the place again, she answered, "Of course, honey. I just need to put some things away. I'll be there as soon as I'm finished."

# Latte: The Club

Meagan was thrilled to have Mikey home and have her bed all to herself again. She texted Allison and Lisa that she was back on carpool duty so to meet her for lattes if they could.

"You're late." Lisa moved her briefcase from the chair next to her for Meagan to sit.

"Sorry, sorry. I had a big Goodwill run that couldn't wait." Meagan took her seat.

Allison was watching the door as Mr. Mustache walked in, saw her, then turned around and walked out. "You must be thrilled to have Mikey back."

"You have no idea. Anyone heard from Rose?"

"Not a word." Allison smiled and gave Mr. Mustache a little wave as he turned around before getting into his car.

"I think she blocked me," Lisa said. "I started texting her every day what we were all doing. This way, when she comes back we don't have to spend so much time catching her up."

Meagan frowned. "What if she never comes back?"

Just then, a man in blue jeans and a white T-shirt walked to the condiment table next to them with two drinks in hand with a few food items balancing
on top. He wasn't a big man, but his presence was felt. Broad shoulders, golden beige skin, about average height. He first caught

Lisa's attention and then Meagan's with his huge, electric green eyes. Lisa whispered, bringing Allison on board, "I just creamed my new La Perlas."

"You wear La Perla?" Allison looked shocked

"Nordstrom Rack, baby." She reached over, took Allison's napkin from under her drink, and wiped her face. "I miss my dirty underwear."

Meagan and Allison refrained from responding.

"I'm serious. I know I'm young for menopause, but I can already feel my body changing and now I miss my discharge."

"You can have mine," Meagan said.

It was too early for Allison to come up with anything funny to say, so she kept it serious. "You can get cream for dryness. Haven't you seen all those commercials?"

"I didn't say I was the Mojave Desert. I just said I missed my dirty underwear."

Meagan was listening while keeping her eyes on the hunk at the counter. Something about him was familiar— she just couldn't pinpoint it. He finished up with the sweeteners and headed their way. As he passed their table he did a turnabout, directing his attention right at Meagan. "I'm glad to see you safe and sound in the daylight."

"Excuse me?"

"I'm the police officer who found you moon bathing. I'm sorry if I creeped you out following you home, but I wanted to make sure you made it safe."

Meagan wanted to die right there and then. Had he seen her masturbating? Was this a big joke? "Well, thank you. I appreciate your service."

"I was on duty Saturday night, but today I'm just a civilian like everyone else. If you'd like to grab a coffee sometime or a glass of wine, here's my number." He laid a business card down on the table.

"That would be nice."

He reached across the table to shake her hand, "Steven."

"Meagan."

And out the door he went.

It took Meagan a moment to come back to the table and realize that Lisa and Allison had just witnessed all this and were very amused.

"Damn, he was a hot one," Lisa said. "Are you going to call him?"

"I think I might."

"What about Josh? I thought things were working out so beautifully with the two of you," said Allison.

Meagan picked up the business card, stuck it in her bra, and smiled at Allison. "Always good to keep your options open."

# Chardonnay: The Club

Allison hung up the phone with Izzy and sat quietly while a tear slowly worked its way down her face. Then she picked up her phone and group texted Meagan and Lisa. *"I got fired.* 🙁*"*

Meagan shot back
*"What!"*
*"NO!"*

*"What happened?"*
*"I'm sorry.* ♡     *"*
Allison texted back. *"I guess Miss Home Wrecker is done crying and is now in revenge mode. She called the salon and told Izzy she was going to Yelp the shit out of the salon about me."*

Meagan wrote back, *"That's bullshit. She can't do that!"*

*"She can and she did. My bad.* 😌 *It goes against our client privacy clause."*

*"What, that her asshole is ugly and you told her?"*

*"No, that I hollered that at her in public."*

Lisa saw the text and joined in. *"STFU, Fuck her, that little bitch. She got you fired?* 👆*"*

*"Yes,"* Allison wrote. *"I'm going to go watch a movie or eat something.* 🍕 🍩 🍦*"*

*"Where's Tom?"*

*"Boston. Home tomorrow."*

Time passed as Allison tried to forget about the salon by binge watching episodes of *Friends*. Just when she had stopped ruminating, Higgins began barking uncontrollably. It was just past 10:00. Allison went to the dining room window and hid behind the curtain, scoping out the grounds. Her heart pounded. A large van, dark in color, was stopped in her driveway with its engine running and headlights beaming towards her backyard. She considered going to the phone to call the police, but then she heard familiar voices and doors shutting. Higgins continued to bark.

As the van pulled away, Allison spotted Gomez behind the wheel. Then out the of shadows she saw Lisa and Meagan walking up the driveway with their arms full, carrying sleeping bags and pillows.

Allison didn't know whether to laugh or cry. As they came closer, she saw that Lisa had a bottle of wine in one hand and what looked like bags of popcorn and potato chips. Meagan also had wine, along with her favorite Carole King *Tapestry* CD. Allison opened the door and they filed in, first Meagan, then Lisa.

"Where do you want us? I can't hold on to this stuff much longer." Meagan walked straight past Allison and flopped on the staircase.

"Sorry we're so late," Lisa said. "Gomez is our DD tonight if you don't want us to stay." She handed Allison the bottle of wine in her hands. "Shitty wine for you wine snobs, but it was all I had in the house."

Allison grabbed three wine glasses and led the girls upstairs to her bedroom, careful not to wake the children. They sat on the floor in a circle around a bowl of barbecue potato chips and a bowl of Skinny Pop Popcorn. Allison laughed at Meagan's old CD. "Girl, I'm almost a decade older than you and don't own a CD player."

Allison pulled up a Sonos app on her iPhone and turned on the Carole King station.

"What are you going to do now?" Meagan asked. "Get another job?"

"No. I loved working and believe it or not, I really enjoyed the spa atmosphere. It was alive and the customers were all so nice. I'm thinking of taking some business classes over at the community college, and maybe when the kids get a little older I'll open my own place."

"That sounds wonderful," Meagan said.

"Yeah. You can call it 'Human Landscaping.'" Lisa pointed a finger to the sky.

They laughed and Higgins began barking again. Afraid he would wake the kids, Allison tried to hold the dog, but he jumped out of her hands and ran down the stairs barking even louder. Allison ran after him while Lisa and Meagan went to the bedroom window to look outside. A small car was parked on the street in front of the house with its engine running. A moment later the car turned off, and Rose climbed out of the driver's seat.

"Oh my God. Oh my God." Meagan panicked. "What do we do?"

"We go hug her. Come on." Lisa flew down the stairs.

Allison was standing with the door open in disbelief as she watched Rose walk up the drive. Allison turned to Lisa. "Did you text her you guys were coming over?"

"Yeah, but I didn't expect her."

Rose arrived at the door and looked at the three of them standing there. They were more beautiful than she remembered, dressed in their PJs with messy hair. The girls stared back at her, wearing her gray terrycloth robe and slippers, hair high in a ponytail, and not a touch of makeup. She was stunning, and they sensed a difference, an air of confidence that radiated from her face and in her posture. Yet she still possessed the same tender kindness of Rose.

"I'm sorry my husband's mistress got you fired."

"All I care about right now is you and seeing your beautiful face in my doorway." Allison wrapped her arms around Rose, hugging her tightly. Meagan and Lisa jumped in for a big group hug as tears ran down all of their faces.

Moments later, it was the four of them sitting on the floor around an empty bowl of barbecue potato chips and half a bowl of popcorn.

"Do you want to talk about it?" Allison asked.

"Well, there's not much to say because there's so much to say. We're in therapy. I don't know where it will go or what the future holds for us." Rose looked at the girls one by one with conviction. "You know I would walk out the door in a minute if it were just me I had to worry about, but I owe it to the girls to at least try."

"Do you love him?" Meagan asked.

"I love him deeply. He's the only man I've ever loved. That's why it's so confusing."

Allison leaned in and lowered her voice. "What does he want? What's his excuse?"

Rose wanted to get defensive, but she didn't know why. It was all still so confusing. "Well, he's been living in the basement ever since I let him come back home. He's desperate to make it work and he's being so wonderful."

"Yeah, they all always are," Lisa said.

Rose shot Lisa a look. "Of course he said it meant nothing and he never thought I would find out. He never wanted to hurt me, blah, blah, blah."

"How did you find out?" Meagan asked.

"I knew something was up. He seemed to have one Wednesday night dinner meeting after another. Then one day I was holding Dahlia. We were laughing and cuddling on the big chair in the sunroom and she said I smelled like her teacher. I don't know why, but I just knew something was up. I thought about how she was always cancelling our meetings and how one time at dinner Frank got weirdly defensive with Dahlia when she called her teacher mean."

Rose took a sip of her wine and looked out the window, fighting back tears. Lisa, Meagan, and Allison remained quiet. Rose continued, "So I stopped wearing my perfume to see if he still smelled like me."

"Wait," Meagan said. "He bought her the same perfume he buys you so you wouldn't smell her on him?"

"Fucker," Lisa said.

"Yeah. It only took about a week and Ana and I both could smell my perfume all over his clothes."

Allison shook her head in disbelief. "Almost pretty smart."

"No, he's not too smart. I guess one night his phone died, so he called me from the hotel to tell me he was running late. I called back and got the front desk. Some Dougy kid spilled the beans without me even asking much."

Lisa squinted her eyes and moved in closer to Rose. "Did you have to pay him, this Dougy kid?"

"What? No. Why?"

"Nothing. Continue."

"That's that. My head was spinning. I was trying to figure out what to do, but then you guys showed up, so I had to act."

"Sorry," said Meagan.

"Sorry," said Allison.

"I'm not sorry," Lisa said. "I would do it again tomorrow because I thought it was the right thing to do for you."

"You guys must've been dying when I told you I was doing the bunny plug. I just wanted to see his face when I walked in wearing that costume since I knew she must have worn it for him."

"Oh Rose, I'm so sorry," Allison said. "It must have killed you when I was talking about her."

"Yes, it sucks. Even if we move forward, something is forever broken."

Lisa bit down on the inside of her mouth to restrain herself from going batshit crazy on Frank and spoke calmly. "I say you even the score and go find yourself a nice piece of ass. Then you go back to him."

Rose smiled thinking about her sweet bellman.

Lisa rethought her response. "Don't listen to me. I've been screwing up so much lately."

They all looked at her, puzzled.

"You guys were right about Mary Jane. She was in the closet at the party. And I've found alcohol on her twice."

"What are you going to do?" Rose asked.

"We have her in therapy right now, and we're just going to love her."

Lisa stared at each one of them with great intensity. "I know she is hurting. I know I am a safe place for her to take out the anger but when does a mother say enough? How much do we take for their sake? When are we doing more damage than good by allowing them to shit on us?"

"Lisa, you're a great mom," Meagan said. "Mary Jane will be fine."

"Yeah, well, she hates me at the moment and thinks I'm the worst mother on the planet."

Allison reached over and squeezed Lisa's hand. There was a moment of silence and then another.

"Josh and I broke up," Meagan blurted.

"I'm so sorry, sweetie," said Allison. "What happened?"

"I have to confess something, but please don't be mad at me." Meagan hugged her knees tightly and closed her eyes. "I made Josh up."

"I don't get it," Rose said.

"He was my imaginary boyfriend who was supposed to help me find love."

Rose and Allison tried to smile, but Lisa sat with a smirk on her face. Meagan looked at her. "What, you knew?"

"Yes, I knew. I've known all along."

"How and why didn't you say something?"

"For starters, ever since you started dating him, you must have used that stupid expression 'manifest this and manifest that' a hundred times. Plus, you would never let a guy trash your house like that. I don't know. I just knew."

"Then why didn't you say something?"

"Because I loved the way he made you feel. I loved the way you let him love you."

Meagan stared at Lisa for a second and then burst into tears.

Lisa continued. "Meagan, look at yourself. Even your pajamas changed."

Meagan looked down at the pretty, soft pink cotton nighty trimmed in lace that showed her curves and thought about the huge, flannel men's T-shirt she had worn when the girls had all gone away together for a night the year before.

"It's the first time since I've known you that you're not hiding behind some tent dress. And look how beautiful you look."

Rose and Allison simultaneously muttered, "You do."

"I just feel like such a fool, and I didn't mean to lie to you guys, but I had to believe he was real to make it come true. Not that it got me anywhere."

Allison put her hand on top of Meagan's and squeezed it gently. "Meagan, Lisa's right. I've noticed such a change in you since you've been dating Josh. You seem calmer, more at ease with yourself."

The girls remained quiet, gazing at Meagan while she looked at the floor, pulling at the carpet. Rose reached over and placed her hand on Meagan's leg. "I think Josh was real in the sense that he showed you how to love yourself."

Lisa felt tears welling up in her own eyes and couldn't take it. "Allison, do you still have the other joint? I think it's time to dance!"

Allison, Meagan and Lisa took a couple of hits off the joint while Rose enjoyed more wine. Allison blasted Fleetwood Mac, "The

Chain," throughout her bedroom, disregarding the sleeping children down the hall. They danced their asses off practically screaming the lyrics, *"never break the chain"* while grabbing each other's hands. U2, Beyoncé and Madonna kept them moving but Tina Turner's Proud Mary took everything they had left to give.

Exhausted, they collapsed on the floor. They killed all the wine in the bedroom and left nothing of the chips and popcorn. They filled Rose in with more details on everything she had missed over the last month and they laughed. They laughed about Meagan's imaginary boyfriend and the cop catching her masturbating, they laughed at Allison's description of Mr. Mustache's little pecker with his mound of white pubic hair, and her smoking the wrong joint. And they just about wet their pants when Rose demonstrated herself hopping around the bedroom with bunny ears on her head along with a cotton tail sticking out her ass and the priceless expression on Frank's face. When their sides hurt and their eyes were tired, Rose and Allison climbed up on the bed and Meagan and Lisa laid out their sleeping bags on the floor at the foot of Allison's bed. Allison turned out the lights and opened the curtains to let in the moonlight.

In the darkness, Rose spoke. "Do you think it's my fault? Was I doing something wrong?"

Allison rolled over and hugged Rose. Lisa and Meagan jumped onto the bed and found space to lie down by Rose's legs.

"We were there with you, Rose," Meagan said. "You're a great wife."

"Rose, don't do that to yourself," Lisa begged. "My mother blamed herself for my father's infidelity. She felt unworthy and her life sucked, but she also did damage to me and my brother. It's not good being raised by a mother with low self-esteem. Don't do it, Rose."

"Lisa's right," Allison said. "And if there was something Frank was unhappy with, he could have talked to you about it."

"We all need to stop beating ourselves up so much," Meagan said.

Lisa stared up at the ceiling, her eyes adjusting to the darkness. "It's my turn to pick tomorrow, and my challenge this month is self-care. We all need to be good to ourselves if we expect to be our best for our families."

Allison loved the concept but needed more clarification. "How do you earn points?"

"Anything you do for yourself is a point. I mean, if you take a nap, buy yourself flowers, get your ass to yoga, or say no to something you never had the courage to before."

Meagan propped herself up on her elbows. "Get your nails done, buy yourself something special, play soothing music while you houseclean...?"

"Yup, they all count as points. Anything and everything you do for yourself counts, even getting a mammogram or your teeth cleaned."

"Oh, I likey, I likey this challenge. What's the bonus?" Meagan asked.

Lisa thought good and hard. Allison, Rose, and Meagan stayed quiet, anticipating what she might say. They all knew she was working with one friend who had just dumped her imaginary boyfriend, another friend on the verge of divorce, and one who had just been fired.

"The bonus this month is to forgive yourself."

"What?" the other girls all said.

"Oh, please. Don't fuck with me. We all know we beat ourselves up daily. 'I need to lose weight, I was too tough on the kids, I don't deserve him...'"

Allison was very impressed with this side of Lisa. "Are you taking spiritual awakening classes without telling us?"

"Ha ha. I'm serious, and we're just going to have to trust one another on earning the bonus. If you feel at the end of the month you have stopped the negative talk inside your head, you get the points."

Rose's whole face lit up in the darkness. "God, I love you, Lisa. And I love you, Meagan and I love you, Allison."

Allison reached for Rose's hand, "I love you."

"Me too."

"Me three."

# Latte: The Club

Gomez pulled up in the driveway just as the Uber was dropping off Tom. They laughed when they saw each other both carrying a tray of lattes.

"Great minds think alike," Tom said.

"I'm just so happy the four of them are together again."

"You got that right."

Plus, you know what day it is, right?" Gomez smiled so big.

Tom knew exactly what he was talking about. "I thought I was the only one who had figured that out. I was afraid to mention it to any of you guys in case the girls found out we knew."

"Oh no, never." Gomez said. "I wouldn't risk them ending their little club for anything. Lisa is so competitive, we've gotten some spunk back in the bedroom ever since they started."

"I love that they care enough to try, to have a club."

The two men reached the door and could hear the girls awake upstairs giggling. Tom looked at Gomez. "Ready?"

"Ready."

Heading up the stairs, they called out in unison, "LATTES!"

# Reading Group Guide

1. Rose's family often plays the game "Rose and Thorn" to share what their best and worst part of their day was. In relation to the book, what was your "rose" and what was your "thorn"? Was there a scene you enjoyed most and one you didn't relate to or enjoy as much?

2. Each woman in the book has very distinct and different personality traits. Which character do you see yourself in most and why? Are you a mix of a few of them?

3. Lisa is struggling with her preteen daughter Mary-Jane. Do you think Lisa handled disciplining her properly? What do you think her next steps should be?

4. Lisa, Meagan and Allison were faced with the difficult decision as to whether or not they should tell Rose about Frank's cheating. Do you agree with the way the women handled the situation or what do you think they should have done differently?

5. Meagan is struggling with adapting to Mikey's dad who recently came back into their lives. Do you think Meagan did a good job in her efforts to create and allow for a relationship between Mikey and his father?

6. At the end of the book, Rose reveals that she and Frank are in therapy and that she does not know what the future holds

for them as a couple. Do you think her marriage can survive the betrayal?

7. Allison is not sure what Tom would think of her waxing another man's private area so she chooses not to share the details since he is not specifically asking. Do you think that is okay or is she being untruthful?

8. In the last scene, the women decide to make the next month's challenge be that they must be more forgiving and kinder to themselves. How do you feel about this challenge? Do you think challenges should all be specifically focused on spicing things up with their partner? Do you think this challenge may ultimately have positive effects on their relationships with their spouses?

9. Meagan struggled with body image issues quite a bit in the beginning of the book. Do you think it was obsessive or common in today's world?

10. Rose had a titillating experience with Joey in the hotel room after he rescued her the night before. Do you think Rose should have slept with him, or pursued more than she did?

*Start your own club!*

Visit our website to get your own Latte to Chardonnay Club
started today!

**www.lattetochardonnay.com**

# Books By Tricia LaVoice

Dear Martha, WTF

Wishes for a
Mother's Heart

Wishes for the Grieving
and Healing Heart

Wishes for the
Heart

Helmets and Hoses

Made in the USA
Coppell, TX
20 March 2021

52027128R00144